ASSORTED MALIGNANCIES

DALE W GLASER

LVP
PUBLICATIONS

Cover Art by Susan Cipriano, Cover Design by Lycan Valley, © 2023
LVP Publications

The Demon Wrestler (appeared in How the West Was Weird v.2 May, 2011)
The Lengths That He Would Go To (appeared in Eldritch Embraces March, 2016)
Rendered By Her Deeds (appeared in Under a Dark Sign October, 2015)
Red Screamy (appeared in Electric Spec May, 2016)
Another Night in Paradise (appeared in Final Masquerade November, 2016)
Bottom Feeder (appeared in Trysts of Fate February, 2017)
Vitriol (appeared in New Realm February, 2016)
The Half-hidden Face (appeared in Cheapjack Pulp March, 2016)
The Trap (appeared in Creepy Campfire Quarterly April, 2016)

Printed in the United States of America

Lycan Valley Press Publications
1625 E 72nd St STE 700 PMB 132
Tacoma, Washington 98404
United States of America

First Printing

ISBN-13: 978-1-64562-008-2

To my amazing wife, Nora, who encouraged me to get back into writing and never stopped cheering me on, even once she realized that what I really liked to write was stories that creep her all the way out.

ACKNOWLEDGEMENTS

This book would not exist without MJae Sydney, publisher of Lycan Valley Press Publications. From accepting a couple of my short stories to appear in Lycan Valley anthologies, which led me to believe we might be on the same wavelength, to walking me through the process of pitching a single-author collection when I had never done so before, to patiently putting up with all my questions and check-ins during the entire production process, she is a great editor to work with and a credit to the indie horror community.

Special appreciation in respectful memory of Stacey Turner, who was taken from us too soon. Stacey selected my story *Another Night in Paradise* for the *Final Masquerade* anthology she edited, which was my introduction to Lycan Valley, and the rest is history and in your hands now.

Russ Anderson and Joel Jenkins have my eternal gratitude for publishing some of my earliest pro works and thus setting me on the path that got me here.

I'm always thankful for my friends. I don't want to out anyone, nor leave anyone out, but they know who they are, the ones who've spent countless nights playing RPGs with me, who've celebrated Halloween with me, who've gone to midnight movie premieres with me, and basically demonstrated and nurtured every geeky influence that shows up in one way or another in my off-kilter little tales of fiction.

Similarly, my family deserves special recognition. My parents for surrounding me with books and putting them in my hands at a young age, my siblings for sharing life's journeys with me, my children for giving me fresh eyes through which to see the world. And most especially, my wife, to whom this book has already been dedicated. Still, she merits the final word on acknowledgements, as I would neither live the life that I do, nor be the person I am, without her constant love and support.

INTRODUCTION

I've been writing stories since I was about seven or eight years old, and even at that young age it was only partly for my own amusement, while the other part was a ploy for attention and praise. The first effort I can remember was an extremely generic bit of high fantasy that involved several warriors entering a deep dark cave and slaying the monster within. I brought the story to school and asked my teacher if I could share it with the class, which she allowed, and so I stood in front of the blackboard and gave a dramatic reading which went fine until I approached the climax, and suddenly, hearing things out loud, realized how I had really gone all out in describing the blood and gore resulting from hacking up an abomination with swords and axes. This got a mixed reaction from my classmates, and I distinctly remember self-censoring on the fly, changing the line on the page from "blood flew through the air and guts spilled out of the wound" to "blood flew through the air and more spilled out of the wound" aloud, because I worried "guts" was too gross for my fellow third graders.

All in all, it was a positive experience which clearly did not put me off either writing or sharing my work with an audience. I've basically been chasing that high ever since, but I've also been wrestling with that inherent tension between what's cool and what's gross, what's exciting and what's dangerous. As I attempt to compose an introduction to the stories that follow, I find myself thinking about that tension a lot, primarily because it is still very much unresolved. I'm not sure if I should find it surprising that my first collection of fiction should be filed under "horror" or if it's the most natural and predictable outcome imaginable.

The main genre I consumed when I was growing up was heroic fantasy. Star Wars, Flash Gordon, He-Man, The Hobbit, the Chronicles of Narnia, the Dungeons and Dragons Saturday morning cartoon, and anything else that remotely had to do with brave and noble heroes on quests for glory and righteousness. I was a happy kid with a stable home life who yearned for adventure not as an escape from the bad but as the next level of good. Not enough to actually go out and do anything about it, but enough to gravitate toward the books and movies that offered vicarious thrills, and to idly daydream about being one of King Arthur's knights or some kind of swashbuckling space pirate.

So all the way up through junior high school I drew my own comic books where my friends and I were transformed into superheroes, and I turned in stories of international super spies for my English composition assignments, and if anyone had anticipated a writing career ahead of me they might well have thought I was on track to be a purveyor of remixed myths and fairy tales that could easily spawn lines of action figures. Anyone including me, I should hasten to add. If anyone had offered me a guarantee on that line of work when I was twelve years old, I would have jumped at it.

Then as I got deeper into my teen years, I found horror. Or possibly horror found me. As an older adolescent I was still fundamentally a happy kid and was slowly developing a sincere appreciation for not just how stable my home life was but how rare a thing that was in the world. But I was being subjected to the same biological social pressures as my peers, to prove myself as a worthy mate. In the old stories that meant leaving home to find one's fortune; in the suburbs of the late 80s and early 90s, that meant watching scary movies and not being a wuss about it. And it worked its way into my writing, too, as seemingly overnight I wanted to write about ghosts and visions of madness more than magic swords of destiny. I'm sure it was all part of my nominally maturing outlook, a way of processing my place in the world and all of my hormone-driven feelings about it. I don't think I ever made it all the way to being a full-fledged cynic, but I definitely became more aware of darkness than ever before.

Except maybe that's not exactly right, either, because there's no such thing as light without darkness. No Star Wars without Darth Vader, no Hobbit without Smaug, no struggle to defend the good without an encroaching evil to defend against. Monsters, blood, the shadows lurking beneath the surface, those are elements of almost every adventure, including the one I made up for myself and my classmates in third grade. There can be no heroic fantasy without horror.

But horror can stand on its own. Heroic fantasy is aspirational, while horror tends to be a reflection of our lived experiences. That's one reason why heroic fantasy tends to utilize secondary world settings, or at least exotic locales in distant times, whereas horror is almost always set here and now. Basically, all literature gives us humans, poor long-suffering thinking animals that we are, a way to confront the things we worry about, the things we don't understand, the things we straight-up fear. Heroic fantasy lets us do so comfortably by layering in separation between us and our problems, separation in time and space and behind the shield of the valiant paragon of courage. Horror lets us do so viscerally, stripping the problems bare and shoving them in the reader's face. So it wasn't so much that I pivoted away from one kind of storytelling and into a very different kind. I figured out part of what made the stories work all along, isolated that, and dug deep.

That is not everyone's cup of tea, and that is perfectly fine. But if you are holding this book and you've made it this far, I have to assume that I need not apologize for what comes next: a one-man show that ranges from mildly shiver-inducing to disturbing. There is fantasy, but not many heroes to be found from here on out, and when they do appear, they aren't always guaranteed to win the day. Some of these stories are bleak, and some of these stories are nasty; some are cool, and some are gross. All of them are mine, and all of them emerged as brief stops on the path that started with a kid bent over a sheet of paper on the coffee table, figuring out how best to enter a monster's lair. I'm still walking down that path, and I hope you enjoy what I've encountered so far along the way.

—Dale W. Glaser
  October 2021

Contents

THE TRAP

"Hey, DEMON!" AN EAGER voice called out.

Corin Garry stopped in his tracks, turned around, and crossed his arms over his chest, a slow and deliberate performance that also took care not to snag any of his black, press-on talons.

"What?" he snarled, compensating with guttural ferocity for having removed his plastic fangs.

They pulled up short within a few feet of him, two boys no more than eleven years old, in semi-disheveled costumes; the light-haired boy in the black *gi* had been wearing a ninja mask earlier, as Corin recalled. His dark-haired friend still wore his bone-embossed gloves and polyester reaper's robe, but the hood had fallen back to reveal his unadorned face.

"That haunted house was so boss!" Reaper said. He let his plastic scythe fall to the crook of his arm, reached his free hand into his bag, and pulled out a Tootsie Pop.

"Thank you so much," Ninja said, with the earnestness reserved for heartfelt gratitude, absent from mumbled thanks prompted by parents. "Nobody around here ever does anything that awesome."

Corin couldn't help but grin at that, despite the expression tugging at the spirit gum holding his demonic half-mask in place.

"You're welcome, little dudes," he said, in his normal voice.

"You gonna do it next year?" Reaper asked, Tootsie Pop bulging in one cheek.

"Probably," Corin said. "If we all still live here."

Someone coming up from behind bumped Corin's shoulder. "Nice hair," Alyssa said.

Corin shook his head, tossing the mask's cascade of black nylon strands. "This old thing?" he asked. "My real hair was longer, in high school."

"Yeah?" Alyssa asked.

"By graduation," Corin confirmed. "Cut most of it off after I got to college. Too much hassle."

"Because you stopped showering before classes?" she teased.

Ninja and Reaper had been staring at Alyssa since she approached. Finally, Reaper recognized her. "No way, it's the girl in the TV!"

The boys had to be younger than Corin had thought, ten years old, maybe nine. Alyssa was a gorgeous fairyland vision: hair swept up off her long, slender neck and piled in a dirty blonde flounce atop her head, shimmering blue eye makeup rendering her green eyes more come-hither than usual, lips glossed iridescent pink, clear straps of diaphanous wings clinging to bare shoulders, mini dress showing off cleavage and curves, glittery tights sheathing shapely legs. But Ninja and Reaper's matching expressions conveyed no lust, only the curiosity and awe of boys beholden to cooties, not beauties.

Alyssa gave Reaper a quick glance and polite, yet confused, smile. Her eyes flicked to Corin as if seeking a proper introduction. Then her brow knitted as a haunted, faraway look fell across her face. She looked back at the boys, stricken, back at Corin again, and started shaking her head, rhythmically, relentlessly. "No, no," she chanted, closing her eyes. "No, no, no," she repeated. "No!" Her eyes flew open, pleading and drilling into Corin's. "You promised! You promised I would never have to think about that place again! Never! No! Noooo!" The last was the keening of a forsaken soul.

"Yo, let's get out of here!" Reaper said, smacking Ninja's shoulder as he spun on his heel. Ninja was already in parallel flight. They whooped as they sprinted across the common green, children pretending to be in mortal danger, but Corin heard an undercurrent of genuine fear as he watched them go.

He looked at Alyssa, who was smiling, kittenishly pleased with herself. "Yes?" she asked innocently.

"I… was not expecting that."

"And…?"

"And, I am impressed."

"And…?"

"I think I'm in love," he half-sighed, half-laughed.

"Idiot," she grinned, pushing him away. "I take it the haunted house was a hit?"

"Big time, and obviously in large part thanks to you," Corin said.

"Well, I'm glad you guys had fun."

"That's why I moved down here," he said. "You theater kids know how to have a good time."

"So why aren't you at the after party?" Alyssa asked.

"Dave made, like, six hours of mixed CDs, but Becky asked if we'd put on the Donnas. Who are not in the mix," he explained.

"But they're in your car?"

"Well, a copy of their CD is," he admitted. "If the four ladies are actually in my car, I might not be back for a while."

"Shame," Alyssa cooed. "So, I have to walk the rest of the way by myself?"

"Unless you come with me real quick …"

"I wouldn't want the Donnas to think you were taken," she said with mock solemnity. "Besides, these heels are cute but killing my feet. I gotta get inside in the fewest number of steps possible."

"I'll buy you a drink once I get back," he promised.

She threw a scoffing *ha* back over her shoulder. Corin continued in the opposite direction. Streetlights glowed as the twilight shadows deepened. He leaned across the driver's seat, ejected the CD and didn't bother to locate the jewel case. Holding the disc on one finger like an ill-fitting silver ring, he jogged back, taking the steep front steps two at a time.

In just a few minutes, he had missed a small wave of arrivals. Mitch's cousin, Lisa, dressed as a slasher surgeon, hospital-green scrubs and cap liberally splattered with fake blood; her boyfriend, Steve, kitted out in an ironically ill-fitting sexy nurse costume with matching bloodstains; two of Blake's co-workers, who either hadn't heard or hadn't believed that it was a costume party.

Blake was working the bar, his face still painted like a demented jack-o-lantern, although, he had shed the heavy black leather biker jacket. Corin held the CD out to him. "One sec," Blake said, cracking open a can of soda and finishing a cocktail. "Seven and seven for you," Blake said, passing the drink to the co-worker to his left, whom Corin was gratified to see had at least worn an orange t-shirt with GENERIC HALLOWEEN COSTUME block-lettered across the chest. "And you wanted...?" Blake pivoted to his other colleague.

"G and T?"

"Right, right," Blake nodded, taking the CD without looking. He swapped bottles, whiskey for gin, with one hand, and fed the disc into the stereo with the other. Corin, Blake and Mitch had thrown enough house parties to know that the stereo belonged behind the bar, where only authorized persons could operate it. A moment later, the opening riff kicked in. From a corner of the couch, Becky shouted, "Woo!" Corin was already injecting himself back into the party, crossing the room to Lisa and Steve.

"Hey," he yelled above the music, shaking Steve's hand. "Long time!"

Steve nodded. "How ya been, man?"

"Good, good." Corin looked around restlessly, scanning the faces in the gathering. "You guys good? Drinks?" Steve and Lisa both held up full beverages. "Cool. Be right back!" He headed for the back door.

The townhouse's deck was so small it felt overcrowded by the half dozen assembled partygoers, including Mitch, in torn clothes and werewolf makeup. Cigarette smoldering in the corner of his mouth, he was giving a light to a girl dressed as a go-go dancer, standing next to another smoking girl in a nearly identical costume. Corin didn't recognize either of the go-go girls. Alyssa stood by herself, in the far corner, leaning against the railing. Corin moved to join her.

The deck shook as heavy footfalls bounded up the stairs, and Paul appeared, dressed in jeans and a white tank top with a red cape tied around his neck and a beer in each hand. "Cor-blimey!" Paul boomed as he spied Corin; he never tired of making that play on Corin's name. Paul handed one bottle to Alyssa and offered the other to Corin. "Beer?"

"What about you?" Corin asked.

"I'll get myself another. Take it, take it!" Corin accepted the bottle and Paul thundered down the stairs, cape flying out behind him.

"I didn't know he was coming," Corin said, twisting off the bottle cap.

"Captain Wife beater? No, me neither," Alyssa sighed. "That get-up of his is so stupid." She attempted to open her beer barehanded, gave up, and then plucked at her skimpy costume to gather enough material to palm the cap. Corin silently held his hand out, took her beer, opened it, and passed it back. She tipped it toward him appreciatively and they clinked longnecks.

She was lying about Paul. Neither Blake nor Mitch would have invited him. Corin couldn't understand why Alyssa wouldn't simply admit having mentioned the party to Paul, unless their perpetual cycle of reuniting and splitting again was nearing another reconciliation phase. Paul reappeared and Alyssa's shifting body language gave Corin the confirmation he hadn't really needed. "Be right back," Corin excused himself, retreating inside.

Already, more costumed revelers had joined the scene, none of whom Corin knew well, if at all. He looked around the room and saw nothing but conversations, already deep underway, circles already formed by Mitch and Blake's friends, and friends-of-their-friends. Blake was constructing a complicated, layered drink, for an audience surrounding the bar. The consummate theater techie, always happiest building something, like the bar itself, a stage prop he'd kept after a summer production, or like the deceptively simple structures that had transformed their garage into a hall of horrors.

A flush of envy and isolation roared through Corin, propelling him through the crowd, toward the door to the basement. He descended the staircase and passed through the garage door at the bottom, entering the now empty haunted house.

Blake had framed out two rough, freestanding walls, a long one and a short one, at right angles to each other, all in one day's vacation from work. With the evening hours of children trick-or-treating past, the pine two-by-fours, draped in slashed black garbage bags and decorated with cobwebs, had been pulled all the way into the garage, the door rolled down. Earlier in the afternoon, the structure had jutted out into the empty driveway. A child walking up the driveway would see the left side of the garage blocked off and the right side open. Younger or fainter-hearted children could collect candy from a bowl at the bottom of the front steps, near the open side of the garage. The brave ones could enter the garage, proceed all the way to the back, walk a one-eighty hairpin around the temporary center wall, and follow it out to the dogleg exit. The horseshoe path took the trick-or-treaters past a cinderblock utility alcove, converted into a cage with spray-painted plywood and dowels, also Blake's handiwork. Corin had played the demon in the cage, slavering and growling and trying to grab children through the bars. In the back right corner, Mitch had hunched and lunged as a chained werewolf; in the opposite corner, a jumbled pile of televisions and electronic junk were stacked on a table. Down the other side of the garage, the trick-or-treaters proceeded to Blake, the punk-pumpkinhead handing out candy and ushering the children back into the night.

Corin approached the televisions; his major creative

contribution to what was otherwise a borrowed idea. The annual Halloween haunted house garage was a Donnelly family tradition from Mitch's childhood, one which Alyssa had taken part in many times, growing up right around the corner.

Corin and Mitch had gone to Mitch's parents to raid their basement for haunted house props and supplies: old chains, rubber bats and rats and spiders, strobe light and smoke machine. In the back of the basement, Corin noticed multiple television sets gathering dust, several of them with built-in VCRs. He asked if they still worked, and Mitch explained they had been replaced by newer models, not damaged, with enough interrogation in his voice to prompt Corin to explain what he was thinking.

"The garage has four corners, but there's only three of us, since Alyssa wants to come to the party in something cute and doesn't want to change out of a monster get-up, right?" he began. "So, we set these up where Alyssa should be. We put in some videos of horror movies and just let them play. Not really graphic ones; the classics. Your dad collects *Universal Monsters* movies, right?"

"They aren't going to work perfectly," Mitch warned. "This one, for sure, had squiggles down one side of the picture."

"That's okay," Corin said. "Don't you think? If the TVs are a little bit off, kinda broken, that just adds to the ambience. Neglect and disrepair, man. It's the video equivalent of cobwebs in the windows or moss on a tombstone."

"Maybe. But then, this one is older than VCRs," Mitch kicked a set with a faux-wood case. "I don't think you could even hook one up."

"We can work with that," Corin said. "We just have it on, showing snow. It'll be super-creepy, like Poltergeist."

Back at the townhouse, unloading the televisions, along with the rest of the gear, Mitch mused aloud, "We could make a movie, too, with my camcorder."

"Totally," Corin agreed, inwardly cursing for not thinking of it. "You think Alyssa would be in it?"

"Our little diva? She'll do it, if it's good material."

"Like what?"

"You tell me, hoss, you're the writer," Mitch had delegated.

In the main set's inert screen, Corin could see his own spectral reflection. He didn't see a writer, he saw a temp who did clerical work for slightly more than minimum wage, dressed in too tight Lycra and wearing a prosthetic hook nose and horns. He pulled the mask off, spirit gum stinging as it tore away from his cheeks, and felt profoundly foolish. What had he thought? That Alyssa would want him if he proved he was just like them, that he could join their garage troupe, wear a costume and get into character and put on a show? Had he honestly, for one moment, expected that near the end of the party, sitting on the couch, Alyssa would lean over and start kissing him deeply, with yearning, while stroking his fright wig? Or that she would sit on the edge of his bed and wait patiently while he ditched the costume and took a jar of Noxzema to the red greasepaint on his face? Stupid moron.

Corin reached behind the televisions, felt for the surge protector, toggled its power switch. The screens came to life, slowly, long-neglected cathode tubes warming up. The central monitor, the largest in the group of four, became a slightly brighter shade of dark gray, with yellow-green letters reading A/V in its upper corner. The TV to the right, cocked at a forty-five-degree angle against the central set, was somewhere in the middle of the *Creature From the Black Lagoon*. The TV to the left, flat on its side, was the antiquated static-only set, and the small TV surmounting the sideways set and the central one, in a crooked straddle, showed the end of *Frankenstein*.

The central television was connected directly to a camcorder wedged into the angular space beneath the *Black Lagoon* set. Corin pressed 'Play' on the camera. Alyssa's crying face appeared in close-up on the big screen, her makeup in ruins, bloody welts at her right temple and on the left side of her neck.

"Let me out! Let me out! Hello? Anyone? I don't belong in here! Please let me out! Please!" She banged her fists on the screen, sobbing. "Somebody get me out of here!" she wailed.

Alyssa had, of course, thrown herself into the role, once Corin had suggested the basic concept he'd come up with; not a narrative movie, but a character – another prisoner in the hall of horrors, like the demon and the werewolf. Alyssa insisted on improvising for several minutes without the camera running, brainstorming with Corin, then managed a single, uninterrupted fifteen minute take. Alyssa was born to perform and could turn it on at will. Given the slightest time to compose herself and get into the zone, she was devastating.

She still looked beautiful, magnetic, even with multiple fake wounds and runny mascara streaming down her cheeks. It wasn't that the thought of her being terrified or in pain turned Corin on, but the power of her performance. Alyssa was insanely talented and possessed of so much passion that she could evoke exactly what he had envisioned and make it real. That passion made her incandescent to him, regardless of the subject matter. He wanted to incorporate himself into it somehow, any way that he could, and always had. From the day they had met years ago on campus, an English major seeking actors to put on a one-act play he was writing for class, and a drama major trying out for extra credit, Corin had wanted to give Alyssa the perfect words to speak, the quintessential character to play. Anything that involved mingling her passion with his, on stage, or in private.

Corin drank some more beer, barely tasting it. It was too late for him and Alyssa; even in college it had already been too late. He cast her in his play, but the parts had already been written before he met her and the deadline for the assignment left no time to re-write for her. They never collaborated again. And she had already been on-again, off-again with Paul by the time she met Corin, too. She had no reason to look twice at Corin, with someone taller and fit, and with a real career in IT consulting locked in her personal orbit, and her locked in his. Which left only this: a slapdash home movie to liven up a Halloween lark; the closest Corin could ever get.

His beer was emptied. He briefly considered heading out back for another one, but watching Alyssa's inspired and virtuosa-freakout, he had no desire to be interrupted. Instead, he turned off the overhead lights, leaving only the irregular glow of the four TV screens. He could still hear a steady murmur from overhead, so he turned up the televisions showing actual movies. If this was the only way he could be alone with Alyssa, he wanted the illusion of perfect solitude.

On screen, Alyssa threw her head back and screamed. The recording was close to the end, and Corin told himself that when it ran out he would rejoin the party, salvage what he could of the night. He could claim he had turned on the televisions on impulse and been drawn into watching Alyssa against his will, but restarting the recording of her from the beginning would be a conscious choice to wallow in pathetic misery. And although a very large part of him wanted to, he had enough pride to stop himself from giving in to it. He hoped.

Alyssa continued calling for help that would never come. For the haunted house, they had balanced the volume of all the televisions so that Alyssa was audible, but just barely; her voice bound up in the mix of hissing snow and dialogue and music, just as her image was imprisoned in the confines of the screen. With *Frankenstein* and *Black Lagoon* turned up even louder now, Alyssa was drowned out. She almost seemed to realize it, as she stopped calling for help, only crying and slapping her open palms against the screen in abject frustration. The screen effect was a nice touch, courtesy of Blake, who had obliged Corin with a large, clear sheet of Lucite from his set-building stockpile. Corin had filmed Alyssa through it, removing the need for her to mime the front surface of her cage. Now, in the playback of her recorded gestures, fatigue was setting in, as the blows of her hands came slower, weaker. Her forehead thudded against the screen in defeat.

Corin didn't remember her doing that when he had filmed her.

How could he *not* remember? He had been just as riveted by the live performance as he was by the recording. He might have been a little distracted, since they were in her bedroom, and the backdrop was one of her black silk bed sheets, which Alyssa claimed was for special occasions. Certain thoughts, neither unpleasant nor entirely unbidden, had entered his mind, and might have distracted him. But he would have remembered a gesture as dramatic as her forehead hitting the screen. Wouldn't he?

Corin tried to remember what came next, how close the recording was to hitting the end. He had no idea. He stared at Alyssa's larger-than-life face on the screen. She stared back at him, her breath hitching, as if all her tears were spent, exhaustion overtaking primal terror. *Imaginary primal terror*, Corin reminded himself. He had given her the idea of being trapped inside a television, a tiny, isolated, solitary confinement, and she had run with it, but it *wasn't* real. No matter how distraught, how destroyed, Alyssa looked on the screen, it *wasn't real*. It wasn't her, it wasn't even an image of her, it was an image of a fictional character they had co-created and hadn't even bothered to give a backstory or name. Corin felt a twinge of retrograde guilt.

Alyssa's lips were moving, and some of the hopelessness had faded from her eyes, replaced by something compelling. Corin was inexplicably curious about what she was saying; the same word over and over again. Alyssa swallowed hard and spoke again; if the television had not been muted, Corin knew, her voice would have been louder, more insistent. She had a strong voice. He wanted to hear it.

The set filled with static had a silver knob the size of a pushpin, which he turned to the left until it clicked and the screen went dead; the snow condensing to a fading dot of light. The sets showing the monster movies had square power buttons, inset flush along their front frames, but Corin found himself reaching for the volume controls and turning them all the way down. He didn't necessarily want to be alone with the recording of Alyssa, he just wanted to hear what she was saying. When Richard Carlson and Colin Clive had been silenced, Corin found the buttons on the central set and turned the sound up.

"Corin?" Alyssa asked, her voice raw from screaming. "Corin?"

It was a different version of the recording; that was the only explanation. His mind might have wandered in Alyssa's bedroom, he might have drifted in and out of a daydream or two, but he could have been visualizing her naked and writhing in graphic detail and he still would have noticed if she had begun calling *his* name. Corin didn't know when Alyssa had recorded the additional footage, or why; most likely, Mitch had put her up to it, as a joke.

He reached over and behind the television to grab the camcorder and turn it off. He disconnected the coaxial and pulled out the camcorder, half-tempted to smash it on the garage floor, which would serve Mitch right. He stepped back, and the sight of Alyssa peering out at him froze him in place.

Alyssa onscreen.

The disconnected camcorder, in his hand.

No feed to the television.

Alyssa *onscreen*.

"Corin? Can you hear me?"

The amplified terror in her voice was painfully real, an icicle plunging into the base of his skull, making him blink, as cold pooled behind his eyes. Corin dropped the camcorder, not in anger, but because his limbs had gone numb, as if he were having some kind of waking dream, the kind where a monster was charging up behind him and he couldn't run, couldn't even move.

"Corin," Alyssa pleaded. "I don't know where I am, how I got here, I'm so freaked out right now. I think I see you out there. Is it you? Corin, please answer me!" Hysteria crept back into her voice, climbing through the upper registers, over the last few words.

He had to stop the video. He could hit the power button on the television, or flip the switch on the surge protector, but either of those would require getting close to the screen where Alyssa was trapped; a prospect that made his stomach pitch like the thought of wading into a river full of piranhas. Then he remembered the circuit breakers, behind a panel near the garage door. Corin edged along the fake wall, ignoring the cotton cobwebs tickling the back of his neck and the way the polyethylene clung to his clammy palms.

He reached the panel, opened it, and looked back at the television. Alyssa was staring at him, *directly* at him, and even when he turned away, he could feel her eyes on him like frozen barbwire scraping the back of his neck. Corin returned his attention to the decal affixed to the inside of the panel. In the distant, phosphorescent glow from the television screens, he found the grid square labeled GARAGE. His finger counted off circuit switches and pushed the twenty-third one.

Frankenstein went dead instantly, as did *Creature from the Black Lagoon*. The central screen remained bright, the only illumination in the garage, which had become a mausoleum, dark and silent, except for Alyssa's ragged breathing, and Corin's, mimicking her. No more noise drifted down from the party. Corin knew, with bone-deep certainty, that if he were to try the garage door, or the door back into the townhouse, neither one would open. Or, if they did, what he would see on the other side would be anything but the driveway or the Berber carpet of the basement hall.

He was already trapped – trapped in a miniature, haunted house – trapped with a television that had trapped Alyssa. Some alternate version of Alyssa, terrified of the inescapable, willing to be with Corin as a final, viable option. Maybe that was the Alyssa he deserved. Maybe he should embrace being trapped, so that he could finally embrace her.

Corin bent over and picked up the camcorder. His momentary fears that the short drop to the concrete had damaged it were allayed as soon as he thumbed the power button and the green diode appeared, floating in the darkness like an unmated firefly. He approached the televisions, reached over them, and felt for the coaxial cables attached to the main set.

"Hold on, Alyssa," he muttered shakily. "I'm coming."

He re-plugged the cables into the camcorder. The large screen went dark, not because it had finally turned off but because it was now showing exactly what the camera in Corin's hands could see; the featureless floor of a dark garage. He rotated the camcorder, aimed it at his face, which appeared on the television screen; sweaty hair matted, cheeks and chin and eye sockets smeared with crimson. He stared into the lens as if it were the black barrel of a shotgun. And when he pressed the record button, it was not unlike pulling a trigger.

SCENT

"COME, HENDRIX, COME ON, BUDDY!" Stephen Mills stood by the front door and jingled the leash, and Hendrix trotted over and sat obediently with his fuzzy chin uplifted. Stephen clipped the leash to the dog's collar, and led the way out the door.

Stephen enjoyed walking his dog, most of the time. A walk in the morning and a walk before bed gave his days a structure they might not otherwise have. There were weekends he would have wasted half the day sleeping in, or nights he could have stayed out too late at happy hour, except for Hendrix counting on him to get up or come home on time.

Clipping on Hendrix's leash and wandering through the grassy areas of their development (not his alone; Stephen thought of many things, like the two-bedroom townhouse, as belonging to both himself and his pet) had allowed Stephen to meet his neighbors, especially when their young children ran up and asked if they could pet the dog. Hendrix was a good-natured enough mutt to sit and flop his tail contentedly against the ground, and patiently endure the small hands that barely glided over his fur or patted the top of his head, and that tiny act of connection made Stephen feel like part of a community.

Hendrix had even helped Stephen meet his last girlfriend, when they had taken a walk in the park and Stephen found himself striking up a conversation with Becca Ryden, who had noticed Hendrix first, of course. The saying about women loving puppies and babies was true. The fact that things with Becca hadn't worked out wasn't the dog's fault at all, and his owner didn't nurse any grudges.

So usually Hendrix's twice-daily walks were part of a comforting routine, with inherent fringe benefits, and on warm summer evenings or crisp fall mornings the walks were a pleasure. But on dark, damp, cold, rainy January nights, there was nothing enjoyable about the experience. On those miserable nights, Stephen often wished the job could simply go without doing. Tonight was one of those nights.

Snow would have been better than rain, even if it that meant the night were colder. Snow tended not to fall as hard or feel as invasive. A white layer of snow on the ground and white layer of winter clouds overhead also made it much easier to see the dog droppings and scoop them into a plastic bag. But the clouds were dark above and the chill rain came down in fat, splattering droplets, and Stephen walked behind Hendrix with his head held down, his chin tight against his breastbone, trying to keep the rain out of his face. He was thwarted from time to time by gusts of winter wind that drove the rain sideways to spray his eyes and his tightly clamped lips. Stephen owned an umbrella, but kept it in his car, parked in front of his townhouse. He and Hendrix had set out from the back door of the house, for what Stephen had expected would be a quick dash, since both dog and man hated the cold and the wet about equally. But Hendrix was intent on taking a longer walk tonight, and the mutt's brown and black fur was soaked and slicked against his skin, and Stephen trudged behind him obligingly because Hendrix was a good dog and deserved a long walk if he wanted it. Stephen simply hoped it wouldn't be much longer.

Hendrix tugged insistently on the leash, his nose low to the ground. He had the scent of something, which always amazed

Stephen. Stephen was smart enough to know what anthropomorphism was, but fell into it more often than not regardless. Sometimes when he was sitting on the couch watching television and Hendrix padded over and set his chin on Stephen's knee and looked up at him with big, limpid green eyes, Stephen saw a soul inside the animal and thought of Hendrix as a complex, if inarticulate, four-legged person. Then they would go outside and Hendrix would catch a scent and instinct would take over, and Stephen would realize how differently they perceived the world, smells versus sights being only one example.

Stephen refused to exert too much control over Hendrix when they took their walks. He held tight enough to the leash to keep Hendrix from chasing rabbits at full speed, or to tug him past piles left by other dogs. But on a night like this, when they were alone in the open grassy area behind the townhouses, Stephen was more than willing to let his dog lead the way and simply follow along. They had the night to themselves, as all their neighbors were staying out of the cold and the rain. Stephen figured that if Hendrix smelled something and wanted to follow it to its source, he could indulge his dog. Hopefully, once the curiosity had been satisfied, Hendrix would attend to his doggie business and they could both get inside and dry off and warm up.

Staring straight down, with icy rain running down the back of his neck, Stephen remembered the few times he and Becca had walked the dog together, when she had started spending nights at their townhouse. Becca had actually asked Hendrix, always the intermediary, if she could sleep over the first time, and Stephen had answered on his dog's behalf, asking for her to join them on their pre-bedtime constitutional in exchange. At the time, Becca had agreed good-naturedly enough. But she had never really had much patience for the walks. The last time she had joined them had been a rainy night, which was enough to put her off altogether. The next night, the extent to which he enjoyed walking Hendrix alone was Stephen's first big clue that things with Becca were heading for an ending.

Hendrix surged forward, snuffling the ground unflaggingly, and yanked his master out of his recollections. Stephen wondered, not for the first time, what exactly dogs smelled on a rainy nights like tonight. Maybe it was the absence of scents that caught the dog's attention, the rain washing away all of the olfactory evidence left behind by the neighbors and the other neighborhood dogs and the family of foxes Stephen could sometimes see from his bedroom window early in the morning. Maybe Hendrix was determined to find a familiar scent. But no, that didn't seem right, since Hendrix had been hauling on his leash in more or less a straight line, not an exploring zigzag. It wasn't a scent Stephen's dog was looking for, it was the source of the scent.

As it had been almost since they had set out, Stephen's downturned field of vision was a dark, featureless smear of rain-drenched grass bisected by the fabric of Hendrix's leash. Suddenly there were larger shapes, bouncing as the rain pelted them, horsetails and saplings. Stephen and Hendrix had reached the tree line where the townhouse development ended and the woods began, and Hendrix was still pulling hard and sniffing hard, drawing Stephen in.

For a few seconds Stephen thought about turning around. The walk had already taken longer than he had expected, and he was sick of being cold and wet, and the farther they went into the woods the longer it would take to get back to the house. Not to mention the real possibility of tripping over a root or a rock or something in the untended areas between the trees, ending up bruised or bloodied and covered in mud on top of everything else. There was no good reason to let Hendrix have his way on it.

Except that Stephen had been working late all week in a desperate attempt to keep a project on schedule, which left Hendrix at home alone longer than he was used to. And it had been cold and rainy this morning (although it had been a little warmer, and the rain had not been falling quite so hard) and Stephen had taken Hendrix on an abbreviated walk then. Stephen thought of all the sacrifices Hendrix made, subsisting on dry dog food rather than fresh meat, and submitting to baths, and restraining himself rather than jumping up on company, and it was anthropomorphism again because Hendrix didn't think of those things as sacrifices or think at all, but Stephen thought of them that way and thought he needed to balance the scales. He followed Hendrix into the woods.

A few yards in there laid a large fallen tree trunk, surrounded by empty beer cans and beer bottles and cigarette butts and snack-sized bags of potato chips and McDonald's and Taco Bell wrappers. Some of the garbage was practically ancient, cans bleached bone white and bottles half-buried in the mud, but some was clearly more recent, the foil interior of a bag of Lays still shiny, the lipstick on a Camel filter still visible, as if a group of teenagers had been sneaking drinks and smokes just the night before. Stephen figured that Hendrix had finally found what he was looking for, maybe an irresistible bit of ground beef still stuck to a burrito wrapper.

Hendrix ignored the party trash completely. He strained on the leash, heading deeper into the woods. Stephen followed.

Deeper in the woods, the trees were taller and broader. Stephen was still soaked and freezing, but the rain no longer reached him here, and he was actually grateful to Hendrix for pulling him into the cover of the trees. He rolled his head on his neck to work out the crick that had developed while holding it down. He looked around, but in the darkness the depths and distances of the woods were hard to make out. He tucked his head down again, finding the ground less disorienting.

Stephen realized that he was going to have to be cautious once Hendrix finally found what he was looking for. When that happened Stephen knew Hendrix would come to a stop, and either try to eat something or mark something. In either case, when they both stopped it would be easy for Stephen to lose track of which direction they had been heading. He still believed Hendrix was pulling him in a straight line, more or less, and the way back home through the dark, deceptive woods would be a straight shot in reverse. As long as he didn't get too turned around when Hendrix stopped leading.

Could Hendrix lead him home? There had been a few times when Stephen let Hendrix off his leash. It was a lot like parole: time off for good behavior. And usually Hendrix was angelic, staying close to Stephen even without the tether on his collar, fetching a stick picked up off the ground, or a ball if Stephen had the foresight to bring one. But occasionally a rabbit or another dog would catch Hendrix's attention and Hendrix would race off, and Stephen would call Hendrix's name until he came back. And Hendrix always came back. Hendrix knew where they lived, and it didn't matter if it was dark or pouring down rain, because Hendrix could find his way. Any dog could.

Would he want to? As soon as the question occurred to him, Stephen dismissed it as ridiculous. Why wouldn't he want to? Was there any reason to think that Hendrix would prefer to spend the night on a bed of soggy, chilly leaves in the middle of the woods, rather than in their townhouse on his oversized doggie pillow? At the moment Hendrix was surging through the undergrowth, straining at his leash, snuffling at the muddy forest floor, but any second now he would find the source of his fascination. And once that happened, once Hendrix was finally done with his walk, the dog would be in just as much of a hurry to get back as Stephen. Maybe more.

All of that made perfect sense, but the thought would not stop nagging in the back of Stephen's mind. He couldn't shake the sense that he and Hendrix were lost and might not make it home. No, not might. The sense that they would not make it home.

Stephen forced himself to look straight ahead, from side to side and back over his shoulder. The woods looked exactly the same in every direction, impenetrable, inescapable, charcoal slashes of tree trunks against the velvet black of night. All the detail had gone out of the world, washed away in darkness. Stephen could hear his sneakers snapping twigs and squelching through saturated earth, and Hendrix's paws scratching through the leaves and grasses. He could hear Hendrix's persistent sniffing of the ground, and his own surprisingly rapid breathing. Other than that, the woods were silent.

Stephen halted. "Okay, Hendrix," he said, "that's enough. Let's go back." Even to his own ears, Stephen sounded unconvinced. The gnawing unease he did not want to acknowledge could barely edge out the desire to make up his shortcomings as Hendrix's owner, the desire he had been nursing all day at the office.

Hendrix exerted himself against the taut constraint of his leash, and Stephen had to take a step forward, another step deeper into the woods, to steady and brace himself. Stephen rotated his wrist to wrap the leash around his hand a few times and pulled Hendrix back. Hendrix strained again, standing up on quivering hind legs and pawing at the cold, sodden air. The dog whimpered insistently.

Stephen marveled at the strength in Hendrix's muscles, that a creature only a quarter of Stephen's weight could hold his own in this tug-of-war. Of course he had powerful little legs, the bursts of speed he showed at a flat-out run left no room for doubt on that. Just because Hendrix was gentle and submissive almost all of the time didn't mean that he was weak or easily dominated. When they played catch and Hendrix was excited, he could clamp down his jaws with savage force that made prying out a tennis ball almost impossible. He had been bred to be a pet, but all dogs had been bred from wild, rough, violent animals, hadn't they? That ancestral creature of the wilderness was still inside of Hendrix. And now Hendrix was in the wilderness. And Stephen was in it with him.

Stephen thought about forcing Hendrix to turn around and dragging him all the way back to the townhouse. But if Hendrix put up a fight, that would be exhausting as well as heartless. And if Hendrix refused to cooperate, then Stephen couldn't count on his dog to lead him home. Or Stephen could acquiesce, follow Hendrix a little bit further, surely only just a little bit further, and once the dog was satisfied then both of them could go home.

Stephen started walking forward, practically dragged along by Hendrix. Even though Stephen was no longer offering any resistance, Hendrix continued to whimper. "It's okay, buddy," Stephen said, wanting it to be true for both their sakes.

Then Hendrix stopped, and Stephen stopped behind him. All four of the dog's legs were locked rigidly, and his wet ears stood at attention. The ground in front of his forepaws gave way to a pitch-dark gap in the earth, what looked like the opening to a massive underground burrow.

"What are you hunting, Hendrix?" Stephen asked.

The growl came from behind Stephen as if in answer, low and deep and imposing. The sound was too big to come from a fox or a coyote, which might reasonably live around the area, too big for a bear, which had no business here at all. More than anything, the hungry, greedy, self-satisfied growl was too easy for Stephen to hear anthropomorphically, as belonging to something with instincts and primitive urges but also thought and will and malice.

A stygian hole that went deeper than Stephen could know lay before him, and an angry and impossibly large beast had somehow prowled up behind him, between him and home. Stephen ran to his right, blindly crashing through the woods, pulling on Hendrix's leash. Everything around him seemed to shake violently, but Stephen couldn't tell if it was because his heart was pounding hard enough to rattle his eyeballs in his skull or because the beast was thundering behind him in pursuit. Stephen simply ran.

When the claws dug into his back like a row of sharpened meathooks, Stephen screamed and shut his eyes. The weight of the beast was on him a moment later, driving him down to the ground. The impact blasted the air from his lungs and drove the claws deeper into his body, where Stephen could feel them scraping his ribs and puncturing his lungs, ripping open pure pain that would define the last few moments of Stephen's life. His last coherent thought, before his whole world became agony and fetid stink of predator's breath was that he hoped Hendrix would run away, faster than he had ever run before.

The beast lay on the ground, with the body of its prey between its talons. It placed one claw on the prey's stomach to hold the carcass in place, and used another to snap off ribs, one by one, exposing the glistening red heart. The beast dug out the heart, tore a section of leathery meat from it, and passed the section to its companion. The second, smaller beast took the heart meat and bit into it.

"Tonight is the perfect weather for hunting," the larger beast said, then rent the heart with its fangs and bolted down a bloody chunk. "The rain makes it easier to find the kind of food I most enjoy. Do you understand?"

The smaller beast swallowed its mouthful of heart. "Most humans stay indoors on a night like tonight. Fewer come out. How can fewer make it easier?"

"So long as the few that venture out are the right variety, all the others may stay in their dens. It takes a special breed of human to indulge a pet on a night such as tonight," the larger beast said, before slurping another blood-slicked strip of heart meat between its teeth.

"Dogs make good lures," the smaller beast said.

"They do," the larger beast agreed. Another pause, another meaty smack of tongue and teeth against the dwindling remains of heart meat. "Humans are so sensitive to the weather, most of them are less likely to put the happiness of their pet above their discomfort in the wind and rain. But the few who still defer to the will of an animal even as they shiver and curse the elements … ah, those are feasts. A night like tonight might yield no prey at all. But if it does, then that heart will be utterly delicious."

"What will you do with the dog?" the smaller beast asked, eyeing the last scrap of heart between the larger beast's claws.

"Turn it loose," the larger beast replied. "Sooner or later another human will find it, and care for it, and grow to love it, perhaps so much that the human will follow the dog anywhere through any kind of weather. The only thing better than a potential lure is a proven one, one that already knows what to do when it finds our scent."

THE HALF-HIDDEN FACE

I ARRIVED AT THE OLD CHURCH, a dark mass of fieldstone and slate jutting from the top of a hill near Lake Beryl, and spotted the couple waiting for me just inside the black wrought iron fence encircling the grounds. The man, Henry Waddell, I had met previously, but it was the woman who waved in greeting as I reached the end of the steep and winding road that was effectively one long driveway for the church. I parked my Corolla next to the only other car there, an Infiniti. The black luxury sedan gleamed like it had just been driven off the showroom floor; my ride was a dingy gray and sported a cracked front bumper that probably wouldn't survive a carwash.

As I got out of my car, the woman strode through the gate and closed the distance between us. She was offering her manicured hand before I had a chance to shut my door. "Mr. Oakes! I'm Lydia Colm."

"Pleasure. Call me Kellan," I told her, entirely out of a general aversion to formalities. It's bad business to flirt with a client's main squeeze, but Lydia seemed like she'd appreciate my friendliness in response to her own. I had already determined that keeping Lydia happy was one of Waddell's main goals in life, and making both of them happy would be mine, at least until I got paid.

Waddell joined us and gave me a perfunctory handshake as well. "Thanks for coming. Drive all right? Find the place okay?" he asked. He was no longer nervously twisting the button that strained to keep his sport coat closed over his protruding gut, as he had the entire time we'd met in my office, but that was because his fingers were occupied interlacing with Lydia's. The eyes behind his dark-framed glasses and the set of the mouth dwarfed by his round, ruddy cheeks still conveyed a forlorn discomfort. I instinctively wanted to put Waddell at ease, but since I had been hired to settle a matter of some dispute between the couple, I wasn't sure if I would ultimately make things better or worse.

"No snags," I assured Waddell. I looked towards the church, taking in the old graveyard full of small headstones, inscriptions eroded and overgrown with lichen. A single gnarled willow grew in the middle of the grave markers. Beyond that, dense trees enclosed the site, framing it like the edges of a fairytale illustration. The old growth treetops stretched higher than the steepled bell tower of the church. The grounds were isolated, a small grassy island amid a sea of foliage that would be spectacular come fall, when Lydia Colm might become Lydia Waddell, depending on what was about to happen. The church had been built long enough ago that it probably qualified as a historic landmark, but it had survived the relentless march of progress mainly thanks to the undesirability of its location. I was sure it had seemed only appropriate to the pious founders, placing the house of God as close to Heaven as the terrain allowed. But it was much more cost-effective to build strip malls and McMansion developments someplace flat than someplace conical, and the areas of least resistance had therefore been targeted instead. I could hear my mother's voice and a lifetime of lectures about the balanced and peaceful coexistence modeled for us by nature above all as I appraised the site, but family bias aside I thought I had it more right than not. "The church really is lovely," I said.

"I think so too," Lydia said, nudging Waddell with her shoulder.

"I never said it wasn't," Waddell defended himself.

"Shall we take a look at the carving?" I asked.

"Yes!" Lydia beamed. She led the way into the church. I looked to Waddell, who gestured to insist that I follow her while he brought up the rear.

The church was cool and dim, sunlight filtered through the recessed stained glass windows. The same irregular pattern of the fieldstone walls was visible from inside, and the carpet was a deep moss green. Lydia strode down the aisle quickly, turned left, crossed along the front pew, and stopped at the baptismal font in the corner beside the pulpit. She stood next to it, already projecting something like pride of ownership, as Henry and I caught up.

The font was a single piece of sculpted stone, not entirely out of place within the dark gray masonry of the church. Clearly it was of different, more ancient origins, a product of late Iron Age Europe. Hard to say how it had come to make the passage to the new world; the church had no records relating to the provenance of the font, and I had been hired to shed the light of my expertise on the subject.

I squatted down in front of the font, orienting the level of my sightline with the carvings around the outer wall of the basin. Bas-relief figures of various biblical icons stood out, the lion lying down with the lamb, workers in vineyards, birds nesting in the branches of the mustard tree. And dominating the front of the stone ring was the graven image of the Green Man. The demonic face looked completely out of place in a church, although I supposed that from farther away than a few inches the gray carving would blend into the monochrome surface of the font, the details too fine for the seated congregation to discern. Up close, though, it was high-grade nightmare fuel, appropriate enough for a primitive, awe-inspiring forest spirit. From my vantage point I could make out everything, the wicked curves of the leaf blades that made them look like devil's horns, the wild and merciless gorgon eyes, the gaping maw that would readily swallow a soul if it weren't already disgorging a riot of vines that fed back into the monstrous tangle of vegetation that formed the shape of the face. It was the ferocious bogeyman I always feared would look back at me if I gave in to the temptation to check what was in my closet or under my bed in the middle of the night. At least, that was the form my childhood boogeyman took; if you weren't raised by a practicing druid priestess, you might have had a different experience.

The whole reason Henry Waddell had hired me, out of all the private investigators around, was because I knew a thing or two about the druids who venerated the Green Man. Actually I know close to everything there is to know about druidic lore, since I was raised to be one. I struck out on my own to become a private investigator only after a couple of formative decades immersed in the tradition failed to convince that it was the life path I wanted to be on. But even after declaring my independence, the reputation attached to my name remained. Technically it was the reputation of my mother, Foltchain of the Oak. Being the son of a renowned and powerful druid brought me a fair amount of side business in between routine cases of surveillance and process serving. The side business tended to involve talking crows landing on my windowsill, or lutins climbing up through the vents of the old brownstone where I leased part of the upper floor. One time a water nymph named Lerna flowed right out of the tap in my private bathroom to ask for my help in a property dispute over a semi-sacred glade. But every once in a while, amidst the normal men and women with their mundane problems and the forest folk with their unique ones, a human walked through the door of my office with a problem only a druid's son could properly address.

I looked deeper into the stony snarl of the Green Man carving. I didn't want to, the fearsome repulsion was threatening to drive me not just away from the font but right out of the church, but I had a job to do and I wasn't a child anymore. The artistry was old, anyone could see that. More important, it was authentic. It had been fashioned by someone well-versed in druidic lore, not an expert in copying but an actual druid. The difference was that the former might have gotten every nuanced line of the leaves and vines exactly right, but in the end would have left only exquisitely crafted stone behind. This was different. This was power, invoked with sacred intent. This was real, and more worrisome than I had bargained for.

I straightened up and turned back to Lydia and Henry. I had a strong urge to tell them both that it was a clever forgery. I could make something up, say I could see telltale signs of modern masonry tools, or insist that a certain combination of leaf edge patterns indicated a more recent interpretation of the iconography. I wanted to shield them both from harm. But I would have been lying, invoking a kind of blasphemy, an invitation to the trouble I was trying to avoid. "It's real," I nodded.

My honesty was immediately rewarded with a grin from Lydia. Henry had the look of a man who knew that trying to argue the point would be futile, somewhere between feeling beaten down and honestly relieved that the matter was settled. "Thank you for your help, Mr. Oakes."

I didn't bother to answer, since Lydia had thrown her arms around Henry's neck and I doubted he would have heard me. Instead, I flashed a sidelong look at the font, and at the Green Man. I felt as though I had barely escaped some kind of trap, but I still didn't like the way the shrouded old god was glowering at me.

Even though I could have made the drive home that same day, Waddell insisted on putting me up in a nearby hotel overnight. He had already paid for my room, and handed me the key outside the church. I chalked it up to his high-income lifestyle, which left him accustomed to not feeling like he had gotten the best service or products unless he paid through the nose for them. I felt no guilt accepting his largesse, figuring he'd probably write it all off as tax deductions related to real estate investments. And the thought of clean sheets and blackout curtains was more enticing than my bachelor apartment any day.

I stretched out on the king size bed and turned on the television to kill some time before the monumental decision of room service versus poking around the local restaurants. I flipped through the channels but nothing grabbed me, meaning nothing pulled my attention away from trying to figure out exactly what was going on with Lydia Colm and Henry Waddell.

I ran down what I knew, based on the conversation Waddell and I had had in my office, when he had explained exactly what services he required and why. Lydia was fascinated with the Green Man, had been ever since she spent a summer abroad in France and visited the abbey-church in Vendôme. Even though it's significantly easier to find historical examples of the Green Man in Europe than here in the States, Lydia enjoyed spending weekends letting Waddell drive for hours to remote folk art museums or rustic immigrant communities trying to locate the few that managed to migrate across the Atlantic.

Waddell specified her interest was in real Green Men, not the cheerful poly resin masks mass-produced to be mounted on backyard trees above the hammock, or the Jack in the Green on a keychain sold at the local New Age crystals-and-incense shop. The thrill of the chase drew Lydia, trying to find authentic Green Men amidst the appropriations and reinterpretations, the homages and the tchotchkes. She was convinced they had found one in this remote church in the woods, and wanted Waddell to buy it for her.

I picked up on a few things that Waddell hadn't said outright, but hadn't tried very hard to hide, either. I could tell he was smitten with Lydia. I could also tell that rather than ask himself how a guy like him got lucky with a girl like her, he already knew the answer came down to his net worth. I wasn't one to judge, not with my personal life and financial stability perpetually in poor-to-nonexistent shape.

I could also tell that he thought Lydia's fixation on the Green Man was ridiculous, but he was willing to indulge it within reason, like the weekend hunting expeditions, but not without limits, and buying an antique stone font was near that boundary. He had tried to talk her out of it by observing they had no place to keep the font. She had countered that he could go ahead and buy the entire church. He had upped the ante by saying that if he did that, they might as well get married there. She went all in and agreed, even offering to forego a traditional engagement ring if he would buy the church, font and all. Waddell hadn't been bluffing. He wanted to marry her and could afford the church, especially once some inquiries around town revealed that the old stone structure was no longer being used regularly; a more modern and more convenient downtown facility now housed services for the faithful. The site was good for picturesque photo ops but most of the locals believed it would be demolished sooner or later.

Waddell had been out-argued but put one final condition on the deal: an independent verification of the Green Man's authenticity. That was the gig he offered me, and I accepted in part because I wanted to make sure Waddell wasn't being completely scammed by a goldbricker. Another part of me wondered, if it was a scam, what Lydia's angle was. The rest of me thought it sounded like easy money.

Not only had it turned out that Lydia wasn't scamming Waddell, that the Green Man font was as real as they get, but Lydia didn't seem much like a goldbricker. Now that I had seen them together, it wasn't totally laughable to think that she loved Waddell, that she wanted to marry the man and not just the money. And Waddell wanted to be with her, too, and the demands that got me involved were more an example of what a control freak he was than any reluctance to seal the deal with Lydia.

Still, if Lydia was into Waddell, then I was left to wonder why she hadn't backed down about the font when he balked. If she wasn't trying to pull something over on him, I wasn't sure what was motivating her. Her Green Man safaris made for as good a hobby as any, but her obsession with owning one had to go deeper. The explanation I kept circling back to, the only one I could think of, was that her interest wasn't art, or history. It was the powers that were the birthright of the druids.

I could tell from the moment I met Waddell that he didn't

believe in little woodland spirits, or the Green Man, the granddaddy of them all. I couldn't fault him for that. Most people are skeptical of anything remotely spiritual or unscientific, entertaining the possibilities only if their own experiences happen to stray outside of official common knowledge, wandering into some cultic ritual get-together, a chance encounter with a satyr. Waddell didn't seem the type to deviate from the gated community and business district paths enough to so much as catch a glimpse of a stray sprite. Nothing chases away the woodland folk quite like the regular use of modern landscaping equipment. For the purposes of the job, as far as he was concerned, that didn't matter. Somehow, he had heard about a connection between myself and druidism, and decided I was the man for the job. All he really wanted was someone who would give him a little cover for his decision to make a wildly romantic gesture and buy his girlfriend a church.

But maybe Lydia believed in the Green Man, and the worship of his terrible potency. And if so, taking ownership of the font might just be the first step in attempting to tap into forces no one should engage with recklessly. I wondered if Lydia knew what she was risking.

The phone rang. Waddell invited me for a toast in the hotel bar, to celebrate the fact that the church had accepted his offer on a handshake deal. The money had already changed hands, and the paperwork would be finalized and filed within days.

I was never one to turn down a drink, but once I got downstairs, I wondered if this would have been a good time to kill the streak. Waddell slumped morosely on a stool at the end of the bar. He had shed his sport coat and the sleeves of his polo shirt dug into the puffy flesh of his arms. He saw me approaching in the mirror behind the rows of bottles, looked back over his shoulder and saluted me with barware that was nearly empty. He turned around to get the bartender's attention, then held him in place until I arrived and placed my own order for a seven and seven.

Waddell slid me a check for my services rendered as I settled onto the stool beside him. I pocketed it as he asked, "Opposites attract, or common ground?"

"Pardon?"

"What do you think makes it work?" Waddell clarified, not exactly slurring but with a fuzzed edge in his voice. "Do people work better together when they're different or similar?"

"I think it depends," I said.

The bartender unobtrusively dropped off our drinks and retreated to the far end of the bar. I took a sip and waited for Waddell to go on. "Lyddie and I... don't agree on much. Like each other's company, but what we do—how we spend our time—it's like taking turns. Dragging each other along. She calls it 'getting me out of my comfort zone'."

"Allegedly a good thing," I said.

"She says I'm not very good at it."

I picked up my glass, but a bad feeling was spreading through my gut and putting a sour taste in my mouth that wouldn't mix well with whiskey and soda. "You think she was planning something like this for a while? Buying the whole church to get the font falls well outside your comfort zone?"

Waddell stared at his drink with guilty eyes. He and Lydia were supposed to present a united front, and he'd failed. "I ... I don't see the fuss over some sculpture, however old it is. I thought maybe ... maybe she wanted to show me she could make money, find something undervalued, buy for a little, sell for a lot ... but I don't care about that. She was just so ... insistent?" He looked to me for a lifeline.

"I think she wanted to keep it," I said.

"Well, she got what she wanted, gotta hand it to her for that," Waddell said, raising his glass toward me.

I declined to reciprocate the gesture. "Where is she right now?"

"Lyddie?" Waddell blinked, then frowned as he realized I was going to leave his proposed toast hanging. He took a gulp of his drink and said, "Sleeping. We were getting ready for bed... and I... I knew I wouldn't be able to sleep, not after just making the most boneheaded real estate deal of my life. Not without a little help."

He sloshed his cocktail meaningfully.

"Did she suggest you get yourself a little help?"

"Did she...?"

"Was it her idea that you leave the room?" I pressed.

"No, I... I mean, she might have mentioned that I sounded like I could use a nightcap but I was thinking the same thing..." Waddell protested unsteadily.

"Mr. Waddell, listen to me," I said. "I don't think your girlfriend's interest in the Green Man is just some hobby. She doesn't want to own it to start some collection. She wants to possess it because she thinks it's powerful." Waddell made an effort to keep his gaze on me but he was playing catch up in his mind. I pressed on anyway. "She's right, it is powerful. There's ... magic, for lack of a better word, in that font. Powerful magic. Dangerous magic, more dangerous than I think Lydia realizes. And I think there's a good chance she's up at the church right now, that she kicked you out to get some liquid sleep aid so that she could run off to the church without you noticing."

"That's... that's... " Waddell was rummaging in his pocket and couldn't find the object his hand sought and the proper word to finish his thought at the same time. He pulled out his cell phone, called Lydia's, and hit her voicemail. He asked the bartender for the number of the hotel's front desk, dialed it, and asked to be connected with his room. More unanswered ringing followed. He set his phone down on the bar and frowned at its inert screen.

"We have to get to the church and stop her," I said.

"No," he shook his head. "No, she's not at the church, that's ... crazy. Let's... let's just finish our drinks, I'll call her again in a few minutes, I'm sure she's fine..."

"She's not fine, not for long," I said. I pulled out the check he had given me. "Look, I will bet you my payday that she is up at the church. If I'm wrong I'll hand this right back to you. But I doubt I'm wrong. I'd go see by myself but I have a feeling she'll listen to you sooner than me. So come on."

Waddell swirled his drink. "Bottoms up," he said before

downing what remained in his glass.

"I'll drive," I said, leaving my drink where it sat. Waddell sulked as he followed me out of the bar.

I pulled up next to Waddell's car, angled carelessly in front of the church, and killed the engine, wondering how I was going to motivate Waddell out of the shotgun seat. But Waddell snapped into action and was out of the car before me, leading the way to the church entrance. I grew painfully aware of how little I wanted to go back in there, my heart racing and my breath ragged. I took an extra second to pull my SIG Pro from the glove compartment and check the safety before I followed.

A pair of burning candles on the altar gave off just enough light to make the immediate area around them visible, but most of the church was in shadows. Lydia was in front of the baptismal font, with her back to us, luminous in a white nightgown. She must have bolted from the hotel the same minute that Waddell had hit the lobby, running down a stairwell to a side exit while he rode the elevator down. She turned around as Waddell passed through the front door, and started to ask, "Henry? What …?" Then she caught sight of me over her boyfriend's shoulder, and her eyes narrowed to venomous slits. "You."

"Lydia, stop," I said, drawing a bead on her along the sight of my gun and slowly walking down the aisle. I tried not to let my face betray the fact that I had no desire to hurt her. Unfortunately, an empty threat of harm was the only leverage I had.

"You," she sneered at me, "were just supposed to be some flake who would back me up, collect your fee, and hit the road." She never took her eyes off me as she slowly backed around the font, ultimately positioning herself in the corner behind it, shielded by it. "You weren't supposed to catch on."

I advanced steadily, trying to think of a better way for it all to play out, my brain refusing to cooperate. The closer I got to the font, to the Green Man's frozen primal scream, the more I felt like

I was going to pass out. I reached the front pew with little black hinkypunks dancing in my peripheral vision.

Staring me down, Lydia dipped her hand into the font, lifted it and let water trickle through her fingers to splash back into the basin, the basin that had been dry that afternoon. I doubted the ancient font was connected to any plumbing, and even if it were, Lydia wouldn't fill it with tap water, not if she knew what she were doing. She would have gone to a nearby stream, a babbling brook lined with stones and tree roots, and filled some container with water that hadn't been filtered and stripped of its leaf bits and algae, insect eggs and fish scales and frog slime. I was gradually accepting that Lydia knew exactly what she was doing. Or she thought she did, which was worse.

"Lydia, it's not too late to walk away," I told her, my mouth dry.

"Mr. Oakes?" Waddell prodded from somewhere behind me. I ignored him, steadying my breathing and tightening my grip on the gun.

Lydia smiled tauntingly and closed her eyes. She cupped her hand and lifted a palmful of water up over her head. Tiny rivulets ran down her golden hair, one tracing its way from her scalp down the delicate line of her nose, collecting in a fat droplet at the tip. She licked it away.

"Mr. Oakes?" Waddell tried again, closer now. I looked back over my shoulder to tell him to stay clear, and his backhand connected solidly with my jaw. I went down with the church spinning around me, landed against the base of the altar. "I don't appreciate you pointing a gun at my lady."

"Thank you, Henry," I heard Lydia say while my eyes were still shut against the pain throbbing through my skull. "Please know that I never lied about loving you. I never, ever wanted to hurt you. But some things are bigger than love. Please understand."

"I understand," Waddell assured her. He sounded unsure of himself and uncomfortably needy for her affection, the way I imagined he would have sounded whenever it was Lydia's turn to get her way and he was trying to be a good sport. He didn't sound drunk at all.

"No, you don't, my darling," Lydia said. "You can't understand because we're all trapped in a legacy of willful ignorance. If mankind hadn't lost their way, if the covenant had extended unbroken... I wouldn't have had to lie about any of this. But the lies were easier for you to believe than the truth. It doesn't matter, not after tonight. Not after I receive the Green Man's blessing."

I pried my eyelids open just enough to see her plunging both hands into the water, cupping them and lifting them up. I caught snatches of the baptismal rite of Blodeuwedd as she recited them in a low, lilting voice. My eyes flicked to Waddell. He had picked up my gun and pointed it in my direction with his finger on the trigger, but his attention was fully on Lydia. A satisfied smile dimpled his babyface cheeks. Lydia brought her hands to her lips and drank the water in a great gulping swallows, tilting her head back.

The candles on the altar flickered, as if something invisible yet powerful had moved through the church. Shadows reeled chaotically against the walls, churning up another wave of vertigo. I waited for it to pass, forcing myself to keep my eyes open.

Lydia filled her lungs with a deep breath, triggering a coughing fit. She bent over the font, her wet blonde hair hanging down against the sides of her face like curtains. She coughed and coughed, and it wasn't the sound of phlegm or water tickling her throat, it was the rattle of something more solid lodged in her airway. Waddell made no move to help her.

"She's choking," I managed to say, my tongue feeling swollen and heavy.

"Yes, she is," Waddell agreed.

Lydia was doubled over the font, gasping for breath and hacking air out against the obstruction, as she raised her head to look at him. Two bright green shoots were emerging from her mouth, growing rapidly in length as they snaked down her cheeks and past her chin. Leaves budded and unfurled from the tendrils.

"H-h-he-en..." Lydia tried to say through the plant matter disgorging from her mouth, but it came out as little more than a garbled cry. The shoots emerging from her mouth multiplied, now four runners, now six. Her eyes widened as two more green sprigs began to grow, one from the outer corner of each eye, with rivulets of blood running down Lydia's face as the branchlets pushed through.

And still, Henry Waddell appeared supremely unconcerned, a curious onlooker at best. "You knew," I said, as new profusions of leafy vegetation sprouted from Lydia's hands and forearms where the water had bathed her flesh. "You wanted her to do this. You drugged me. Had the bartender put something in my drink. So I wouldn't stop her."

"I doubt you could have stopped her," Waddell shrugged. "But once I realized how much you understood, I knew you needed to be eliminated." He threw me an annoyed look. "If you had just finished your damn drink, we wouldn't be having this conversation."

"If you had shot me by now, we wouldn't be having this conversation," I pointed out, pushing myself up from prone to a seated position.

"Pulling the trigger myself would be a desperate option," Waddell told me. "One I hardly need resort to now that I have my very own primeval force of nature to command."

The foliage encasing Lydia's arms crept higher and higher, past her elbows. Her mouth was now a permanent O, lips prised apart by shoots too numerous to count, curlicuing through the air. Trembling slips of green grew from her nostrils as well. The shoots from her eyes were tracing up along her temples and across her forehead, and tendrils newly emergent from her ears poked up out of her hair like verdant antlers. The front of her white nightgown was becoming deeper red as blood flowed from her ears, her nose, her eyes, her mouth, down her chin and neck. I realized I was waiting for her to close her eyes, for either the pain or the fear to overwhelm her and shut her down, but she never so much as blinked as the greenery consumed her from the inside out.

The clinging leaves and vines garlanded her body like a second skin, and when more than half of her body had been transformed, she stepped out from behind the font. She walked towards Waddell, moving with a weird but stately grace, leaving a trail of bloody droplets on the floor as she proceeded. Her hair was completely obscured by leaves, as was most of her face, except her eyes and her teeth. Her eyes remained wide and blue, seeing everything in new ways that I could only guess at through some combination of stories my mother had told me and my wildest imaginings. Her teeth were changed, larger and wider and more pointed, like a bear's, and stained with chlorophyll.

Waddell backed into the aisle, clearing the way for Lydia to approach me. But it wasn't Lydia, not anymore. It was the embodiment of something not at all human, despite the corporeal shape it took and the body it had co-opted. Call it the Green Man or the Green Woman, it didn't really matter, it dwelled outside gender constructs and beyond everything that we animals know about life. The weirdest deep-sea jellyfish has more in common with humanity than the Green Man ever did or would. And it turned away from me, to the aisle.

"No, no, no," Waddell chided her. "First things first. Mr. Oakes needs killing, followed by burial in a shallow grave in the woods, both of which I am delegating to you."

The Green Woman gave no indication that she understood him as she proceeded slowly up the aisle. Waddell wheeled on me, shoving the muzzle of the pistol closer to my face. "Why isn't she listening?" he demanded.

"She won't listen to you, or anybody, not any more," I answered. "She can't."

"She has to!" Waddell said. "Tell me what to do!"

"Tell you how to get her to kill me?" I asked.

"You're dead either way," Waddell sneered. "I would think getting to go at the hands of the tree-god would be a dream come true for someone like you."

I let my silence speak to my skepticism about that theory.

"I need that thing. I need the edge," Waddell said. "If I can control it, I will make sure that it only comes forth when I say so, and disposes of people who on some level deserve to die. But if I can't, it's going to do whatever it pleases, kill whomever it stumbles across. Isn't that right? How do you feel about that?"

I felt incensed about that, almost as incensed as I was at Waddell for using hypothetical innocent victims to bolster his own argument. But he was angry, too, and he was starting to get a look in his eyes that I recognized, the look of someone who feels a steadily rising urge to pull the trigger the longer they hold a gun in their hand. "You have to ... reestablish contact with her," I said. "Eye contact, physical contact, as much as you can. You can't just dictate to her."

Waddell narrowed his eyes at me, weighing what I had said. He glanced up the aisle, where the Green Woman had nearly reached the front doors. He hurried after her, grabbed her shoulder, stopped her in her tracks.

"Lydie, please," he said, the cutthroat ruthlessness banished from his voice, the obsequious suitor restored. He stepped around her, putting them nose to nose. He grasped the sides of the Green Woman's face, barrel of the gun flattening the leaves on the right side of her head, his fingers digging deeply into the left side's vegetation. "I know what you wanted from the Green Man. And I know this ... rejuvenation ... was not what you expected. But remember who you are. Remember us. Remember me, and trust me, and I'll take care of you. I promise."

The Green Woman wrapped the fibrous bundles that had once been her hands around his throat. Green runners constricted around his fleshy double chin, elevating the man so that his twitching feet drummed only empty air. Waddell clawed at the Green Woman's wrist and forearms, drawing beads of sap but no other outward reaction. The Green Woman had her back to me, but I imagined her staring at him with her bulbous blue eyes, indifferent to his shocked indignation and his difficulty breathing.

The stalk arms of the Green Woman bent, drawing Waddell close enough for their mouths to meet. The moment their lips touched, the candlelight in the church intensified, as if the flames on each wick were intensified by an influx of ritual energy. I could see the sharp-edged foliate covering of the Green Woman, shining like malachite in the firelight, and I could see the soft pale skin of Henry Waddell's arms as he began his own transformation. His dermis blanched and sagged, deflating like popped balloons, then darkened and grew pitted and crumbled away to dust. In a matter of moments his musculature and skeleton completely decomposed, and his clothes fell to the floor of the church amid a scattering of mineral remains that glittered like pixie trails.

I watched the Green Woman glide out of the church, to fade into the surrounding forest, her proper domain. When she was gone, I waited a full minute sitting on the edge of the dais, then got to my feet and retrieved my gun.

As I walked from the church to my car I listened to the woodland night sounds, the near-mindless crosstalk of crickets and frogs, the occasional yip of a fox, the unceasing flutter of wind through the leaves in the canopy. I didn't hear anything that sounded like the Green Woman, not that I expected to. I thought for half a second about sticking around trying to tie up loose ends, but realized that would be pointless. I knew what Lydia Colm and Henry Waddell had done to each other, but I'd never know why, exactly.

Those kinds of questions were moot, anyway. Henry Waddell was dead and Lydia Colm no longer existed. Eventually the police would come looking for them, but any clues they might find at the church, Waddell's clothes and car, Lydia's blood, none of it implicated me. Even the hotel room and the bar tab were on Waddell's credit card. I hadn't accomplished much other than bearing witness to a couple's self-destruction, except maybe limiting the fallout and keeping the casualties to a minimum. As I ghosted out of town, I had to tell myself that was enough.

Annual Review

JOHN NIEDER STOOD UP FROM HIS CHAIR and hit the familiar Ctrl-Alt-Del key combination to lock his workstation in one swift motion. His head swiveled, taking in the rows of cubicles on either side of his own, but no one else looked up to catch his eye. Apparently no one else had gotten their own copy of the email that had appeared in his inbox a moment ago, the brief message that filled him with some deep, nameless foreboding.

Annual Review Resolution Process
Bourman, Adele <abourman@vaunted.com>
To: Nieder, John <jnieder@vaunted.com>
Wed 1/22/2020 9:51 AM

Please drop by the Human Resources suite at your earliest convenience to discuss.

Best regards,
Adele Bourman
Human Resources Manager

Vaunted Financial Services—Safeguarding Your
Overall Worth
127 Mortimer Sq. 66th Floor New York, NY 10109
Mobile: 212-555-1074

John knew "at your earliest convenience" was corporate-speak for "right now, unless you have a world beater of an excuse" and that knowledge had immediately brought him to his feet. Still, as he left his cubicle row and turned left to make his way to the area occupied by HR, he felt he probably had a grace period of at least a few minutes. More than enough time for a quick detour to the kitchenette, to fortify himself with coffee and gather his thoughts.

The kitchenette was narrow, with a countertop running its length and two sets of cabinets, above and below the counter. Opposite the countertop was a bulletin board permanently dominated by a laminated poster giving notice of various state and federal labor statutes. At the kitchenette's far end stood a water cooler, and atop the counter were two coffee makers, one a state of the art bean-to-cup computerized behemoth, often offline and in need of maintenance, the other an old fashioned two-pot station that reminded John of a college gig waiting tables at a local restaurant. Amazingly, the bean-to-cup machine was in working order today. John placed a cup on the tray and selected a small light roast from the touch screen.

As he listened to the beans grinding through the machine, John tried to anticipate what would occur once he reached Adele Bourman's office. Annual reviews had just concluded last week, and his had gone very well if he did say so himself. His manager, Pete, had offered him nothing but positive feedback, and John had taken great satisfaction in feeling that his strategy for the review's self-assessment portion had paid off. Free to award himself any scores across the various categories, John had opted to lowball everything, figuring that Pete wouldn't be able to resist the opportunity for managerial input, happier to raise artificially low scores than to chop down artificially high ones. Sure enough, Pete had mentioned multiple times in the review meeting that John had been too humble and too hard on himself, and John was positive the final scores had come out more in his favor than they would have otherwise.

So he had gotten a glowing annual review, and happily signed off on it. What could be in need of resolution? John had never heard of a resolution process for annual reviews, had never known such a remedy existed. In his experience, annual reviews were a pro forma affair, conducted every January and then forgotten about except in rare circumstances. Someone asking for an extended sabbatical, or pushing hard for a promotion or a raise, could appeal to the paper trail of annual reviews. But otherwise, they were just an exercise in rule-following and box-ticking.

With a hiss of steam, the machine finished spitting coffee into John's cup. He added a splash of cold water and drank the coffee black, taking a first sip as he left the kitchenette. Unbidden, the thought came to him that annual review files might serve another purpose: building a case for termination. Surely, John told himself, that wasn't the meaning behind the email. He might have subtly manipulated Pete into giving him the highest scores he could get, but he hadn't tricked him into a good review that he didn't deserve. John knew he did good work, and Pete was happy with the results. No one other than Pete had the authority to terminate him. Did they?

The entire sixty-sixth floor was a large U-shape, with John's cubicle somewhere on the U's east side, the reception area and conference rooms along the short south side, and HR located near the executive suites on the west side. John passed row upon row of co-workers, none of them sparing him so much as a glance as he passed. These were people he considered friends, including Tom Pfefferman, for whom John had bought several rounds of liquid lunch on the day his wife served him with divorce papers, and Mykayla Downing, who always dragged John up to sing karaoke with her at the annual Christmas parties. Could they not feel the discomfort and nerves radiating off him as he passed by? Or were they already trying to distance themselves from the dead man walking?

He turned the corner and smiled wanly at the receptionist, Cheryl, as he approached her station of brushed nickel rods and frosted glass plates etched with the Vaunted logo. Cheryl was on the phone, but smiled back at him and raised a hand in a quick wave. That made John feel a little better. Surely, if he were about to be canned and security was waiting to escort him out of the building, someone would have given Cheryl a heads up about the potentially fraught fallout. It would have been easy enough for her to pretend the phone call was occupying her attention entirely, and since she didn't have to smile and wave, she must have wanted to, or at least had no reason not to.

The dizzying spiraling out in his mind hadn't quite finished when John suddenly found himself right outside of Adele Bourman's office. It was an inner room, with glass walls separating it from the office and solid walls between it and the floor's central elevator lobby. Only the highest level execs got true window offices with views of downtown Manhattan, but it was still a nice perk to have a door to close for the semblance of privacy, John thought, as he knocked in what he hoped was a carefree way.

"Come in," Adele called out.

John opened the door and smiled at the manager of human resources. "Hey, I just got your email. You wanted to see me?"

"Yes, thank you, John," she nodded. "Close the door and have a seat."

John did as he was bid. The chair in front of Adele's desk had molded plastic arms, and he rubbed the bends in them with his thumbs.

"As I indicated, this is to do with your annual review," Adele began what sounded like a rehearsed speech.

"Yeah, I thought my review went pretty well this year," John cut her off, doubling-down on the only play he felt he had. "Thought it was a done deal, at this point."

Adele's tight lips twisted in an expression that was, by technical definition, a smile. "Your review went well," she acknowledged. "You received one of the highest annual review scores of anyone in the entire company."

"Oh." That sounded so much better than whatever John had been expecting, he was at a loss for a proper response.

"In fact," Adele went on, "your score ranks at the Paragon award level."

"Oh, wow," John exhaled, feeling something like a shiver of pleasure from sheer relief. "Oh, man!" he laughed, "you have no idea how nervous I was walking over here! I thought there was some kind of problem with my review!"

"Well," Adele said, dipping her head slightly, "as it happens, there is a slight issue in need of resolution."

"There… is?" John asked. He did not immediately revert to panic, but was deeply confused.

"You understand how determining the Paragon award works?"

"Sure," John shrugged. Adele looked at him expectantly, as if he were back in elementary school and she were the teacher who had just called on him to explain a frog's life cycle or how to convert mixed numbers to improper fractions. "Whoever has the highest annual review score in the entire company, as long as it's above four-point-seven-five, is designated a Paragon." He felt that answered the question of determination, of what calculation went into handing out the award. He did not add that it had always seemed to him to be a mixed blessing. On the upside were some immediate, concrete rewards, including a nice-sized spot bonus, some stock options, and three extra paid vacation days, as well as some longer-term less tangible benefits, such as getting on the fast track for bigger, better clients and, ultimately, promotion. The downside was that the Paragon was under a microscope for the entire year, until a new award was handed out after the next round of annual reviews. The Paragon was expected to live up to the honor, to mentor others, to tackle special assignments with relish and volunteer for committees with flair. None of that really mattered, anyway, as only a fool would turn down the Paragon award.

Adele seemed satisfied with his answer, at any rate. "We began the program eight years ago," she expanded, "and we have had six Paragons since. One year, the individual with the highest score was Brandon March, who had already won the award two years earlier, so there was no new Paragon designated. Another year, no one in the entire organization scored above the four-point-seven-five threshold."

John nodded. "That was the year the Harrington account imploded and almost took us all down with it," he remembered.

"Yes. Other than those exceptions, the process has worked as intended. A Paragon for each year, most years, the occasional year with none. What we have never had—or had never had, before now—was two Paragon-eligible employees at the same moment."

John felt his eyebrows rise involuntarily.

"You received a four-point-nine-three," Adele said. "Quinn McLallen also received a four-point-nine-three."

"Good for her," John said, and meant it. He wasn't particularly close with Quinn but knew that she was very good at her job in the marketing department. The last time he had run into her she had just started spearheading an international ad campaign. Winning the Paragon award could easily be a stepping stone for her to a title change, director of overseas brand awareness or something, maybe eventually a division of her own, with new boxes reporting to her in the org chart.

"It is unprecedented," Adele said, in a way that made John uneasy.

"Well, look," he offered, "if this is about, you know, how we share the award, I mean, I'm fine with splitting the bonus. Or the paid time off. I mean, obviously, it's not really about all that," he hurriedly added. "It's just an honor to be recognized. Such an honor."

Adele regarded him critically. "I appreciate your point of view on the subject," she said. "Unfortunately, they…"—and here she inclined her head slightly, indicating the offices beyond her own, the seats of power occupied by the company's chief officers —"regard the situation in different terms. Precisely opposite terms."

"I'm not following you," John said.

"The money is trivial," Adele said, "as is the vacation allowance. I'm sure it would not surprise you to hear that very few of the previous Paragons utilized all their standard paid time off, let alone dipped into the bonus days."

"Okay," John said.

"The entire reason the Paragon awards were instituted," she went on, "was for the benefit they could provide to the entire company. Not as a compensation incentive, which could have been handled any number of ways. Rather as a method of modeling our core values, which would otherwise be abstract and difficult to convey. When a supervisor identifies a deficiency in one of his or her direct reports, they..."—this time she merely lifted a finger, angled to point in the direction of the chief officers' offices —"would much rather the supervisor say 'I'd like you to be as detail-oriented as Brandon March' or 'I need you to go above and beyond as habitually as Katherine Delacroix' than leave the definition of the lacking value up for interpretation."

"All right," John nodded.

"They..."—finger point—"feel that having two Paragons at once would dilute the efficiency to an unacceptable level. Between supervisors not wanting to give offense to either you or Quinn by choosing one over the other to model desirable values, and the direct reports undermining the intended message by comparing the two of you. Both of you arrived at your identical annual review scores by different measures, which in itself could breed ... confusion."

"Well, how about this," John said, "Quinn can have the title, she can be Paragon for the year and all that goes with that, and I'll just take the bonus." He grinned to show he was being a good sport.

"I'm afraid that won't work, either," Adele said, unmoved.

"Won't work for them, you mean?" John asked, tilting his head in the direction Adele had pointed. She nodded. "I'm afraid I'm out of ideas for a suitable resolution, then," he told her.

"That's perfectly all right," she said. "I didn't ask you to drop by so that you could suggest a resolution. A resolution is at hand. I merely needed to inform you of it." With that, she stood and began to walk around her desk.

"Oh, well, good, that's great, thanks," John stammered, awkwardly rising to his feet. As Adele reached for the doorknob, John felt certain he was about to be dismissed, and his mind raced for some way to ask what the resolution was going to be, without looking like an idiot who hadn't managed to follow the thread of the conversation. But rather than standing aside and gesturing John out of her office, Adele preceded him through the door.

"Follow me, if you would, please," she said over her shoulder, and John acquiesced. After a few steps he realized how strange it was to be walking behind her, and lengthened his strides to draw even with Adele. They walked toward the reception area, where Cheryl was once again too focused on a phone conversation to interact with passers-by, and Adele pushed through the glass doors to the elevator lobby. She pressed the down button.

"So this resolution, it affects me and Quinn about the same…?" John probed, partly out of curiosity and partly to fill the silence as they waited for the elevator.

"Yes, I spoke to her earlier," Adele said. The light over one elevator glowed and the steel doors slid open. Within the elevator, Adele bent at the waist slightly, to wave the combination ID badge and magnetic keycard on a lanyard around her neck at a sensor mounted below the floor buttons. The sensor's green LED blinked and Adele pressed the button for BB2, a floor John had never been to but which he surmised was at least two levels below the building's ground level entrance. The wordless melody of a muzak version of "Wind Beneath My Wings" burbled over their heads as they plummeted an eighth of a mile straight down.

When the elevator doors opened again, Adele stepped out into a cramped hallway and John saw no choice but to follow. The surfaces were all gray concrete, the only decoration a foot-high stripe of chipped red paint bisecting the walls. Occasionally there were black doors, windowless and knobless. and about as often there were bare lightbulbs buzzing in wire cages. Adele passed several doors without comment, until they came to one with an ornate pull handle, shaped like what looked to John like some kind of Swiss army knife style combination letter opener and church key. A sensor was mounted on the wall beside it, and Adele once again flashed her keycard. John heard a heavy thunk of bolts falling and Adele opened the door, which gave on a stairwell.

"Where...?" John started to ask, but Adele ignored him and descended the stairs. The hallway had been cool, its close air heavy with excess moisture that became rivulets of sooty condensation on the walls, but the lower John descended along the stairs, the more it became outright cold and dank. It reminded him of the walk-in freezer at that long-ago restaurant, including the smell of too much food left waiting overlong. The difference was that in that freezer's chilly confines, the tang of overripeness mixed with recognizable food odors, while here the rot was disturbingly unidentifiable.

John began to entertain the idea of interrupting the seemingly unending trek, of stepping forward as they approached the next door and throwing his arm between it and Adele, refusing to let her open it until she explained where they were going and what they would do when they got there. But there was no next door. The stairs ended at the opening to a short hallway, more of a crude tunnel carved through strata of stone, and at the far end was an unbarred cleft that gave on a massive, enclosed space.

John stopped in his tracks as he exited the tunnel. The subterranean cavern was so huge its upper reaches were lost in shadows. John tried to calculate how far below ground they actually were, two elevator levels below the lobby plus however much farther down the stairs had taken them. He'd lost count of how many flights and switchbacks they had descended, but it still seemed impossible that such a colossal area could exist beneath the city streets. It must be a trick of the light, he decided, the weird green radiance that provided scant, flickering illumination around the perimeter. John's eyes scanned for whatever the source of the green light was, more status LEDs, or possibly chemical glow lanterns, but saw only a half dozen metal braziers ringing the cavern floor, low green flames within them. He realized there were no electrical cables anywhere in sight, no water pipes, nothing interrupting the excavated geology beyond iron age bowls of fire.

John took a step toward Adele, who turned around and held up an admonishing hand.

"No need to follow me any further," she said, and pointed somewhere behind John. "You will find what you need there."

She turned her back on him and stalked away, fading into a shroud of semi-darkness. He could just barely detect her movement as she ascended a curving staircase along the cavern's inner wall. John turned in the direction she had indicated. He spotted a wrought iron rack supporting three poles standing on end. Each pole was over six feet long, and resembled the handle on the door in the hallway off the elevator, though at this scale they no longer brought to mind desk accessories or kitchen implements. The pointed ends were sword blades, flanked with vicious barbed hooks that looked like monstrous claws or fangs.

Reflexively, John turned back to look for Adele, to demand some kind of explanation as to what any of this had to do with resolving the annual review situation. He could no longer see any sign of Adele, but did notice another figure on the cavern's far side: Quinn McLallen. John imagined that when Quinn had arrived at the office that morning she had been wearing some variation on her usual attire, but she must have shed half of it. Her feet were bare, as were her arms, high heels and blazer discarded, leaving her in only a dark colored pencil skirt and lighter hued camisole. Her long blonde hair was piled atop her skull in a messy bun. She was pacing back and forth in a tight circuit like an animal in a zoo enclosure, occasionally bouncing in place on the balls of her bare feet before resuming the back and forth, and she was holding one of the bladed poles, as well.

One of the weapons, John told himself, there's no two ways about it, they're weapons, I'm standing in front of a weapons rack and I'm supposed to pick a weapon, Quinn already has picked a weapon, because we're supposed to fight. She's not pacing like an animal, she's limbering up like a boxer, a prize fighter, we're going to fight for the prize of who gets to be this year's Paragon. It was an insane, yet inescapable, conclusion.

From all around the cavern's upper reaches, a sibilant chorus echoed off the rocky dome. Quinn took this as a signal to advance on John, and John felt it too, the urgent demand for obedience, for bloodletting. The hissing mass was hungry.

Even so, John refused to accept the inevitability of it. He held up his empty hands as Quinn approached. "Hey, Quinn," he said in his most reasonable voice, "I don't know what they told you, Adele barely told me anything, but we can work this out like …"

As he had been speaking, he hadn't been quite sure what comparison he could make or what ideal he should appeal to. That they were adults? Professional colleagues? Work friends? It didn't matter, because Quinn wasn't listening. She brought her weapon to bear, swinging it in a two-handed overhead swipe, and all John could do was throw himself to the side to avoid being chopped in half. He felt a bright stinging line drawn down the outside of his right hip, and heard the clang of Quinn's blade striking the rock floor. At the same time, the green flames flared and rose higher as if their fuel had been replenished. John landed awkwardly on his left side, scraping his elbow and knee on uneven protrusions, but the blunt ache of those impacts was quickly swallowed by the hot bloom of pain spreading along his right thigh. Blood ran down his leg and soaked into his trousers.

John twisted his head in time to see Quinn charging at him, weapon held high and ready to drive down through his chest. He groped blindly for the weapon rack, fingers wrapping frantically around the haft of one of the implements, but couldn't dislodge it from the crossbars. Quinn stabbed at him, her face twisted in fury, and John barely drew his legs up in time to kick out at the plunging blade. One shoe sole connected with the hook flanking the main blade, while the other smacked Quinn's knuckles.

The double kick was not enough to disarm Quinn, and barely broke her stride. But it was just enough to make her miss, and to gain John a moment's respite. As Quinn recovered her balance, he scrambled up to his feet and braced himself against the weapon rack. "Quinn, seriously, this is crazy. I don't care about the Paragon award, you can have it all, I don't care!"

Nevertheless he was already lifting a weapon from the rack, knowing that his words would have no effect on Quinn. She was almost close enough to strike again but had resumed walking side to side, sizing him up and shifting her grip on her weapon back and forth. John held his weapon to the side in one hand, its head resting on the cavern floor, and held his empty hand out as if awaiting her response, whether it came in the form of words or an attack.

Quinn appeared to be of a similar mindset, waiting for John to commit to an attack first. John dropped his head in resignation, then joined his hands on the haft of his weapon and brought it up as powerfully as he could, like a hockey player trying to get a surprise wrist shot past the goalie. The blade and its jagged side barbs, which made John think crazily of the hungry jaws of a termite, raced toward Quinn's head, but Quinn ducked low and the blade missed. Simultaneously, Quinn lashed out from her crouched position, cutting deeply into the flesh of John's lower leg. He staggered away from her, reeling and in fresh agony. The green flames rose higher again, burning brighter. John knew that if Quinn's blow had been a few inches higher, it would have hit his knee and likely crippled him.

John lifted his weapon and held it in front of his chest defensively as he limped backward. Did Quinn hate him so much that she relished this opportunity to savage him? He tried desperately to remember if he had ever inadvertently provoked her in any way, a joke taken out of context, a last slice of pizza scarfed at product rollout Lunch and Learn, anything. But nothing explained her hostility toward him.

Quinn was taking her time, knowing she had the advantage and pondering the best way to fully exploit it. John watched her, trying to discern her approach and the best way to protect himself, but couldn't help but be distracted by the shadows cavorting up the cavern walls. Now that the eerie green pyres extended far above the braziers' rims, new subtleties of the cavern had been revealed. Stone balconies jutted from the inner surface, upon which stood robed figures watching the struggle between Quinn and John intently. These were the ones who had whispered the primal command to fight for supremacy, and who now avariciously awaited the outcome.

The feel of so many greedy eyes upon him made John's skin crawl, but worse, it made his present situation sickeningly real in a way it had not been before. The chill in the air, the smell of death and decay, even the wounds he had sustained had all felt like components of a nightmare that could still end on better terms. Surely someone would come and restore order, putting a stop to this madness, or else he would wake up tangled in his sheets and out of breath but no worse for the bizarre stress-induced dream. But the presence of a leering audience convinced him that this was no anomaly of circumstance or imagination. Viscerally, John confronted the concrete possibility that he could die, here and now.

John squeezed the haft of his weapon and moved toward Quinn. He exaggerated his limp, practically dragging his leg behind him, to lull Quinn into overconfidence. She planted her feet and bent her knees, a portrait of tense anticipation. John took a deep breath and pretended to stumble as he put weight on the leg he had been dragging. He bent at the waist and stutter-stepped closer to Quinn, then recovered and slashed with all his might at Quinn's center mass, fully prepared to drive the blade in deeper with all his weight behind it once it found purchase in her flesh.

The gambit did not work. Quinn was ready to parry his clumsy attack with the bladed head of her own weapon, and after knocking it aside she followed through with the butt end of the haft, cracking it across the base of John's skull. He saw stars, felt his fingers spasm open and distantly heard his weapon clatter to the cavern floor, the sound subsumed by riotous hissing from above. John tried to regain his bearings and turn toward Quinn, knowing the only way he could ward off her next strike would be to face it head on, but he was so disoriented that the mere act of revolving in place toppled him.

Sprawled on his back, his vision began to clear. The green fires raged in swirling columns that reached the cavern ceiling. In their emerald brilliance John could see the hissing figures arrayed around the subterranean arena's walls, now in a frenzy of excitement. Sleeves rolled down upraised waving arms, revealing scaly limbs and fingers tipped with claws. Hoods fell back from reptilian heads with blazing slitted eyes and wide mouths baring fangs. A huge graven statue had been set into one of the cavern walls, metallic surface glinting in the green firelight: a girthy man seated on a throne, arms wrapped around several bags overflowing with coin on his lap, a crown of horns above slitted eyes. Instinctively John knew the statue was Mammon, and the reptilian creatures were the demon's servants, and servants of the executives of Vaunted Financial. Or perhaps they were the executives, their true forms visible now. It would explain so much.

Quinn loomed over him. He opened his mouth to beg her not to do it, but stopped himself as his gaze met hers. Tongues of green flame were reflected in her eyes, each one a darting phantom. John saw the elite gymnastics camp where Quinn wanted to enroll her daughter and the college application essay coach she had researched for her son, saw an addition built onto her house for her aging father-in-law and a wine country tour of southern Europe with her husband, saw tailored clothing that would enhance her image and the seeding of an scholarship fund that would enhance her social regard. The Paragon bonus and the career path it opened up were stepping stones to those objectives, which she carried in the steely set of her jawline and the heaving breaths rocking her torso and most of all in the fleeting green flashes in her eyes. Quinn knew what she wanted and John knew absolutely nothing would stand in her way. As she brought the weapon down and pierced his heart, John knew that against all of Mammon's promises he never had a chance.

PRESERVATION

WE COULD WAIT THEM OUT. Entropy was our ally. Zombies reaved the Earth, so we hid and waited. For however strong, savage, unstoppable, the zombies were necrotizing tissue. Dead flesh and bone, animated yet decomposing. We pledged patience, enduring while the zombies decayed. We forgot about formaldehyde. Zombies didn't rise the moment life's spark fled, they sat up on funeral homes' steel tables, veins filled with tissue fixatives. So obvious in hindsight. When the first zombies attacked, they drew close and claimed their victims easily, because they hardly looked dead at all. Smooth skin, rosy cheeks: their makeup was *flawless*.

Bottom Feeder

Tyler came to, cold and wet and in pain. The sensations allowed him to realize he was awake since his eyes were no help. He blinked several times, trying to clear stinging saltwater from his field of vision, which remained inky black. He wanted to rub his eyes, but his hands were tied together on the far side of the wooden pole against his back. His shoulders alternately burned and ached from being wrenched backwards, depending on whether he allowed the muscles to relax as much as they could in their awkward posture or tried to pull his wrists free of the plastic zip ties digging into his skin and locking them together. He was sitting on sand and stones in a few inches of water. Small waves lapped at him, chilly enough to put a dull numbness in the back of his legs. Water dripped from overhead.

He shook his head back and forth, still trying to clear his sight. He caught glimpses of light on either side, and craned his neck trying to get a better view. The sources of the illumination were far away.

Slowly, his vision cleared and adjusted to the dark enough for him to differentiate shapes in the shadows. A solid surface overhead blocked out the night sky and made the area immediately around him as dark as the bottom of a pit. The surf on either side was only slightly brighter, reflecting a sky heavy with rain clouds.

He was under the pier. What was he doing under the pier? It hadn't been his idea, not this time. He had given up on fooling around under the pier long ago, until Hannah had brought it up again.

Hannah. Hannah had taken him by the hand and led him toward the pier, and after so many times that he had suggested they find a little privacy there, only for her to demur that it wasn't nearly private enough, he had been helpless to resist when she took the lead. When she pushed him up against the pylon and pinned his pelvis with her own, grinding into him while her hands went to his neck and her mouth found his, he was overwhelmed. When her grip around his neck had tightened all he could think was that he never wanted her to stop. She had pulled away and he had tried to think of something appropriately sexy to say that would heighten the mood. Truthfully, he was more concerned in the moment with heightening his own mood, since Hannah already seemed plenty revved up on her own, enough to have caught him off-guard and unprepared, and the last thing he wanted was to miss this golden opportunity because he couldn't respond.

While he had been formulating the most seductive dirty talk he could, Hannah had slammed the back of his head into the pylon. He had seen stars, the kind that whirled and reeled around one another like little glowing white bumper cars. That was the last thing he remembered before waking up here.

His legs felt stiff, and he drew up his knees to flex them. His heel dragged over something sharp, probably a broken seashell, but it brought to mind the claw of a crab, snapping defensively at his flesh. He had been traumatized by stepping on a crab when he was four years old, and the old fear was a constant presence in the back of his mind whenever he came to the beach. Now he was overwhelmed with the sudden, irresistible conviction that a crab was going to scuttle along, bump into his leg and pinch it, sink the teeth of its pincers into his flesh where they'd stay embedded like the rusty blade of a tiny knife. What if the crab nicked him somewhere near a major artery and he lost a lot of blood? What if he got an infection?

Jesus, what if it nipped him right in the nut sack? It might, he realized, if it crawled up between his legs, because not even a layer of hibiscus-patterned poly and nylon mesh would protect his sensitive bits. His board shorts were gone. When had he gotten naked? How?

The question was outweighed for the moment by the very unimaginary presence of a sand fiddler side-walking towards his junk, brandishing its oversized claw like some tiny fiend wielding a wicked meat hook. He saw himself trying to crush the thing between his legs, but that would never work, he realized. The crab's shell would protect it, and having his inner thighs cut to ribbons by its claw or the spikes of its shell would be only slightly less shocking than … he couldn't even finish the thought. He pushed himself up, hard, his back scraping against the pylon as he awkwardly maneuvered his feet underneath his torso. Wood splinters and barnacles left his back slashed and bruised as he forced his way upright. He slipped, his foot gliding back out across the surface of a large algae-slimed rock, and landed hard on his bare ass with a splash, but he shuffled up the pylon again until his feet were flat and stable and his legs were straight. He gasped for air, worn out from the terror-fueled exertion. He wanted to bend over with his hands on his knees while he caught his breath, but the zip ties on his wrists prevented him. He settled for letting his head hang down so that his chin touched his sternum.

He came back to the question of where his board shorts had gotten to. Things had been moving fast with Hannah, but not that fast. Or had they? No, he was sure that the naked threshold had not been crossed. He would have remembered. Despite the fact that many times, up to and including today, he had seen her in a bikini that left almost nothing to the imagination, complete nudity was still a rare treat, like the time last summer when she had finally let him have sex with her. That was why he was always hinting that they should get busy at the beach some time, when she was already most of the way to naked. If Hannah had asked him to take off his board shorts, he would have said her first or no deal. Otherwise he would have been suspicious that she was just trying to punk him.

That must be what this was all about, he realized in a burst of relief. She had been punking him all along. Get him under the pier, knock him out, tie him up, strip him out of his shorts, and enjoy the humiliation when someone found him letting it all hang out, that must have been the plan. Even as he thought it, a memory came to him, sitting against the pylon with his head ringing, his hands tied, Hannah yanking his board shorts down over his hips. That had happened. And Hannah had been saying something, hadn't she? He couldn't remember. Maybe he hadn't been able to hear her at the time. Had she hit him twice? Stunned him, tied and stripped him, and then knocked him out cold? He could have a concussion. He could have brain damage. If he did, then so would she when he got his hands on her, the little witch …

A tickle on the top of his foot made him kick his leg so hard he aggravated an old knee injury he had suffered on a hard slide into second base a couple seasons back. The joint throbbed angrily. He shivered even as he told himself it was nothing, just the waves washing something up over his toes, probably a piece of seaweed. Nothing to freak out about.

At least Hannah's plan had failed to hit its ultimate goal. Being tied up naked was not ideal, a huge and literal pain in the ass thanks to the cuts and abrasions the pylon had made when he had wriggled upright against it, but no one had seen him in this state. The area underneath the pier was exactly as private as he had always tried to tell Hannah it was, and at this time of night, with the rainy weather, the entire boardwalk and beach were deserted. He told himself that meant Hannah would be coming soon, wondering why he hadn't shown up after being cut loose by a surfcaster or called from the police station or something. She would come, because she didn't want him to spend all night tied to a pylon, did she? She had punked him but she didn't want to cause any permanent physical harm.

Did she? What had she been saying as she stripped him, before she knocked him out? Tyler wished he could remember, or at least most of him did, while a tiny, disquieted gut feeling told him the answer was nothing good.

Something pricked his right heel, and there was no doubt in his mind that it was a crab. A tiny one, probably, but alive and apparently unhappy about the human feet taking up space in its habitat. He lifted his foot in a reflexive jerk, stared down at the lapping water and tried to see where the crab was. But the waves were opaque as oil. He stomped his foot down, on the off chance he might squish the thing, but as far as he could tell his sole only drove a deep impression in the wet sand. His feet fidgeted in the muck nervously, toes burying themselves under the sand almost with minds of their own, like they had when he was a little kid. He felt strangely reassured, his ankles providing smaller and less fleshy targets, until he remembered that crabs could burrow under the sand as well. He shook his feet free.

Maybe he had just imagined the pricking at his heel. People's minds played tricks on them in the dark, especially if they were dehydrated with low blood sugar and had a mild freaking concussion. His loss of consciousness had not been restful, he felt exhausted and his nerves were shot, he was being paranoid … and another crab claw scissored at the insole of his right foot.

"Shitfuck!" he hissed. Then, much louder, as loud as he could, he yelled, "Help! Somebody! Anybody! Help me down here! Help!" There was no answer.

How could Hannah want to hurt him? They had met when they were little. That first summer, when his parents and hers had rented either side of a duplex for the same week, and both families had hit it off so well, he and she had been in between first and second grade. He hadn't paid much attention at first to Mr. and Mrs. Maris, since Hannah had been such an ideal playmate, just as interested as he was in climbing the rocks of the jetty and exploring tide pools. Gradually Tyler had come to realize that Mrs. Maris always seemed to know the night before when bad weather was coming, making rainy day plans with his mother in advance. Mr. Maris and Tyler's father would sometimes disappear for a morning, gone fishing, a friendly competition that Mr. Maris always won handily. Whenever his father would ask Mr. Maris his secret, he would only laugh and say, "Ask my wife some time." But that was all background, adult stuff, penetrating Tyler's awareness only because Hannah, her mother and her father were three of a kind, people who never seemed to be vacationing at the beach so much as returning to it. The sea belonged to them, and they belonged to the sea. But it was Hannah he was always drawn to, the skinny little girl with the hair that glittered like sun-struck sand.

They'd had their ups and downs summer by summer but by freshmen year of high school, when their parents had gone in together on buying a timeshare, he felt closer to Hannah than anyone else in the world. And he knew she felt the same way, and that their bond was strong enough that it was no big deal for teasing to morph into flirting in direct proportion to their physical development. It seemed harmless enough the first year, until they both spent eleven and a half months replaying every conversation back home, and then spent an excruciating two weeks dying to find a way to be alone together. That last night, when they were fifteen, they walked to the end of the boardwalk, sat on a salt-stained, rusty-legged bench and kissed for hours. The summer after that, last summer, they convinced their parents to go out for a grown-ups dinner while they stayed home to watch a movie, and they had sex with each other for the first time, in his bed upstairs. Hannah had worn nothing but her silver cowrie necklace, the one her mother had given her when she turned twelve.

A nip at the littlest toe on his left foot, more than a nip, like someone going after him with wire cutters. He yanked his foot away and slammed it back down again immediately, momentarily convinced he could smash a crab's exoskeleton barefoot with sheer rage, not caring if the cracked fragments of crab shell would slice his foot bloody. He struck nothing but sand and water. The little bugger was fast, and viciously territorial, but if it kept antagonizing him and couldn't figure out he wasn't going anywhere, it was going to wind up dead.

Another jab needled his ankle, just inside his left Achilles tendon. "Shit!" he cried again, followed by another louder "Help me! Somebody!" which was met with unbroken indifferent silence. A sharp pinch assaulted his right big toe. His legs were spread with his feet at least a foot and a half apart, which meant that he had just been clawed by two different crabs in rapid succession. How many crabs were there under the pier? Was it mating season or something?

Crabs. Mating. Now he remembered what Hannah had said while he was trying to shake off the first bounce off the pylon she had given his skull, while she was looping the zip ties around his wrists and cinching them tight. She had been behind him, that was why he couldn't picture her saying it. She had leaned over his shoulder and put her lips against his ear, and even amid the mounting sense that their tryst was going horribly wrong he had felt a tingle in his groin from the way her soft breath tickled. And she had said … she had said …

"You gave me crabs, you asshole. So now I'm going to give them to you."

Maybe he had been blocking out what she had said because it called to mind what had not been one of his proudest moments. His doctor had confirmed a bad case of pubic lice late last September, which he assumed he had contracted from Kayla Bonnatale on Senior Skip Day. Although it might have been Jess Myerson on Fourth-of-July weekend. Definitely one of those two. And he had known, on some level, that he should let Hannah know that when they had slept together in August there had been a risk he'd passed them on. But she had been a virgin before that, and he knew she assumed he had been too. How could he tell her he had caught something she might catch without her realizing he had caught it from someone else before? Was he supposed to take the romantic idea that they had lost their virginities to each other away from her? That seemed too cruel to her and too unpleasant for him to contemplate. So he had let it go as a little white lie of omission. Maybe she'd dodged the STD bullet, maybe he hadn't passed the pubic lice to her. And if he had, she'd find out on her own soon enough. Once he had finished the month-long course of treatment, and gone through all of the nasty oily brown pube shampoo, he had put the entire incident out of mind.

But nobody had dodged anything. Hannah had gotten her own diagnosis and figured everything out. Well, maybe not the part where he wasn't a hundred percent sure which skank had given him the crabs to begin with, but then again, maybe she had. Maybe she thought even worse of him, and assumed he had been banging a hundred percent of the girls back home. Maybe that explained why she was pissed off enough to risk fracturing his skull while leaving him bound and naked someplace where she knew the crabs would be plentiful and feisty. Because she had known, hadn't she?

A nip at his right ankle bone, another nip at the middle of his left outsole. A third crab crawled over his toes, along the top of his right foot, and snapped at his shin. He danced crazily, shaking his legs, sending droplets of blood flying into the incoming tide. "Shit, shit, shit!" he screamed, the last expletive rising to a falsetto that would have been mortifying if he were not preoccupied with avoiding the biting claws. And still, no one was within earshot to hear.

He flexed his arms desperately, trying to tear free of the zip ties, but the sharp plastic edges dug excruciatingly into his wrists without showing any sign of weakening their hold. He knocked the back of his head against the pylon in frustration, and was rewarded with a fresh bloom of nauseating pain throughout his skull. Then he had an idea. He braced the sole of his left foot against the pylon, just beneath his tailbone, then braced his right foot beside it. He squeezed his arms against the pylon and managed to hold himself up with his feet out of the water. "Ha ha, fuck you, crabs," he growled. "Or go fuck each other for all I care. But I know you're not gonna climb straight up a pole." He also knew that he couldn't perch halfway up a pole for very long, either. His arm muscles were already starting to quiver, and a burning knot was forming between his shoulder blades. But he felt optimistic about the plan all the same. He would have to pace himself, put his feet down for brief intervals, just a few seconds here and there and then back up the pylon. He thought he could manage the pylon shimmy for a couple hours, and then the sun would come up and surely someone would come back to the pier, someone who could hear him calling for help and cut him loose. Maybe even before then the seagulls would scare off the crabs at dawn.

His mind flashed back again, not to what had happened after Hannah had lured him under the pier, but what had come before. They had walked up the beach together to get Italian ices, and on the way back Hannah had stopped to lift a crab shell out of the wet sand, picked clean by predators and tide. She'd thrown it into the waves like a skipping stone, but before that she'd touched it to her lips, as if kissing it for luck though she held it for several seconds. At the time it had seemed insignificant, meaningless, one of those odd Hannah quirks. But now...

Tyler heard, for the first time since he had regained consciousness, a sound that was not the whisper of the surf or his own harsh respiration. A chattering, clattering series of clicks, like someone pouring out a box of plastic toothpicks, coming from below him. He craned his neck to look down and saw more crabs around the bottom of the pylon. Dozens had formed a double ring around it, with dozens more climbing onto their backs and more still crawling out of the waves and onto their brethren, layer upon layer, rising higher, closer and closer to his upraised feet. They jostled in constant motion, drumming their legs against the strata of shells below, snapping their claws angrily on open air. If there had been any liquid left in his bladder, he would have voided it then.

The crabs were coming for him. For *him*, deliberately, malevolently. He knew with utter certainty that was the truth.

When Hannah had pulled back from that predatory kiss, right before she had slammed his head back into the pylon, there had been a look in her eye, a look like nothing he had ever seen in another human being. The feverish light of forbidden knowledge. She knew what was going to happen to him, not hoped, not expected, but absolutely undeniably knew not just what would happen but how it would happen, too. None of that could possibly be true, and yet. That look, like a girl who could whisper a secret wish into a shell and throw the shell into the ocean with absolute conviction that the wish would be granted.

Tyler screamed, not for help, not from fear or anger, a pure primal howl, the sound of sanity about to snap. He dropped his feet, stomping and kicking at the crabs, scattering them in cascades of shattered shells and fractured claws. The crabs fought back, slashing and pinching, and the saltwater stung his lacerated flesh. Fine, he wouldn't be able to keep his feet out of reach of their living tower, he would have to fight, it would hurt like hell, but he could fight until sunrise, he could fight them off, even if he had to fight hundreds of them, they were just fucking crabs …

A massive hump broke the surface of the water directly ahead of Tyler, fifteen or twenty feet away. It rose and rose, a giant warty mound, wider than it was tall, so that by the time the peak of it was within inches of the underside of the pier, its base at the water's surface stretched much wider than the sides of the pier. The smell of it wafted over him, an exhalation of mineral tang and warm ammonia. The warts squirmed and shifted and rearranged themselves as the shape grew and grew out of the water, and Tyler realized that they weren't warts at all, they were crabs, of course they were crabs, thousands upon thousands of crabs in a giant cresting living wave that was advancing toward him.

Hannah hadn't said she was going to give him crabs after all. "You gave me crabs, you asshole. So now I'm going to give you to them."

The mountain of crabs surged forward, breaking and sliding toward Tyler, an avalanche of crabs that buried him up to his chest in skittering legs and scissoring claws and the weight of ten thousand spiny shells. He screamed, a random string of words, repetitions of "no" and "please" and "help" and "mom" which degraded into wordless shrieking while the swarm of crabs harried his flesh. A crab sunk its claw into the meat between the second and third toes on his right foot, and he tried to kick it away, but the blanketing press of crabs all around him immobilized his leg. Some of the smaller crabs at the bottom of the swarm were pulverized, crushed by the weight above them, and broken bits of shell were embedded up and down his shins and calves like shrapnel. Living crabs tore at his hips and thighs and belly, plunging their claws into muscle, scraping bone at the bottom of his rib cage. Tyler felt a serrated pincer slide around his right index finger, felt it close and sever the digit, felt the tiny mouthparts of several crabs chewing at the raw stump, and had he been able to scream any louder, he would have. But his voice was cracked and hoarse, and the tide of crabs was still rising, covering his chest and his neck and finally his mouth, nose, eyes, completely subsuming him into the voracious mass, the death of a thousand cuts that danced across every inch of his skin. Whatever remains were not devoured by the teeming crustaceans were quietly swept out to sea with the tide after the crabs dispersed, as the rain continued to fall.

ANOTHER NIGHT IN PARADISE

"SORRY I'M LATE," SHE SAID.

Cal looked up at the girl who had materialized beside him, who was already leaning against the side of his and Vinnie's booth, knee grazing his hip where she propped on the cushion of the C-shaped bench, hand familiarly making small circles on his shoulder. She wore the barest smile on her lips, and barely any clothing: short-sleeved pink top, translucently sheer, which came only halfway down her ribcage and was knotted between her breasts, pink thong, chunky Lucite high-heels. Even in the near-dark surroundings, far from the bright pin spots trained on the stage, Cal could see a fiery boldness in her eyes that merited a response.

"Do I know you?" Cal asked.

"Not yet," the girl promised. "But you look like you've been waiting all night to buy a nice girl a drink. And here I am."

In spite of himself, Cal liked her style. Ignoring the baleful expression gathering strength on Vinnie's face, he slid over to make room for the girl. She lowered herself onto the seat with a dancer's grace, a quality one might expect in every professional exotic dancer, but Cal had been to enough strip clubs to know better.

"What's your name?" Cal asked.

"Ariel," she answered.

"Cal," he said, then pointed to his companion. "Vinnie."

"Hi," she smiled.

"Where's your seashells?" Vinnie asked.

"I only wear them on my days off," Ariel answered without hesitation. She had no doubt heard the question, or any number of other mermaid jokes, countless times. Vinnie scowled at being denied the opportunity to explain the gag.

A waitress appeared at the table, wearing an outfit only slightly more substantial than Ariel's, differentiated mainly by the cocktail tray under her arm and her vastly more comfortable-looking shoes. "Another round, guys?" she asked.

Vinnie threw back the last dregs of his drink and nodded as he slid the glass toward the waitress. Cal turned to Ariel. "What are you having?"

"Midori sour, thanks for asking," she said. Cal looked to the waitress to verify she had gotten the order, a put-upon look indicating she knew Ariel's go-to cocktail well enough. Cal sloshed his own glass meaningfully: close enough to finished to be ready for a replacement by the time she came back. The waitress dutifully departed for the bar.

"Ordering for me first, what a gentleman," Ariel teased Cal, earning a reproachful grunt from Vinnie. "He is a gentleman, I can tell," she insisted, caressing Cal's forearm. Cal wondered what to make of the girl. It was a slow night. He and Vinnie were the club's only customers so far, no surprise that they'd be approached as marks. Cal would never take any stripper's come-ons at face value, but the mere fact that he felt the need to remind himself of that made him acutely aware of how good Ariel was at her job. Her fortunes, and those of every girl in her position, rose and fell by creating and sustaining the fantasy image of a woman who loved getting naked, being ogled, and forging a fleeting yet deep bond with whomever her current mark happened to be. Most of the strippers Cal had known either undersold or overplayed, usually because they were drunk, high, not very bright to begin with, or all three. Stripping exploited the ignorant and the damaged, and Cal knew that without being troubled by it. Partaking in vaguely consensual exploitation would not even crack the top ten list of unseemly things he had done.

But Ariel did not come across like most strippers. Maybe she was one of the smart ones, straight and razor-sharp, who could legitimately think of herself as an empowered sex worker, an almost mythically rare breed, but one which nevertheless did exist; the cliché of the girl working her way through college was not a complete fabrication, Cal had found. Ariel didn't slur, or lose the focus in her blue diamond eyes, unlike the strippers whose stock and trade was liberated sexuality in the form of a woman who would roofie herself for your convenience. Calling him a gentleman hinted at some kind of insight into parts of him that were normally hidden under a default denial that chivalry existed.

"This guy," Vinnie pointed an accusatory finger at Cal. "You think this guy's a gentleman? You should hear some of the fucked-up shit he comes up with sometimes."

"Such as?" Ariel asked.

The waitress reappeared, and set the three drinks down around the table. Vinnie raised his glass, slurped a mouthful, and wiped his lips with the back of his hand. "One time he said this bitch was ugly as a candy bar after someone shit it out."

Ariel's eyebrows rose as her gaze slid over to Cal, whose only reaction was to shrug and say, "I don't recall saying that."

"Yeah, man!" Vinnie insisted. "Remember? At Delilah's that one time? This bitch was onstage and you told me to get a load of how she looked like an Oh Henry! shit, on account of her ugly tits. I remember, 'cause of the Oh Henry! part especially. You coulda said she looked like a Snickers shit or Nestle Crunch nipples, fuckin' whatever, who the fuck even thinks about Oh Henry! bars anyway?"

Cal cracked the faintest of smiles, and turned to Ariel. "I remember what he's talking about now. Maybe what I said was fucked up, but it wasn't exactly what Vinnie remembers, either."

"Fuck you and your fucking bullshit!" Vinnie snarled. "That is exactly what you said, word for fucking word."

Cal continued speaking directly to Ariel. "The young lady in question, she had really bad boob-job scars. Malpractice kind of bad, huge puckered seams in her skin..." Cal gestured at the stage, where a stripper was hanging inverted astride the pole, her legs making a wide V. "We were about this far away and I could see them plain as day. So I leaned over to Vinnie and said, 'Those scars on her tits are some O. Henry shit, there.'"

"The fuck did I just say!" Vinnie crowed in triumph.

"The author, Vinnie," Cal said patiently. "Not the fucking candy bar." Returning to Ariel, he said, "I'll concede that it wasn't a gentlemanly thing to say. But how often do you see that kind of irony in real life?"

"Not often, at least not with such blatant visuals," Ariel agreed. "This place might qualify on some level, though."

"Fair point," Cal nodded. The club was called The Paradise, but the dark, windowless space was more like a dungeon, albeit one with an incessant thumping soundtrack, an overripe smell of spilled alcohol mingled with baby powder perfumes, and bodies that writhed writhing in something other than the pain of torture. Cal angled his glass toward Ariel so that she could clink it with her own.

Vinnie slammed his glass down on the table, giving the ice an angry jangle. He scanned the club for the waitress, failed to locate her, and stood up to stalk toward the bar.

"Sorry," Ariel said. "I didn't mean to drive your friend away."

"He's not my friend," Cal snipped.

"No? You guys must hang out a lot. Enough to have stories about each other."

Cal shrugged. "That doesn't make us friends. We don't have anything in common. Well, not much."

"You two work together?"

"Something like that."

"But you're not in the same book club," Ariel guessed.

Cal chuckled. "Yeah, no, Vinnie isn't much of a reader."

"We could have changed the subject."

"Vinnie isn't much of a talker," Cal said. "In fact, that's probably half the reason why he got up and left. He has a very... transactional worldview. He does a job, he expects to get paid for it. He buys something, he expects to get his money's worth. This?" Cal flicked his finger back and forth between them. "Me buying you a drink? Huge waste of money to Vinnie."

"Some people would say strip clubs are a huge waste of money."

"Right. But Vinnie always sticks to the script. He always orders vodka rocks, so he knows the bartender's not ripping him off. He never pays for lap dances."

"Bad tipper?"

"He keeps track of how many drinks he orders, and end of the night when he leaves he'll give the waitress one dollar per drink. Unless she fucks up in any way over the course of the night, in which case, nothing."

"What about the dancers?"

"Nah, he never tips them at all. That's why we don't sit at the stage. And, you know, all of the above, is pretty much why we never go to the same club twice."

"Doesn't sound like much fun. Why bother?"

"As a favor to me, I guess. Sometimes when I've had a rough night I need... something like this."

"Rough night tonight?" Ariel asked, with a convincing enough note of concern.

"Rather not talk about it," Cal said. "So, what about you? You and your co-workers have a book club, talk about early twentieth century American writers?"

Ariel laughed. "You don't have to be a literary nerd to catch an O. Henry reference."

"Mm-hmm. But I don't think your stage name is a Disney reference, either."

"No?"

"Seems more like Shakespeare to me."

"Prospero's servant? That's an.... interesting association. Kind of obscure as allusions go."

"You got it right away."

"Fine, you got me, I'm a lit nerd. And now that my secret's out, I might as well tell you a story. One time I was working at this club and there was this other girl there, she had a ton of ink. But it was all one big tattoo. So picture this: she's kinda tall, like maybe five-ten. Deep tan. Long brown hair she teased out, like, crazy. Big round fake tits."

"Eh, she's losing me," Cal said.

"No, I know, I prefer them natural too. Obviously." She hefted her own breasts as examples. "But she was real lean, athletic, wouldn't have had curves at all without the boob job. Worth the risk of disfiguring scars, right?"

"Maybe. So what about the tattoo?"

"Okay, so, it was your basic tribal, huge though. All interconnected black ink, from one wrist up to her shoulder, down her back, around her hip and down the opposite leg." Ariel gestured up and down her own limbs as she described the locations of the tattoos. "So you know my first thought when I saw her?"

"Tell me."

"If I ever have to do a casting call for an all-girl lesbian porno version of Moby Dick, there's my Queequeg. Second thing I thought was, 'Queequeg' is the worst stage name ever."

Cal laughed. "Yeah, that's pretty bad. Not what she was going by, though, I assume."

"No, of course not. I think she was Roxy or Riley or something like that."

"Worst stripper name I ever ran across was Mirabile."

"That's pretty."

Cal shook his head. "Too on the nose. She was doing the whole Catholic schoolgirl thing, button down shirt, plaid skirt, white knee-high socks, pigtails, all a bit much."

"So she offended your deep religious sensibilities?" Ariel asked. "You think God disapproves of strippers?"

"Ha. I'm the last person anyone should ask about what God approves or disapproves of."

"Because you don't know, or you don't care?"

"I thought we were talking about stage names."

"All right," Ariel drew back almost imperceptibly. "Best name?"

"Best... there was a girl in Atlantic City who went by Vegas, which I could never quite figure if it was stupid or brilliant. Since it stuck in my head I guess I have to go with brilliant."

"Agreed."

"Other than that, I don't know... Ariel's starting to make a run for best."

"Is that so?" she asked, coy yet pleased.

"It's growing on me, maybe," he backpedaled. What the hell was he thinking, flirting with a stripper? He wasn't going to wait around until her shift ended and take her out or try to bring her home. He wasn't even going to establish the rapport a steady customer might develop. He was never going to see her again. Next time he and Vinnie hit a club, they'd pick another. It wasn't a matter of wasting money, or even wasting time, both of which he had fully intended to indulge in as a matter of course. But it was an emotional investment, however temporary and illusory, and an ill-advised one at that.

"Well, your name is growing on me, too," Ariel said. "Although I can't say whether it's perfectly suited for whatever line of work you're in."

Cal snorted. "You don't want to know what line of work I'm in."

She covered his hand with her own. "Try me."

He shook his head. "Some other time." He began to seriously consider leaving soon, quitting while he was ahead. Then he noticed Vinnie, still standing at the bar, his steady intake of vodka punctuated by grunts directed at a stripper who had insinuated herself alongside him. He pointed the pair out to Ariel. "Vinnie might be making a liar out of me."

Ariel glanced toward the bar. Cal wondered if she noticed that

Vinnie had turned around, broad back leaned against the chipped brass rail, elbows braced nonchalantly. He wondered if Ariel would dissect and interpret Vinnie's body language the way he did, and read the way that Vinnie looked around the club trying to spot a better prospect as the clumsy ploy it was, an attempt to gain negotiating leverage over the girl attempting to seal the deal.

"Let me guess," Ariel said. "You told me Vinnie doesn't pay for lap dances, but that's not entirely true. He just does it very rarely. And... oh, no, is he actually haggling with Naya?"

"You are good," Cal said. "He only gets lap dances if he's going to get his money's worth, and that means he sets the price and the girl has to be his type."

"Is she?"

Cal considered Naya, her blonde hair loose and bouncy like something out of a shampoo commercial, her makeup traditional but heavy, her surgically enhanced breasts threatening to spill out of a fringed string bikini top, her denim cutoffs with their button fly already undone and top folded down to better show off the tramp stamp on her lower back and the piercing in her belly button. She was short enough to be girlish without seeming too delicate, curvy enough to have plenty to shake but nothing that jiggled on its own. "Physically, pretty much," he said. "Is she a talker?"

"On the job? Not much more than 'oh, baby, come with me, let's get naughty' and variations on that theme."

"They're perfect for each other, then," Cal confirmed.

Ariel contemplated the twosome at the bar silently for several moments, then fetched a heaving sigh and mused, "They would have the most beautiful babies."

Cal almost choked on the liquor he was swallowing, but cleared his airway with energetic coughing which dissolved into heartfelt laughter. Ariel regarded him with a wicked, tight-lipped smile for a few seconds before joining in, and they laughed together, a genuine shared experience. Then it evaporated. Cal looked again toward Vinnie, to see if the big man had noticed that he and Ariel were laughing. Vinnie would assume, as he always did, and rightly in this case, that they were laughing at him, and that would spell the end of the night. But Vinnie was allowing Naya to lead him away, their negotiation successfully concluded, transaction underway. Cal took a swallow of his own drink.

"The line of work you and Vinnie are both in," Ariel ventured, "is that the thing you like least about him?"

"Not sure," Cal admitted. "But it's up there."

"Is that the thing you like least about yourself?"

"What are you, my therapist?" Cal shook his head. "I didn't come here to talk about my problems... my life. I came to forget about it for a while."

"Forget about your life, or your problems?"

"Same difference."

She slid a little closer. "Maybe it's not good for you to just try to forget. Maybe it'd be better if you told another person about it. Just once. One person you're never going to see again." As if she'd read his mind. "One person who owes you for the drink," she smiled.

He stared at her, daring her to back off, to swerve away from the oncoming collision. She met his gaze, unperturbed. He beckoned with a slight tilt of his head. Their hips were already pressed together, and she could only come closer by leaning her face toward his. He aimed his mouth at her ear. "We kill people."

He pulled back to look her in the eye, and she refused to shrink away. "You say that like you think I've never met anyone with blood on their hands," she said.

"Most people haven't."

"That's just something most people tell themselves."

"You're talking about people who know someone who caused a fatal car crash, or helped someone OD, or stupid shit like that. I am talking about getting paid to murder people."

"And I still say you're not the first person matching that description I've ever met. Although you don't seem the type. Vinnie does. He's a thug, a brute, he's got just barely enough brains to realize he's going to do a certain amount of killing while he's walking the Earth anyway, he might as well get paid for it, maybe even set himself up behind some protection from the consequences. Which means he's mobbed up. Both of you are."

"Ding ding ding."

"But you're smarter than Vinnie. And you don't have the casual killer profile."

"Which you've figured out right after meeting me."

"Am I wrong?"

"...I suppose not. I hope I'm smarter than Vinnie, even if I'm dumb enough to wind up in the same place."

"So how did you get here?"

"Smart people make stupid choices. Smart and arrogant go hand in hand. Smart people think they can walk up to the line, dance on it, but not step over it. Do some drugs, but not so much that it takes over your life. Or only takes over a little. So you need to steal some money for the habit, but not so much that anyone will notice. And you pick your targets wisely, or tell yourself that's what you're doing. And then one day you pick the wrong one."

"That sounds like the answer to how did you end up behind a dumpster with a bullet in your brain."

"Hmp," Cal made the noise of recognizing humor without actually finding it funny. "You don't know how close it came to going down like that."

"So tell me," Ariel urged. "Come on. You're almost there. You're so close."

"They picked me up walking down the street, pushed me into a dark alley. Probably there was a dumpster in there somewhere, at least a couple of garbage cans. And they were going to shoot me, no doubt about that, by the time we were off the sidewalk they had their guns in their hands. I had nothing to lose. Do nothing, bang. Do something, maybe I might get out of it, maybe not, but nothing worse than my brains blown out, right?"

"I can think of a couple worse things."

"So could I. And I did at the time, and I just started talking about it, trying to buy some time, trying to figure out a way out, just babbling really. Nothing left to lose, like I said. I started asking them what the point was, what they would get out of it if they killed me and dumped me in an alley. It wouldn't get them the money I owed them. It wouldn't get them anything."

"It would send a message," Ariel said.

"Right, that's what the one guy said. But I told him that didn't make any sense either. I had no friends at that point, ; no one would miss me if I was gone. Unless they were going to hand out maps to my rat-chewed corpse, no one would ever know how I died, or why. I must have said the same thing over and over again thirty, forty times, coming at it from slightly different angles, over and over, running my mouth to save my life."

"I knew you were a talker," Ariel smiled.

"Well, eventually the guy heard what I was saying, and told me to come with him. Back to see the boss."

"And you went?"

"Didn't think it was one of the worse-than-a-bullet options," Cal admitted. "Not at the time. Now..." He trailed off into his glass, finished his drink.

"The boss didn't kill you. Obviously."

"Right. The guy, I think he was getting some thrill out of torturing me. I had planted a doubt in his mind, that somehow he'd be screwing up if he just shot me and left me dead and anonymous in some back alley. He wanted to make sure the boss was cool with what he had planned, or find out what the boss wanted exactly if it wasn't that. So basically he brought me along to watch him and the boss talk over how I was supposed to die."

"So, how were you supposed to die?"

"Discussion never got around to that. First thing the boss did was shoot the guy, for not doing the job of killing me, for coming back and bothering the big picture man with the little details. Then he reminded me that I owed him a lot of money. Which was one of the points I had made to his recently deceased associate, but I knew all I was expected to do was agree. So I did. And then the boss asked me if I wanted to pay it off by taking a job."

"And you took it."

"I took the lifeline he was throwing me, yeah. I didn't even try to rationalize it, beyond knowing that I'd get to live a little longer by saying yes. You want to hear something funny?"

"Sure."

"This is the part where I should say, 'And I'll never forget the relief and sheer joy of being alive that I felt when the boss stopped aiming his gun at me and put it back down on the desk.' But you know what? I have forgotten it. It's been a long time and I've... it's just gone. I keep doing what I have to do to survive because deep down I'm an animal intent on outrunning death, but there's no upside to it."

"Hilarious."

"Right?"

"So what, the boss killed the guy who was supposed to kill you, and then he needed a replacement enforcer, so he offered to cancel your debt if you took the guy's place?"

"Not exactly."

"Then what, exactly?"

"The boss saw my point, believe it or not. He wanted me in his organization as a consultant, I guess you could say. Obviously he already had plenty of guys like the one he'd just put down, guys like Vinnie. Someone who can find someone that needs killing and make them dead, they're a dime a dozen. But to truly send a message, each death had to be meaningful, understandable to anyone who heard about it, and likely to get attention. Deaths that were so brutal, so personal, they couldn't possibly be written off as accidents or random crimes. Deaths so specific and distinctive they were practically signed and sealed. And deaths so noteworthy they'd make it into the newspapers, get spread around by word of mouth, and become urban legends. Planning those kinds of deaths requires creativity, and the boss's enforcers all had a certain deficiency in that area."

"As did the boss himself," Ariel said.

"Right. He saw the appeal in being as feared as the Devil himself. He had that much vision, at least. But he needed me to make it happen."

"So you don't kill people, you just dream up spectacularly grotesque ways for them to die, and Vinnie executes," Ariel said. "Different jobs, really."

"Don't you think that's splitting hairs?"

"Do you?" Ariel asked.

"I told you, we kill people. Vinnie and I, together. Said it, meant it."

"Regret it?"

"Sometimes." Cal stared down at his glass. "Not enough to do anything about it. If I walk away now, I'm dead, and I don't want to die. But if I keep going I'm..."

"Damned?"

"For lack of a better word," Cal said.

"What better word could there be?"

"A word that doesn't imply a higher judgment, a heaven or hell I don't believe in."

"But you do think along those lines, maybe not right out of Sunday school, but you do think what you do and what you're responsible for, directly or indirectly, matters. For all we know, you might be doing God's work, killing people who actually need killing, sending warnings to people who aren't too far gone yet. Maybe you saved yourself, maybe you were saved, because of some higher judgment."

"Laying it on kind of thick now," Cal smiled crookedly, leaning as far back as he could against the booth's wraparound seat back. "You've already earned your tip from me, don't worry." He realized that none of his amusement was reflected back in Ariel's expression. "What, are you being serious?" he asked.

Ariel shrugged, willing to wait for him to figure it out.

"Look, no offense," Cal said, "telling yourself whatever's in your past is all part of some plan, or whatever, if that's what gets you through the day. That's fine for you and anybody else it works for. I'm not part of any plan other than what my boss tells me to do. Maybe there's a heaven, maybe there's a God, I don't know, but what I do know is God doesn't really get involved here on Earth. Is something waiting for us on the other side? Maybe, maybe not, I don't know, but here in the real world there's little kids with terminal cancer and young soldiers getting blown up ten thousand miles from home, while scumbags like me and Vinnie walk around untouched. No plan, no reasons, just the way things are."

"Maybe you're right," Ariel said. "Feel better now?"

"I'm trying not to feel anything right now," Cal said. "Belly full of bourbon, face full of tits, mind empty, that's the plan," Cal said. "My plan. My reasons."

"Ariel to the main stage! Ariel! To the main stage!" a voice boomed from the speakers overhead.

She slid away, reluctantly, curving her body as if it were being pulled toward Cal and away from him by equal forces. "Gotta go," she said. "But come and see me up there, and we'll see what else I can do for your plan." She shimmied her breasts, a showy move that came across more joking wink than suggestive enticement.

Cal watched her weave between chairs and tables on her way to the stage steps. He looked around for Vinnie and Naya, but couldn't spot them. He pushed himself to the edge of the booth bench and hauled himself to his feet, feeling a little unsteady as he moved toward the back of the club and the men's room. Had he lost track of how many drinks he'd had while talking to Ariel? He'd certainly lost track of time, along with his usual tendency to keep most of his thoughts to himself.

Voiding his bladder was a relief, and as he washed his hands he stared contentedly into the mirror over the sink. It took a few seconds before he realized it was a behavior he rarely engaged in any more. Self-regard and soul-searching were habits he had gradually shed over time, now strangely foreign to him, an indulgent luxury he could neither justify nor afford. And yet, here he stood, meeting his own gaze in the flake-edged glass without flinching, reconnecting with a piece of his past.

In spite of himself, he wondered if Ariel had actually accomplished something. Telling her more than he was accustomed to acknowledging about himself had enabled him to face his reflection for more than a second without wanting to throw up or smash the mirror. A small difference, but a noticeable one.

He stopped pondering before the men's room attendant could have the chance to find his behavior strange. He flicked water from his fingers into the sink, turned around with damp hands ready for the offered paper towel, and realized there was no attendant. Odd. Strip club men's rooms always boasted some older gent with coke-bottle glasses and a red bowtie, ostensibly giving the joint an air of respectability and class but really just ensuring there were eyes everywhere and no part of the club was truly private, no secret space for dancers to be assaulted by customers or busted by vice for turning tricks. But Cal was all alone. Absently he grabbed a paper towel from the wall-mounted dispenser, dried his hands, pulled the door to return to the club floor.

Cal scanned the entire room, not as he would normally feast on all of the hedonistic depravity on display, but the way he would assess a potential target's apartment or workplace, keying in on anomalous details, inventorying anything out of the ordinary. Ariel was on the main stage, gyrating around a brass pole, rhythmically, hypnotically, but he forced himself to note her and move on. At another pole on the opposite end of the stage, a stripper wearing nothing but black vinyl thigh boots stuporously changed poses in time with the music. In the far corner of the club, Cal could just make out Vinnie occupying an overstuffed chair, with Naya draped across his lap, having shed most of her trailer queen outfit. Across the club, two strippers were talking to one another, standing close and taking turns pressing mouth to ear, one dressed like a naughty librarian, the other a down-market lingerie model.

Cal looked for the bartender; she was drying a hurricane glass with a frayed white hand towel. His eyes sought out the DJ in her booth, intently focused on the computer screen that cast ing a pale phosphorescent glow on her face. Cal's eyes swept the club for other customers. There were none.

He and Vinnie were the only men in the establishment.

Cal walked between the empty booths, down the stairs that separated the outer lounge from the inner stage area, and approached Ariel. He stopped at the edge of the stage and looked up at her. She noticed him, smiled down upon him. She worked her way around the pole, placing it between herself and Cal, then dropped into a crouch, her buttocks brushing the backs of her heels. He leaned in, jerked his head for her to come closer. She stretched forward, catlike, and crawled across the stage toward him. She tilted her head to the side so that her tresses brushed the surface of the stage. He brought his lips to her exposed ear. "Ariel really is your name. Your true name. Isn't it?"

"Yes," she answered without hesitation.

"But not after the little mermaid," he went on. "And not after Prospero's spirit servant, either."

She pulled back, looked deeply into his eyes to see what he suspected and what he knew. The expression on her face shifted, minutely but profoundly. A few moments ago she had been playful, teasing, daring him to keep up; now she was somber. They were still connected in a dance, but one that could not end well for both of them. "No," she admitted, shaking her head.

He leaned in again, despite the fact that she was no longer playing along; his mouth found her ear within the fiery curtain of her hair. He could taste the steel piercings lining her helix. "But maybe after the one from Milton."

Her head rolled languidly against his as she took her turn to murmur directly into his ear. "Not after, not exactly. But you're getting warmer."

She stood up, dancing for him, maintaining unnervingly steady eye contact every time the position of her body allowed for it. Cal felt his heart hammering in his chest, the compulsion to flee raging against an utter inability to move an inch from where his feet were rooted, like a mouse giving rapt attention to a cobra. Ariel strutted away from him, looking back over her shoulder, swung around the pole, returned to the edge of the stage in front of him. Fluidly, she turned her back on him, fell to her knees, arched her back until her head was inverted and she was looking at him upside down. Her hips rose and fell in time with the music.

He sought out her ear once again. "So my Hebrew's a little rusty," he said. "I know 'el' means 'of God'. What's Ari?"

She rolled onto her side before she told him: "Lion." From there she regained her feet, hips swaying as she rose. Her fingers reached for her breastbone, for the knot of her top, to untie it.

Past Ariel, in the corner of the club, Cal could see Naya and Vinnie. The big man was slouched low in his chair, the back of which only came up to Naya's waist as she stood behind it. She draped her upper body over Vinnie's head, her stomach against his scalp, breasts brushing his jowls, mouth somewhere around his belt buckle and hands braced on his knees. Cal watched her straighten her back in a long, slow unfurling of her spine, fingernails tracing tiny furrows up Vinnie's pant legs and the sides of his shirt. Then the nails sank deep into his ribs, drawing viscous blooms that glowed purple-black in the dim.

Naya flexed her arms and opened Vinnie's chest. His face became a scream of pain and rage, although the sound didn't reach Cal's ears; Vinnie's punctured lungs too breathless to produce more than a wheeze. He would die here, but for now the agony continued unabated as his hands shook weakly, his head trembling side to side in mute protest. His eyes went wide, anger draining and replaced by abject terror, as Naya walked slowly around the chair and climbed into his lap on her knees. Her hands dripped with dark.

"Don't worry," Ariel said, with heartbreaking sincerity, somehow drawing Cal's attention away from Vinnie, back to her face. She smiled at him beatifically. "He was unrepentant to the very end, and he died reaping what he had sown. You've made your last confession. It really is as good for the soul as they say."

"You're still going to kill me," Cal said.

Ariel nodded. "But you won't feel any pain. I promise."

She had finished teasing apart the knot, and the front of her top fell away from her breasts in twin diaphanous cascades, gossamer flares of sheer purple that spread and stretched and became wide wings of light the color of the dawn. Ariel reached up above her head as if to take hold of some glint of light coming from the mirror ball, and then the glint of light was the edge of a sword, and the sword was swinging towards Cal's exposed neck like the promise Ariel had made, the promise of no pain, the promise of a kind of absolution and the end of all pain.

And in the end Ariel was true to her word, as all angels must be.

After The Inferno

THE SERE SKY, ALL DIRTY DUN CLOUDS like an ancient vaulted ceiling of crumbling stucco, appeared indifferent to the one-man rotaplane as it bobbed beneath it like a brass bumblebee. Bertram Lyman was equally indifferent to the sky, focusing all his energy on cranking the foot pedals that kept the push-propellor spinning and the bellows pumping updraft to the lift blades. His thighs burned with the effort, and the soles of his feet were developing blisters of surprising intensity; this was the farthest he had ever attempted to take the rotaplane, by an order of magnitude at least. His eyes were fixed on the rotaplane's dashboard compass, a wobbling sphere floating in mineral oil under glass, which indicated his heading continued to be roughly three-hundred eighteen degrees, north-northwest. He was nearly there.

The quality of the ground, several hundred feet below, began to change, from the gentle ripples with their telltale salt-stains that had once been the floor of the Irish Sea to the craggy outcroppings which were the erstwhile Emerald Isle's coast. It was emerald no more, of course, every hillock reduced to gray ash-smeared soil and barren black rock. If, however, the tome that Bertram had discovered and translated was true, then the island might yet conceal a treasure worth more than emeralds, more than diamonds or gold or even precious water itself.

Worth could be a subjective thing, of course. What Bertram considered an invaluable resource was regarded as danger to be avoided by others. But Bertram cursed those others for fools, just as he cursed his feeble legs for weak and useless things as they faltered in their rhythmic revolutions and the rotaplane began to tremble unsteadily. He steeled himself and bore all of his will into each pedaling downstroke, and yet his disobedient mind sparked with stray thoughts, futile wishes for just a small bit of phlogiston. It was not the first time he had made such a wish, and he was sure it would not be the last. He had wished for fuel more often than he had taken the rotaplane out on salvage sorties since the Great Inferno, and he had flown so many salvage sorties he had lost count.

If he had been able to cure himself of coveting phlogiston, then his present course would have been markedly easier. Despite its retrofitted foot pedals, the rotaplane still bore the weight of a theoretically functional compressor engine as well as a not inconsiderable fuel tank. The one-man craft would have been less of a trial to keep aloft by pedaling had the engine and fuel tanks been removed, but Bertram could not relinquish his hope that the machinery would run under its own power once again someday. And he would not have been flying this particular route were it not for the slender hope of finding fuel once he landed.

No one knew how the Great Inferno had started, exactly. Any witnesses to that cataclysm's genesis would have been incinerated immediately, in the moment of ignition when the heat was most intense. But in its aftermath, when the survivors had dug themselves out of the drifts of char and cinders, speculations and hypothetical reconstructions had provided an acceptable account of what must have happened. The phlogiston refinery in Sunderland had suffered a terrible accident. Some blamed human avarice and sabotage, but any reasonable individual would admit that the suicidal act seemed unlikely to have been the result of mere greed. In any case, when all of the refinery's phlogiston had ignited at once, the firestorm swept outward with devastating speed and unquenchable hunger. Every other source of phlogiston in the world had fed into the conflagration, in escalating waves of flame.

The Great Inferno had raced across the land in all directions, devouring everything flammable. Stone and metal survived, but wood and other plants burned to ash, from farmer's crops and wild forests to the timbers of houses, bridges, ships. When the Inferno reached water, it vaporized it; every schoolchild knew that phlogiston was inextinguishable by water. Or had known, when chymology and thermodynamic engineering were still regarded as necessary, vital pursuits, and not despised as the root cause of the world's ruination. Now life had little room for anything other than daily survival, the struggle to find scarce food and water, and fuel when invoked at all was a symbol of hubris from a grim creation myth.

Bertram rejected such binary thinking, finding the very notion that a chemical tool could be all-powerfully malicious as laughable as the idea that it might be omni-benevolent. Simple superstition, as unrealistic as the old Irish legends about Saint Patrick banishing all snakes from the island and driving them into the sea. Bertram far preferred the facts and formulae of science, and knew he could master phlogiston to serve his purposes, if he could only locate a new source.

The indifference of the torpid sky suddenly shifted, as a furious headwind slammed into the rotaplane, upending it as a child would flip a tiddly-wink. Bertram's feet slipped from the pedals, just as his backside would have slipped from the seat if not for the five-point harness securing him at the controls. For a moment the rotaplane was soaring upward, not under its own faltering power but borne on the air currents; then the wind abated and the rotaplane began to free-fall.

Desperate, Bertram found the pedals and began to revolve them, setting the propeller blades spinning, but the rotaplane continued to plummet. Worse, the entire craft was now corkscrewing downward like a falling samara, the spiraling descent nearly as rapid as a nosedive with the added stressors of centripetal force taxing Bertram's fortitude. If not for the rotaplane's bottom-heavy ballast, he might have found himself dropping upside-down, and as good as dead. Even so, he wanted to slacken his limbs, to close his eyes and even let go of consciousness itself. Yet he knew that the imminent high-speed impact with the ground below would translate a moment's inattentiveness into eternal rest. Despite the vertiginous, elliptical tumbling that robbed him of all equilibrium, Bertram fought to regain his bearings. His eyes looked not for the horizon, not even for the floating compass, but for the rotaplane controls yawing wildly back and forth before him. He gripped the handles like lifelines, orienting himself on their relative stability, and stiffened his legs.

A pedal smashed into his Achilles tendon, and he bit his lip at the pain but kept his foot where it was, preventing the pedal from flying around again. He slid his sole backwards onto the pedal, then found its counterpart with his opposite foot. He pushed, gathering momentum, setting the rotors in motion once more. The rotaplane's spill from the sky slowed ever so slightly, and its flightpath of declivity gradually bent from an orthogonal to the ground below to an obtuse angle.

The rotaplane's skids met the ground, still pitched steeply and approaching with great velocity. The rotaplane bounced off the parched surface atop a cliff, inverted itself, struck the ground again, bounced again, skewed sideways, and made a final surrender to gravity. Bertram felt every impact up and down his spine, rattling his skull. When the rotaplane mercifully came to rest, he forced himself to take a deep breath, if only so that he could hear the rush of his exhalation and assure himself even with his eyes closed that he was, in truth, still alive.

After taking in several lungfuls, equal parts air and dust raised by his crash landing, Bertram extricated himself from the rotaplane seat, separating himself from the machine by slow degrees, trying to avoid harming himself or damaging the aircraft further. If all went according to plan, he would need the rotaplane in good working order to carry him back to England, and as far as Bertram was concerned, his plans must continue. Once he was standing beside the rotaplane, he performed a cursory check, examining the framework and the visible moving parts for catastrophic damage. The rotaplane had been dented and bent in places, but nothing appeared ruinous. Bertram nodded in satisfaction and attempted to set the aircraft upright on its runners once more.

The rotaplane was heavy, and stoutly refused his efforts to tip it into its proper orientation. Bertram heaved and shoved in vain for what felt like a promethean eternity. Then he stopped suddenly, freezing in place, eyes wide. He turned his head by minuscule increments to look back over his shoulder, convinced that something had shifted just behind him. Yet nothing revealed itself. The wind continued to rise and fall, redistributing ash and dehydrated silt in drifting patterns, but no other movement was visible, no other sounds audible.

Bertram nonetheless took the opportunity to survey the immediate vicinity for the first time since his crash, looking past the furrow the rotaplane had gashed into the ground. To his back was the cliff face that had once tumbled down to the wild Irish Sea and now merely separated two arid plains of differing elevations. Several rusting hulks stood nearby, two to his left and one to his right, their dull orange hides pitted and pocked. Before the phlogiston storm had turned machinery into the ultimate taboo, such technological triumphs were commonplace. Now they were regarded with the same unease as the graven idols of lost civilizations, left to brood over the desolation in obscurity.

He walked toward the nearest forsaken machine, a shepherd's mate. Once the automated device had rolled back and forth along the grassy verge of the cliff, swinging its carousel of iron paddles to warn sheep away from the treacherous drop. Bertram shimmied the central axle to reach one of the armatures, and balanced atop it. He pulled a socket wrench from his belt and loosened the bolts attaching one of the paddles. He stuffed each bolt into his pocket as it came free, and within moments the paddle fell to the ground. Bertram dropped down, retrieved the paddle, and returned to the rotaplane. Using the paddle as a lever, he righted the aircraft, and continued examining its airworthiness.

The rotaplane would fly again, Bertram concluded. More to the point, it would fly him home, once his explorations had been concluded successfully. All the major parts were intact, and while the propellers were slightly bent he believed they would suffice to cross the ashen seabed and return him to England, providing adequate lift once they were spun by the phlogiston engine. Without the elixir he sought, the rotaplane would unlikely become or remain airborne. For that matter, if he failed to discover the phlogiston he had already promised himself, then he might as well never return to England at all.

Bertram retrieved his haversack from the rotaplane. Using his hand compass and the brittle old map, he oriented himself and his present position along what had once been the island coastline. He did not attempt an exacting calculation, since he would need to make progress inland before attempting to navigate by the ghosts of old, burned-over landmarks. Once he identified what he presumed to be the proper direction to proceed, he set off on foot. After a few dozen strides, he abruptly turned around and ran back to the cliff. He gathered up corroded fragments of the dead machinery and built a rough lean-to around the rotaplane, to camouflage against scavengers. Any truly enterprising individual who came close would see through the mask straightaway, but Bertram reasoned nonetheless that it was better than nothing. He embarked on the course he had chosen for a second time.

The going was slow, the ground uneven and treacherous. The Great Inferno had metamorphosed grass and soil into desiccated ash which clung to unburied loose stones or settled into pits and fissures in the bedrock. Bertram walked as slowly as a first-generation march-nought, establishing absolute certainty in the stability of each footfall before taking another step forward. He made incremental if desultory progress across the desolate terrain, leaving occasional markers to help him retrace his path back to the rotaplane. He saw not another soul, nor any signs of life. It was commonly assumed that Ireland had been completely depopulated, as its less industrialized landscape would have provided few stone or iron bulwarks against the Great Inferno. Had there been any survivors, surely some of them would have made their way on foot across the arid seabed to seek refuge in more prosperous England, yet nothing of the sort had occurred. Bertram grieved for the Irish, in an abstract way, even as he rationalized that taking what he had come for would be easiest if no one remained to object.

Idle fantasies of vast, secret pools of phlogiston passed the time pleasantly enough until Bertram spotted an outcropping a few hundred yards away, several degrees off from where he had expected it. But the surrounding area was essentially featureless, and the discrepancy could easily be explained by his own loose calculation of distance and estimation of direction. The outcropping had to be the structure he sought, and he made for it with as much haste as caution would allow.

Soon he stood before the shape which had caught his eye, a triune of heavy, angular stones which had obviously been shaped by human hands into two plinths and a crosspiece, all framing the natural entranceway of a cave. The pitch black opening into the earth was only five feet tall, and barely wide enough to admit a man's shoulders. In earlier times, the primitive architectural feature would have been obscured by grass, moss, and clinging vines. According to Bertram's map, the entire structure would further have been situated within a dense stand of trees hiding it from the view of unknowing passersby. But with all vegetation incinerated, the denuded rock lay plainly exposed. Bertram stood at the chthonic doorway, hearing a rapid, half-crazed breathing that he gradually came to realize was his own.

Bertram reached into his haversack and pulled out a pair of opera glasses, copper casings inlaid with ivory. With practiced ease, he held the glasses to his forehead, slipped small leather straps from his flight helmet through copper buckle fittings, and secured the device. He lowered the eyepieces to his own sockets and twisted the focal wheel between the chambered lenses. The cave's impenetrable darkness resolved into a distinguishable pattern of monochromatic surfaces, such that Bertram could make out the contours of the tunnel descending deeper into the earth.

The act of donning the occludoscope and the familiar spectral irradiance amplification of its vanadate lenses served to calm Bertram's nerves and quiet his breathing. He ducked his head and stepped between the plinths.

The tunnel meandered back and forth as it progressed ever downward. After Bertram had been walking for nearly a minute, it forked, with the branch to his right inclining back towards the surface while the one on his left sank deeper through the bedrock. Bertram chose the left path. Two minutes later, he noted that the tunnel floor fell away abruptly a few feet ahead. He stepped gingerly to the edge, looked down, and saw a four foot drop to a small landing, followed by another steep drop. Bertram carefully lowered himself down the steps, then followed the tunnel for another minute before encountering a switchback. He was beginning to wonder how long the tunnel could possibly run when his nose caught an earthy tang in the air, something he had not smelled in a long time: the smoke of burning lignite.

Even before the Great Inferno, Bertram had only rarely been in the presence of lignite. As an energy source, it was inferior to phlogiston in every way. Every device in his family home, in his school, in the shops he frequented, all were fueled by phlogiston. Yet once in a great while, Bertram would have reason to visit a farm in the country, or a wharf along the Mersey, and there he might find some poor wretch using the greasy brown combustible for cheap heat. Since the Great Inferno, lignite was just as distrusted as phlogiston, or as bitumen or whale oil or any other flammable substance, for that matter.

Nonetheless, Bertram knew the odor of lignite, and it was indubitably nearby. Silently, Bertram raised the occludoscope to his crown and allowed his eyes to adjust to the near-total darkness. The faintest roseate glow touched the walls ahead, and Bertram felt along the underground corridor in that direction. As he drew closer to the light source and the burnt fragrance in the air, Bertram heard low voices, chanting in unison.

The tunnel floor met the top of a staircase, not a crude, severe sawtooth like the obstacle he had encountered earlier, but a much more accommodating set of chiseled steps, polished smooth. The right-hand wall of the stairway was a solid mass of rock, but the left-hand side was partially open, wrought as a handhold of sorts that ran downward waist-high. Bertram dropped to his hands and knees and crept up to the half wall, peering through the angular gap in the stone.

Below was a large chamber, filled with more wooden furniture than Bertram had seen in one place since before the Great Inferno. All were mismatched: a wingback that would not have been out of place in an Oxford don's private library here, a weather-beaten rocking chair from the front stoop of a farmhouse there, but they had been deliberately arranged with meticulous thought. The layout approximated the inside of a church. Rows of chairs formed simulated pews, with a central aisle running the length of the cavern. A massive slab of rock at the front was surrounded by a crude balustrade formed by scraps of wood, and atop the stone dais was a stout old trestle table repurposed as an altar, with three very fine chairs arrayed behind it, facing the congregation. In an ordinary church, there would be ceremonial candles lit, standing on tall spindles between the chairs or burning upon the altar itself, but none were present in the scene below.

At the moment, the three finest chairs were unoccupied, but three figures in hooded sackcloth robes stood behind the altar, while nearly two dozen others in similar dark shrouds knelt along the perimeter rail. The central figure of the trio behind the altar, arms upraised, droned an unceasing rhythm of Latin syllables, snatches of which Bertram recognized from Catholic services he had attended in his youth as a means of shocking his staunchly Episcopalian parents.

At intervals, just as Bertram remembered, the congregants would make their rote responses as one. Eventually a chant culminated in a prolonged "Amen." As the echoes of the affirmation faded, the congregants rose to their feet. The celebrant, as Bertram thought of him, arched his back and raised his arms higher still, tilting his head back to address the cavern ceiling and through it, presumably, the Almighty.

"Oh Lord, our most righteous heavenly God, we know that we are far from your favor," the celebrant intoned gravely. "Once, you promised Noah that you would never again bring forth in your wrath a flood to punish fallen mankind. We sinners took that covenant for granted, forgetting in our impure hearts that you had made no promise about other elements, and might one day bury us in stony earth, or flail us with roaring wind, or scour us in purging flame. Yet we also know that we are not utterly forsaken. Even now it is by your will alone that the abominations and Oilliphéist and Caoránach, once imprisoned but now freed by the angels' flaming swords, prowl the wilderness rather than seek us in our very homes."

The congregation murmured contrite agreement. Bertram was struck by the oddity of a Catholic priest speaking in vernacular rather than Latin, but quickly realized that he was witnessing the rites of a new religion, a post-Infernal religion. The old Church trappings remained, the habits of papistry died hard, but they had reoriented themselves into new modes, better expressed in the vernacular.

The celebrant continued, "We who were spared the fires of your divine retribution know that we are unworthy, for all are born guilty of irredeemable sin, and all share in the fallen nature of man. We who survived know that your anger and jealousy await appeasement. We who repent shall appease you, while those who continue to turn away from you must be brought low."

"We who repent shall appease you, while those who continue to turn away from you must be brought low," the congregation repeated.

"For your anger is just and right, oh God, and your jealousy is deserved," the celebrant went on, the fervor in his voice intensifying. "You, Holy One, created the burning sun and set it in its place in the heavenly sphere. You, most high, loosed the lightning bolts which sparked the first fires upon the Earth. To you alone, almighty God, belongs the sole right to control all flames, and those who would have usurped your power over fire instead incurred your swift and all-consuming judgment. Those who escaped that divine immolation, and would even now continue to blaspheme your holy dominion over all flames, must also be brought to judgment."

One attendant moved to a corner of the nave and struck an old church bell with a small hammer, and a cold chill ran down Bertram's spine. The Great Inferno had been a tragedy, decimating the global populace and destroying much of the structure of civilization, but its causes were accidental. Bertram rose each morning and faced each day believing that the work at hand was to rebuild from the ashes of the charred ruins all around. To believe that God in heaven would have deliberately set fire to his own creation betrayed a fundamental outlook that Bertram felt sure would drive him mad. To further believe that the all-knowing, all-powerful God had not gone far enough in his destruction …

Bertram's thoughts were interrupted by a panicked voice emerging from the impenetrable shadows on the far side of the cavern church. "No, please, no!" the cries begged. Two congregants all but oozed out of the darkness, ebon robes indistinguishable from the shadows. Between them a man struggled to escape. He was perhaps fifty, with thinning gray hair, broad across his shoulders and chest, round-bellied, bow-legged. He was stripped to the waist, his wrists bound in shackles connected by an iron chain, the ends of which were held by the congregants as they led him up to the altar. "No, let me go! For pity's sake!" the man protested, his voice raw. The acolytes ignored him, maneuvering him into a supine position atop the altar, allowing Bertram to see that the man's ankles were hobbled by shackles and chain as well.

One acolyte pulled the man's hands up over his head, looping the chains through a ring bolted to the floor beside the altar, while his counterpart performed similar motions on the other side to secure the man's legs.

A final tolling of the bell reverberated through the cavern and slowly faded away. The celebrant looked down on the man chained to the altar. "You have sinned against God and against your fellow man, by transgressing into His holy dominion over fire," the dark priest informed the bound man.

"No, never, I never ..." the man protested, straining against his bonds in vain.

The celebrant gestured to an attendant, who turned away and retrieved a quart-sized jar of flint glass. The congregation gasped at the sight of the vessel, and Bertram's eyes widened as he recognized the pale golden liquid within: phlogiston. Reflexively, Bertram clapped his hand to his lips, to stifle a moan of self-satisfied vindication. The map had been true, had led him to his heart's desire.

"Do you deny that this ... essence of the diabolical was found on your property?" the dark priest demanded. The entire church had gone still as a tomb, and the celebrant's voice was quiet, yet crushingly intense.

"Please, please, no ..." the man on the altar gasped, the position of his arms making it hard for him to breathe properly. "I don't know how ... someone else must have hidden it there ... please, believe ..."

The celebrant looked away from the man and out over his fellow worshippers of darkness. "We live in hope of our eternal reward in Heaven, and we fear not the devil in Perdition, for we know that his terrible lake of fire has been utterly drained and brought forth on Earth. Wheresoever we find the last dregs of this unholy fluid, oh God, we claim it in your name and bury it well, to lead us not into temptation and fiery damnation."

At those words the acolyte holding the jar descended from the dais and walked down the aisle. Bertram watched, unable to take his eyes off the vessel. At the back of the cavern, the acolyte drew aside a curtain of the same dark sackcloth as his garb, behind which stood rough brick shelves, lined with jars, bottles, and flasks of flint glass, all filled with phlogiston. The acolyte set the jar among the others, closed the curtain, and returned to the altar, all while Bertram pressed his fist hard against his teeth, heart racing. There was more phlogiston in the secret church than he dared dream existed after the Great Inferno. He stopped just short of thinking of it as a miracle, then realized that the entire scene below him could be considered miraculous. Phlogiston that had not been combusted, wood that had been scorched but not completely reduced to ash, human beings who had been burned and scarred and yet lived. The underground church was a gathering of survivors, both the living and the objects. And yet the men and women huddling in the braziers' smoky light to worship their angry, vengeful God and atone for their supposed sins did not seem grateful for their own survival.

With the acolyte once again at his side, the celebrant looked to the vault above once more. "God, we pray that this sacrifice will be acceptable to you, and will stay your hand from igniting the holy flames which are yours and yours alone to command, or unleashing the savage hellions of the wilderness," the dark priest intoned, as he drew a dagger from his belt and held it above the intended sacrifice's breast. The man on the altar screamed and arched his back, but moved very little as the acolytes manning the chains held fast, increasing the tension in the bonds.

Bertram's horror was overtaken by a sudden, undeniable conviction that this was his best opportunity to take what he had come for. All eyes were on the celebrant, awaiting the catharsis of sacrificial bloodletting. The victim's dying screams would cover any extraneous noise Bertram might inadvertently make. If he could move quickly enough, he could descend, grab the phlogiston, and retreat before anyone had a chance to notice.

He crept down the stone stairs, reaching into his haversack as he went. He pulled out a bundle of tiny brass rivets, connected by tightly wound strands of hemp. Bertram shook the netting loose, holding the edge in his right hand. He looked back over his shoulder just in time to see the dark priest's knife plunging down into the chained man's heart. Ruby droplets spurted from the victim's chest, spattering the celebrant's face, while the man vehemently howled his agony . The priest raised the knife again, his hands gleaming with a sheen of heart's blood, and stabbed once more. The man's cries of protest and pain became awful garglings, choked in blood.

Bertram shuddered involuntarily, whipping his head back toward the shelves. Most of the flint glass vessels were simple, utilitarian shapes, but among the cylindrical canisters and teardrop bottles were several which were practically works of art. One was pyramidal, etched with an elaborate all-seeing eye on one triangular face. Another was almost perfectly spherical, except for a small flat base, and the glass had been colored like chalcedony with swirls of yellow, orange and red. Yet another had been cast in the shape of a rampant lion, with a black rubber stopper clenched in its fanged jaws.

Bertram would grieve for the loss of the more fanciful vessels, but he needed the phlogiston more than he needed to preserve the dead legacy of glass-smith artisans. Working as swiftly as he dared, he began loading vessels into the netting. He avoided those which looked too fragile, or which were only half-full or contained nothing but dregs, yet the vast stores spoiled him for choice, and soon his net was filled with sturdy flint glass jars full of phlogiston. On impulse, Bertram grabbed the pyramid-shaped vessel, stuffed it in with the rest, then drew the net tight and knotted it. He slung his pack over his shoulder and made for the staircase.

His foot had just grazed the bottommost step when he heard a cry from the front of the sanctuary: "Stop, thief!" With the cumbersome pack all too visible from behind, Bertram was in no position to argue. There was nothing for it but to flee, and Bertram scrambled up the stone stairs gracelessly but with inspired swiftness.

A few paces beyond the top of the staircase, Bertram was once again plunged into sheer subterranean darkness, but a smart snap of his head brought the occludoscope back down from his forehead to the bridge of his nose. He could only hope that his pursuers might have forgotten in their haste to bring light sources, costing them precious time as they reversed through inky blackness to fetch … what? Given their eschatological fear of open flames, torches seemed unlikely. Yet they must have navigated the tunnel somehow.

Bertram tried to put the speculation, compelling as it was to his inner engineer, out of his mind as he raced pell-mell through the twisting corridor. He reached the series of drops, now four-foot elevations he was forced to pull himself atop after hoisting the netting up onto each successive landing. He strained to hear if his pursuers were near, but the only sounds he could make out were his labored respiration and the dull thudding of his pulse in his skull. Once he cleared the last elevation, he sprinted up the tunnel. A blindingly brilliant aperture flooded the occludoscope's lenses: daylight. Bertram snatched the eyepiece off his face and shoved it into the haversack caroming off his hip.

He burst through the plinth-framed doorway, breathing in ragged, harried gasps. Running had reawakened all the pains of his crash injuries, and aggravated several. He was now convinced that he had cracked a rib on his right side, and that the fracture was worsening from the exertions of his escape. A dozen yards from the exposed doorway, Bertram stopped, dropping the netting to the ashen ground and bracing his hands on his knees. He closed his eyes, fighting a wave of vertigo, and his mind entered a fugue-like state where time had no meaning.

Bertram had no idea how much time had passed when an angry shout of "There!" roused him from his hunched reverie. His eyes flew open to see three sackcloth figures emerging from the tunnel doorway and heading toward him. Bertram immediately recognized one as an attendant to the dark priest, the one who had held up the damning phlogiston vial. Now he held a smoking lignite lantern. The other two were a gray-haired yet solidly built man, and a woman with long dark plaits, both armed with vicious-looking cudgels. As one, the black trinity advanced on Bertram.

Bertram reached into the net for one of the smaller vessels. He brandished it at his pursuers, who stopped dead, hints of true fear on their faces. The attendant called to him, "You have already provoked us, blasphemer, but do not dare invoke the fiery wrath of our Lord!"

"Is God going to smite me, loosing his thunderbolts?" Bertram taunted. There had not been a single lightning strike recorded since the Great Inferno, as thunderheads could not form given prevailing atmospheric conditions. "I very much doubt that!"

"Fool, you will burn yourself alive, and all of us with you!" the woman hissed.

They were the fools, Bertram told himself. Everything around them had been thoroughly dephlogisticated. Everything except the distilled phlogiston itself. Bertram removed the stopper from the vessel in his hand. He raised the opened container high over his head, signaling his intentions as clearly as he could. The robed trio remained rooted in place. Bertram swung the vessel through the air in a zigzag, sending ribbons of golden fluid in spattering arcs across the ground between himself and the acolytes.

The silent gray-haired man took two steps backwards, while the dark-haired woman let out a dolorous moan like a sleeper in the throes of a nightmare. But the attendant held up his free hand placatingly. "The chrism of perdition cannot blaze on its own," the attendant said with satisfied superiority. "Be not afraid, for …"

Bertram had slipped a Promethean Match from his pocket and dropped it on the ground, at the terminal end of one of the phlogiston trails. He drove his boot heel into it, shattering the ampule concealed within the paper wrapping. Bertram drew his foot back with more force than he had brought it down, nearly falling backwards in violent recoil. The potassium chlorate coating on the glass mixed with the released sulfuric acid, and the paper caught in the exothermic reaction burst into flame. The phlogiston ignited a moment later, great slashes of fire leaping to life between Bertram and the acolytes.

Now the woman did scream, a frenzied high-pitched wail of terror, and the other acolytes yelled and cursed, and the burning phlogiston roared as it consumed itself, but all of those sounds receded quickly behind Bertram as he ran away. He followed his markers, retracing his original path poorly at best, as his boots began to feel as though they were made of lead and his every exhalation became the strained wheezing of an overheated teakettle. He wiped sweat from his eyes with one sleeve until it was soaked, while the other arm, steadying the netting full of phlogiston vessels across his shoulders, cramped ferociously.

Finally Bertram saw the dilapidated hulks of the herding behemoths, and beyond them his rotaplane. Coming upon it now, Bertram realized that his improvised blind for the rotaplane would not have fooled anyone, as the aircraft's continuous lines were obvious through the gaps in the assemblage of rusted scraps piled around it. Nonetheless, the rotaplane stood where Bertram had left it, his escape and salvation. No, Bertram amended, the phlogiston on his back was his salvation, and would speed his escape as well.

Bertram approached the rotaplane and set the netting down. Adrenaline ebbing away, he reached with trembling hands to pull aside the camouflage. He moaned, wordlessly, with every breath that escaped his lips, and his heartbeat echoed louder than ever in his ears. The clamor of his body's recovery effectively masked the sound of the acolyte approaching him from behind. Bertram felt the rush of air a moment before the cudgel connected with the meat of his shoulder.

Bertram fell hard against the rotaplane. Reflexively he turned around, to be confronted by the oldest acolyte's fearsome visage. The man was no longer gray-headed, his hair and his eyebrows singed down to the bright red skin. New burns overlaid the man's previous scars, weeping despairingly. The acolyte raised the cudgel over his head, and brought it down with skull-splitting force.

Bertram threw himself to the ground. Distantly, he heard the thud of the cudgel connecting with metal, as he grabbed a piece of scrap metal lying beside him and jabbed it upwards into the acolyte's belly. The acolyte grunted and staggered backwards as Bertram pushed himself to his feet. He cocked the metal back over his shoulder in a cricketer's pose and swung hard at the acolyte. The unwieldy scrap grazed the man's scalp, rather than staving in the side of his head as Bertram had vaguely intended, but the acolyte cried out in pain all the same. He dropped his cudgel and instinctively covered his burned flesh with his arms.

Bertram cast a glance back at the rotaplane, and froze in disbelieving horror. The blow that he had dodged had turned the controls into mechanical ruin. Uprooted springs and cracked gears spilled out of the smashed navigation panel. The control handles dangled tenuously from a splintered shaft. The rotaplane would never fly again.

Bertram had only a moment to decide on his next course of action, but in his heart he knew there was no choice at all. He grabbed the netting, clutching it to his chest like a newborn in swaddling. He ran toward the cliff, reached the edge without slowing, and threw himself into the air, hurtling forward a few feet before gravity seized him and pulled him downward. Bertram twisted in midair, trying desperately to land on his back and shield the phlogiston containers from the impact.

The desiccated seabed rushed up to meet him, driving the breath from his lungs and violently rattling the flint glass jars in the netting. Shooting stars flooded Bertram's field of vision. Gradually he became aware of a bright, jagged pain in his hip, where he had landed on a sharp stone protruding from the ground. The pain reassured him that he had not broken his neck and died.

Slowly, Bertram rolled over and lurched to his feet, turning his back on the high cliff. He took a tentative step, testing his lacerated hip's ability to bear the stress of walking. He had a long journey on foot ahead to reach Liverpool once again, but he would not be returning empty-handed. That made everything worth the cost.

"Come back!" The admonition came from behind, from the clifftop. In disbelief, Bertram turned around to see the acolyte standing at the edge, beckoning him.

Bertram laughed wildly, which in turn led to a coughing fit that doubled him over. When he stood upright again, the acolyte was still waiting expectantly atop the precipice. "I'm afraid I can't stay," Bertram called up insouciantly. He held the net aloft with one hand, like a trophy, although the weight caused his arm to quiver after a few seconds. "If you want this back you'll have to come after me yourself! But if you don't fancy the dive, rest assured that I will make far better use of this than you! It's not doing anyone any good hidden away in your deep, dark cave church!"

"I don't care about the demon oil!" the acolyte insisted, and Bertram could swear that the man sounded genuinely concerned that Bertram should hear him out. "You must come back!"

"Well and good if you're willing to concede the phlogiston is better off with someone who knows what to do with it," Bertram yelled in return. He started slowly walking backwards, determined to put as much distance between himself and his pursuers as possible, in case they did decide to chase him all the way to Castle Street. "But I can only make use of this fuel by returning it to civilization! Nothing worth igniting it for on your godforsaken isle, I'd wager!"

The acolyte was a small dark figure atop the cliff, growing smaller with every backwards step Bertram took, yet he could see the man stiffen in his sackcloth at the term 'godforsaken'. Still, the man would not give up, beseeching Bertram, "If you try to cross those wastes, you will die."

"Perhaps," Bertram shrugged, exaggerating the gesture so that the other man could see it. "Perhaps not."

"You will, make no mistake," the acolyte warned. "Once, the seas were our protection against monsters dwelling in their dark depths. The same waters that bore up our Lord when he walked upon them bore down upon the serpents and kept them far from us. Now that the seas have boiled away, nothing holds the monsters back. The wastes belong to them. Anyone who treads where the seas once were, walks into the shadow of death."

"I shall take my chances!" Bertram insisted, turning his back on the man on the cliff. He limped slightly at the pain in his hip, and the weight of the phlogiston vessels in the netting further unbalanced him, so that his top speed was barely more rapid than a brisk stroll, but he continued doggedly on his way for as long as his aching, overtaxed muscles could stand it. The granular matter beneath his feet, pebbles and bones and shells, shifted with every step, while the overall terrain undulated in frozen crests and troughs.

Bertram stopped to catch his breath and looked back. The cliffside was distant now, and although he could not be absolutely certain, he was fairly sure the acolyte no longer watched him from the edge. More importantly, the black-robed man was not pursuing him across the floor of the vanished sea. The wastes, he had called it, and perhaps he believed every word he had said about the lethal terrors they purportedly held. As ludicrous as the acolyte's final warning had been, it nagged at Bertram's mind.

Bertram dismissed it all as irrelevant. He had not come this far to study primitive supernatural beliefs or to understand why anyone would take the Great Inferno as a divine signal to regress back into the unenlightened past. The devastation wrought by the phlogiston firestorms had been tragic, a disaster of heretofore unseen proportions, but it had also been an accident, not a curse. A mere setback for human civilization, Bertram believed, not at all glibly, to be learned from and recovered from, and ultimately surpassed. Phlogiston-fueled devices had taken humanity so far, would take them further still. Bertram, with the phlogiston in the canisters weighing down the netting so that the cords bit mercilessly into his shoulders, would build and experiment all the way to mankind's next great leap forward.

He wished he could leap forward to the moment where he was measuring out the phlogiston into vials in his workshop, rested and recovered from the trials of this expedition. This was not the triumphant ending to his adventure that he had originally envisioned. He should be flying in the rotaplane, all but in repose in the control seat while the combustion of phlogiston powered the lift and thrust. He had been quite fond of the rotaplane, and as fatigue settled into his muscles he felt the loss all the more keenly. He looked to the cliff once more, if only to catch a final glimpse of the rotaplane's elegant foils or a glint along its galvanized piping.

Something moved.

Not atop the cliff, but along the intervening ground, the wastes, closer to Bertram than the barren isle. Something shifted along a rise in the seabed and then disappeared into a dry gully. It was not an acolyte, of that Bertram was certain. Probably it was some old piece of flotsam caught in the wind, the tattered sail of a long lost shipwreck, nothing more. All the same, Bertram turned his back on the cliffs once more and willed himself forward, faster.

He heard only the scuff of his boots and his involuntary grunts of pain as the agonizing burden of the netting swung with his gait and chewed his palms bloody. Then another sound reached his ears, a low and insistent susurrus behind him, not the skittering of random debris in the wind but a deliberate and propulsive scrape. It was drawing closer.

Bertram ran, and immediately knew with icy certainty that he could not maintain that pace for more than a few seconds without flagging. He lowered the netting, holding it out to his side rather than against his shoulders. His arm bore the weight for a half dozen paces, and then the netting was dragging on the ground, bouncing and jostling with unsettling clanging chimes, flint glass on flint glass. Bertram instinctively wanted to calculate how much phlogiston he might lose if the vessels bottommost within the netting were to break or shatter, and how likely those broken vessels would be to protect the others from similar fracturing stresses, but such a mental exercise was completely beyond him until he could escape the sheer panic of being followed across the arid seabed by some unseen crawling thing.

The ponderous dragging sound grew louder still, and Bertram knew that whatever was behind him was enormous. He heard the sounds coming from in front of him, as well, and stumbled forward, up another seabed moraine, altering his trajectory subtly while telling himself that the sounds were not quite so loud in this new direction, that a gap could be found.

At the summit, he looked down, and there he saw the monster. It looked like the remains of a snake that had been partially eaten by some ravenous bird of prey, except for two attributes: its size, easily twenty feet long from the blunt point of its head to the whiplike tapering of its tail, and its movement, for despite its deathly pallor and missing chunks of flesh revealing the skeleton beneath, the serpent slithered across the ground. As Bertram watched, the giant serpent doubled back on itself and lifted its head from the dusty ground. A rotten black forked tongue flicked in and out of the denuded reptilian jawbones as the skull's ruined eyes stared directly at him.

Bertram hesitated only a moment before digging a flint glass vessel out of the net. He had no desire to waste any more of his precious treasure, yet his survival instinct overrode his parsimony. He removed the lid and drew a Promethean Match from his pocket, leaning the capsule against the lip of the jar with one end floating in the distilled phlogiston. Bertram cocked the arm holding the vessel, and with his free hand smashed the lid into the Match.

In Bertram's mind, all was accomplished in a single smooth motion: the lid striking the jar, the ampule cracking and mixing its chemical composition, and the vessel hurtling through the air toward the cadaverous serpent. In reality, as soon as the Match broke and flared the exposed phlogiston ignited with searing fire and blinding light. Even as he threw the vessel away, the blaze scalded him from fingertips to elbow, furious heat followed shortly by the rippling, numb cold of shock. Bertram barely saw the conflagrant vessel strike the leviathan and shatter, phlogiston dribbling down the serpent's pallid belly like molten candle wax, before he was running for his life.

He heard the titanic snake thudding to the ground, presumably writhing in its death throes, and continued to run. The sounds of scraping, parting grit harried him, alarmingly steady and rhythmic. Bertram chanced a look backwards over his shoulder. The undead serpent was chasing him, no longer aflame, drawing nearer with every gargantuan undulation.

Bertram stumbled, sprawling in an ungainly heap on the dusty ground. He had a moment to consider, however briefly, that some things remained beyond the ken of science, that the greatest technological disaster of all time might have been survived by monstrosities which already existed far outside the understandings and achievements of scholarship, that even a world laid bare by cleansing fire held unknowable secrets. Then the undead serpent's prodigious fangs lanced through him, and brought his speculations to an end.

SWAG

THE THING IS, I'D MISSED LAUNDRY DAY and was running late. I threw on the free, ugly t-shirt I'd gotten at that presentation on timeshares in Saint Villaret last month. Sure the logo was weird but how was I supposed to recognize it as the secret sigil of a malevolent elder god? Or that exposing it to sunlight would make the sky explode like a fiery ocean of liquid madness to herald the return of Zangooka the Unliving Doom? So sorry I inadvertently unleashed the apocalypse or whatever but it's not like I could leave the house half-naked, could I?

THE LENGTHS THAT HE WOULD GO TO

BYRON WELLER HAD DONE PLENTY of dishonest things while attempting to hook up. There was the time junior year in high school when he had forced his best friend, Amy Gwintney, to drive in meandering circles up and down half the back country roads around town until close to one in the morning. The mobile surveillance had begun because Byron thought he had glimpsed Nathan Robinson's car passing Amy's, recognizing it from the previous summer's theater camp. Since Nathan went to Bridgeford, their rival high school, Byron hadn't crossed paths with him since August, and didn't want to wait any longer to see him and his perfect lips again. But Byron had told Amy that it was Marcus Smith's car they were chasing, since she had the hots for him. That night ended in failure, but was far from the end of Byron's romantically oriented duplicity.

The pattern continued in the middle of his first semester on campus, when he had shown up in the lecture hall for Economics 203 (Statistical Modeling) for four consecutive weeks' worth of Tuesdays and Thursdays, slowly seating himself closer and closer to Trevor Jones each time, until he could almost reach out and touch Trevor's beautiful hair. Byron had never taken Econ 202, or

Econ 101 or any other pre-req class before noticing Trevor and following him to Zigler Hall that first Tuesday. The weekend after his eighth unofficial audit, he very purposefully bumped into Trevor at Psi Nu's Jungle Jam, played it off as coincidental, and made smalltalk about Professor Iovino's annoying speech impediment over flat, warm beers until they progressed to making out on under the back balcony, including much satisfying stroking of that amazing hair. And, of course, there was last summer, when he assumed a completely new identity as Manfred the foreign exchange student in order to seduce the rookie lifeguard at the pool. The deception had probably been overkill for getting innocent, over-eager, all taut muscles Daryl into bed, but proved invaluable when Daryl got entirely too clingy and "Manfred" could conveniently disappear back to Switzerland or Sweden or wherever his fake accent was supposed to have originated.

But far and away, the most ridiculous falsehood Byron had pulled off so far had been pretending that he was interested in medieval and renaissance history, not merely interested but downright obsessed enough to join the campus chapter of the Society for Creative Anachronism, all to spend a little more time with Jerrod Putnam. Jerrod was a year ahead of Byron and had devoted his junior year campaigning for Seneschal of the Barony. Byron hated himself a little bit for knowing what a Seneschal and a Barony were, but learning the lingo that Jerrod lived and breathed was the price he was apparently willing to pay. The SCA meant so much to Jerrod and Jerrod, in turn, meant a lot to Byron. At least, Byron had a strong feeling that Jerrod could mean a lot to him. He was different from Daryl the lifeguard and Trevor the business major and Nathan the cutest Puck in *A Midsummer Night's Dream* ever. Jerrod was cute, too, but he was also more real, attractive to Byron on a more primal, interior level. Byron Weller did not believe in either love at first sight or in soulmates, but Jerrod Putnam had come closer than anyone else on Earth to making him reevaluate the possibilities of their existence.

Jerrod was also a gentle soul, and that made Byron less

aggressive than usual in response, so his original plan to attend a meeting or two of the SCA and then suggest he and Jerrod go off somewhere to exchange sonnets privately had turned into Byron's regular participation in all the club activities and events. Some of it, he had to admit, had been fun, in a deeply dorky way. Overall he was in a holding pattern slowly orbiting Jerrod, afraid of overstepping and scaring him off. He needed an organic moment to present itself naturally, and Jerrod was usually too busy for anything like that to spontaneously happen. But every so often they would exchange a glance or a smile or brush hands and Byron knew he couldn't give up on Jerrod, not yet.

When Jerrod texted him on a Thursday afternoon and asked if he wanted to hang out that evening, Byron thought his slow play was finally about to pay off. He waited twenty minutes, giving his phone seven separate checks to mark the passing time, before texting back that he'd be down. Jerrod texted back "Meet me at the Barony hall at 11" and Byron typed "K" but deleted the letter unsent, reminding himself to stay cool.

The Barony hall was an old pottery studio in the woods, owned by the campus but no longer used by the Fine Arts department. It had in fact been unused so long that it had started collapsing, which allowed the SCA to petition to take over the structure as a headquarters, meeting place, and storage facility. All of that had been before Byron's association with the group, but he understood that Jerrod had been a big part of the reconstruction effort. It was in good physical shape now, but as far as hookup locations went, the place gave Byron flashbacks to high school, furtive kissing and groping in secret neglected places. Without a doubt one of the better things about college was having dorm rooms and off-campus apartments for late night trysts. Couldn't Jerrod tell his roommate to find someplace else to crash, or even just request that he grab a few beers until the bars closed at two? Then again, knowing how much Jerrod adored all the trappings of the SCA, Byron figured maybe Jerrod had a thing for the Barony hall. Maybe his inhibitions were naturally lower among the tapestries. Hey, whatever worked.

Byron left his dorm at quarter to eleven, strolling across the quad with an anticipatory grin on his face that he was not even cognizant of until it abruptly fell when the Barony hall came into view. Standing at the end of the gravel and dirt trail was not Jerrod, but Logan Huff. Byron shoved down all his feelings of disappointment, his daydreams of one-on-one time with Jerrod shattered. He reminded himself that he had been playing it cool so far and could play it cool a bit longer.

"Hey, Logan," he offered nonchalantly as he drew closer.

Logan's eyes narrowed suspiciously at him. He nodded in a way that could have been interpreted as a greeting, or a warning. Possibly both. Byron was willing to abandon the chitchat he hadn't felt like making anyway while he tried to guess what Logan was thinking. Had Logan also been under the impression that he and Jerrod were set up for something like a date? Byron doubted that Jerrod was playing both of them. Jerrod was so sincere, so earnest, those kinds of domineering mind games were the farthest thing from him. Moreover, he didn't see how Jerrod could be into Logan at all. It wouldn't have surprised him terribly to learn that Logan was Jerrod's type, because Logan was a lot of guys' type. He was tall, he had a runner's build. His flawless skin and piercing blue-green eyes were alluring. But Byron never got a gay vibe from Logan, nor any kind of straight vibe, for that matter. Some people were asexual, or so consumed with other priorities that they might as well be, and that was Logan down to the bone. He was always intense, sometimes brooding, sometimes wickedly sarcastic, but never particularly plugged into the same mating rituals as everyone else. As far as Byron had ever been able to tell, Logan never socialized with other SCA folks, and attended the bare minimum number of meetings and events to be considered a member in good standing. He usually spent his time at events reading books from the university's special collection which only SCA members were allowed access to, another of Jerrod's little victories.

Of course, Logan's book fetish still left the possibility of an awkward love triangle, or a love V with three corners and only two sides: Byron lusting after Jerrod and Jerrod pining hopelessly for Logan, who neither noticed nor cared. Byron had never keyed in on Jerrod's attitude toward Logan before, but he resolved to pay attention tonight. While playing it cool, he reminded himself. He slouched casually against the wall of the Barony hall, while Logan stood stiffly and scanned for Jerrod's approach.

Jerrod arrived within minutes, right at eleven.

"Hey," he hailed them both. "Sorry. Hope I didn't keep you guys waiting long."

Byron shrugged.

"I'm still just waiting to find out what's up," he said. "Bit late to be holding court."

Jerrod smiled as he pulled the keyring from his front pocket and started to unlock the door.

"It's gonna be cool. Right, Logan?"

Logan snorted involuntarily and tried to cover it with a laugh.

"Unbelievably cool," he promised, trailing Jerrod through the door. Byron followed, crossing the threshold just as Jerrod was hitting the lights.

The main room of the Barony hall was fairly spacious, and everything in it looked as it had at the last SCA meeting. Overstuffed cushions and Ottomans fished from second-hand stores had been refurbished to look period-appropriate. In the corners, a couple of slant-topped tables, one complete and holding an open illuminated manuscript. The other table was a reclamation work in progress, pale unstained new elements grafted onto the darker salvageable bits of the antique original. Straight ahead was a door leading to the area that had once housed the kilns, when the hall had still been a pottery studio. Thanks to a demolished wall it had been converted to a semi-enclosed forge area used by the armorers to fashion breastplates and shields and other steel equipment. Another door, to their right as they entered the hall, connected to a large supply closet housing everything from cookware to handmade period garb.

Byron watched Jerrod out of the corner of his eye as Jerrod visibly swelled with pride the moment he crossed the threshold. He loved the trappings of romantic chivalry so damn much, and Byron liked him all the more for that unabashed joy. This imaginary pocket of time they collectively escaped into was how Jerrod wanted the rest of the world to function all the time.

If only.

Logan slipped off his backpack and opened it, pulling out a leather-bound book of his own. He surveyed the room until he spotted a small table, which he pointed out to Byron.

"Move that to the middle of the room."

Byron blinked.

"Move it yourself."

Logan had been flipping the pages of the book he had brought, and paused to look up contemptuously. "I am trying to find something quickly. Would you please move the table? And Jerrod, would you please bring out the bowl?"

Every time he said the word 'please' it sounded derogatory.

Jerrod was in motion immediately, approaching a locked cabinet with his key ring swinging around one finger. Byron rolled his eyes a little and moved the table. Logan set the book down without looking up or saying thank you, continuing to skim through the pages. Byron glanced at the text out of curiosity but every line was gibberish. Perhaps Manfred the exchange student would have been able to decipher it.

Jerrod returned with the bowl, which was about the size of a bathroom sink, cast in bronze and inlaid with various stone tiles, forming a mosaic that Byron had never noticed before. He had seen the bowl, which someone had donated to the SCA in the past, around here and there, most recently filled with apples and pears as Kaitlyn Moore had used it as the subject for a still life. The pattern inside the bowl was hypnotic, weird geometries coming together in meaningful imagery just when Byron was about to look away, then dispersing into random visual static when he looked more closely. There was just enough room for the base of the bowl to rest on the tabletop above the spine of the book.

Logan made no acknowledgment of Jerrod's contribution either, which Byron found at least a little gratifying; if Logan were looking to forge any kind of connection with Jerrod, he was passing up some easy opportunities. Hopefully Jerrod would pick up on that as well. For the moment, Jerrod took Logan's fixation on the book at the expense of social niceties in stride. Jerrod was able to take most things in stride, even Cam Hadley's body odor, Byron realized. Cam was a good Marshall, but he worked up a powerful sweat in his padded practice armor, and the resulting funk was impervious to washing away.

Jerrod indicated a couple of nearby cushions and Byron followed him, lowering himself on the brocaded surface while looking expectantly at Jerrod. Once he was settled on the cushion beside Byron's, Jerrod said, "Logan wants to do a demonstration at the next meeting. It's some kind of mystical ritual reenactment, you know, alchemy, hermetic theurgy? He asked if he could do a run-through tonight."

"And he had to do it here?" Byron asked.

"He said that bowl was a perfect prop," Jerrod shrugged. "I guess he wanted to practice here since he's going to do the actual demo here for everyone else."

"So why'd you ask me to come?"

"I thought you'd be interested, since you're into all the occult secrets and stuff," Jerrod said.

"That's a pretty broad category," Byron replied, desperately trying to remember if he had ever feigned an interest in ritual magic or anything remotely connected to it while interacting with Jerrod. A conversation about the DaVinci Code? A joke about Madonna's interest in Kabbalah? A passing reference to Blue Oyster Cult?

Jerrod, as always, was unfazed. "Okay, fair point. I don't know, I just felt like we needed a third person. To avoid any potential appearance of impropriety." He spoke with his customary sincerity, but managed to smile self-deprecatingly at the end.

"Oh, of course," Byron agreed. "We wouldn't want to be accused of anything... inappropriate."

Jerrod chuckled as if he were deliberating whether or not to continue flirting.

"Whoa," he said, "that is a big knife."

Reflexively, Byron peeked down at his crotch, before realizing that Jerrod was actually looking at Logan. Logan had a tight grip on the hilt of a weapon with a blade that was not only large but deadly looking. The phrase "ceremonial dagger" flitted through Byron's mind right before Logan held his open hand above the bronze bowl and slashed his palm with the knife, drawing a bright red line of blood. Logan clenched his fist hard enough to make the tendons stand out in his forearms, as blood dripped rapidly into the bowl.

"Jesus!" Byron yelped.

"Logan, what...? Is that your blood, your real blood?" Jerrod demanded.

Logan spoke, but not to answer Jerrod. The words coming out of his mouth as he stared at the splattered ruby pattern dotting the inside of the bowl were in an unrecognizable language, something harsh and guttural and inherently alien. "*Shtunggli shogg.. uln geb ooboshu s'uhn... nilgh'ri throd... goka hai... goka hai!*"

Jerrod pushed himself to his feet.

"All right, look, Logan, if this is you hurting yourself as some kind of cry for help, let's talk about it, okay?"

Logan ignored Jerrod, throwing open his lacerated hand as he came to the end of the incantation with a vehement "Uaaah!" Byron jerked away involuntarily as blood flicked from Logan's splayed fingers. Jerrod could be as concerned about Logan's mental health as he wanted; Byron was concerned about hepatitis.

The bowl moved. Logan had not touched it, as far as Byron could see, or the table it rested on, but the bowl wobbled back and forth under its own power. The rim dipped on one side, then the other, gradually establishing a circular pattern as the bowl spun on its base, faster and faster. The crimson fluid in the bowl sloshed in the tide of centrifugal force but never spilled, despite the fact that it looked like much more blood than Logan had shed, more than he could have lost while remaining upright.

Logan smiled, but it was a snarl of triumph, the aggressive teeth-baring of violent vindication.

"You never knew," he sneered. "I wasn't sure how far you'd let me get, but you honestly never knew what you had here. Did you really think this was a fruit bowl? Idiots."

Jerrod neither answered the question nor rose to the bait of the insult, as for once he was at a loss for words. The bowl continued to spin with dizzying speed, and from its bottom a glow emanated, a fearfully cold luminescence like distant starlight. The blood darkened and surged, gathering and rising in strange coagulated shapes.

"All of you," Logan growled, "so busy playing dress up, playing make believe, that you never realized you had a piece of history in your grasp, a ceremonial relic for summoning a shoggoth servant. But of course none of you would be prepared to make the sacrifices to control that kind of power, even if it meant the world would be yours for the taking."

Within moments the volume of the blood was more than could be contained. Rather than overflowing onto the table it rose up as sinuously as a hypnotized cobra emerging from a fakir's basket. The substance no longer resembled blood at all. It had become black and viscous with a sheen like the oily smears of color on rancid meat. At the crown of the ever-growing amorphous column, an eye opened, a sphere of bilious ochre with a black pinprick pupil.

Byron and Jerrod both screamed, while Logan laughed mockingly. More eyes of different sizes opened, clustered asymmetrically around the first, most of them similar shades of unhealthy yellow, although one was a bruised purplish-red and another was an unsettlingly brilliant emerald. The grotesque mass continued to expand, its top nearly brushing the ceiling. A fissure split and widened halfway down the protoplasmic column, the edges of the orifice extending ichorous matter into the shape of fangs.

"*Tekeli-li,*" the shoggoth croaked.

"*Tekeli-li hafh'drn WGAH'N!*" Logan shouted.

The dark cylindrical glob twisted around to direct most of its mismatched eyeballs at Logan. Four distinct pseudopods extruded outward from the center of the mass, forming limbs that approximated tentacles and spider legs simultaneously.

"*Tekeli-li,*" the shoggoth cried out again. "*Tekeli-LI!*"

"*Ch'yeh wgah'n! Mnahn'...*" Logan answered, only to be interrupted by the shoggoth lunging for him, pulling the bronze bowl off the table to gong madly against the studio floor. The fanged orifice clamped around Logan's left arm, swallowing everything from the elbow down, while the four inhuman limbs swiped at his head and chest.

Logan screamed in equal parts pain and affronted disbelief, stabbing furiously at the shoggoth with the ceremonial dagger still clenched in his right hand. The blade punctured the quivering surface again and again, spilling oily black fluid that bubbled noxiously where it struck solid surfaces. The abomination's mouth remained closed around Logan's other arm, inexorably drawing him in, until his shoulder was flush with the fangs.

At the base of its black, elongated body, the shoggoth was growing six more limbs, thick and squat like the legs of a tortoise. The thing braced itself on its cluster of lower appendages and whipped around savagely, lifting Logan off his feet and tossing him through the air like a rag doll. Byron watched Logan smash into the front door of the studio, and a part of his brain still capable of anything other than raw shock noted that most of Logan's left arm was gone except for a ruined scarlet stump. Then Byron was grabbing Jerrod by the wrist and pulling him towards the forge.

"What... where...?" Jerrod struggled to speak, dazed.

"Getting the hell out of here, this way," Byron answered. He rattled the doorknob, locked. He turned to Jerrod for the keys, but spotted the shoggoth taking notice of them. He pulled Jerrod away from the door as the monstrosity slung towards them, and bolted for the supply closet. He shoved Jerrod in, pulled the door closed behind them. A massive thud of the shoggoth's bulk against the door followed, but the barrier held. The shoggoth loosed a howl that Byron could hear receding, as the monster retreated back to its unfinished business with Logan.

"Wait, what about..."

"Logan's good as dead," Byron cut him off. "And brought it on himself, frigging psycho. Summoning that... that..." Byron groped for the right description but found none. He tugged Jerrod toward the back of the closet. "Come on, I think we can push through the ceiling back here, maybe crawl out... there's vents in the attic, right?"

Jerrod stood rooted in place. "That thing... what do you think it's going to do after... after it's done with Logan?"

"I don't know, and that's why we need to be as far away from here as possible by then," Byron snapped, awkwardly rearranging collapsed tourney tents in the confined, dark space. "Give me a hand!"

"It could go anywhere, attack anyone," Jerrod reasoned. "We can't possibly warn everyone in time. No one would believe us, anyway."

"Their loss!" Byron retorted.

Jerrod shook his head slowly. "We have to stop it."

"We?" Byron felt his eyes popping. "*We?*" From the other side of the door, a scream reverberated. The indignation and outrage were gone from Logan's voice, leaving only the sounds of mortal terror and excruciating pain.

Jerrod turned away from Byron and reached for the weapons rack, shifting rattan swords along the rails before finally drawing out a rapier. Jerrod twisted the blunted shell casing and rubber cap off the tip, revealing the needle-sharp point beneath. He looked back to Byron and said, "We're the only ones here," before moving back toward the closet door.

"Dammit, dammit, dammit," Byron seethed as he strode toward

the rack and grabbed an axe for himself, a heavy weapon that was one of smelly Cam Hadley's pet projects. Too dangerous for the official melee events, too big for the throwing competitions, the thing looked viciously cool, like something out of Heavy Metal cover art. Maybe Byron had said as much out loud to Cam once, and that was where Jerrod got the idea about his interest in swords and sorcery. Right now all Byron was focused on was his desire to split open a skull with the axe, although he wasn't sure if that skull belonged to Jerrod, Logan, or the monstrosity awaiting them. He also didn't know if the shoggoth even had a skull, or if Logan still had enough of one intact to be split, but he followed Jerrod through the opening door nevertheless.

The shoggoth loomed opposite them in the center of chaos and carnage, gnashing its fangs mindlessly as it probed the edges of the hall's front door with its upper appendages, seeking purchase to pry it open. The floor was strewn with torn cushions, shredded tapestries, and overturned tables, all painted in visceral red and abyssal black. Other than the bloodstains, there was no sign of Logan. No, Byron corrected himself, there was one: a single shoe in the far corner, speckled in clotted crimson.

The shoggoth rotated and undulated toward them. *"Tekeli-li!"*

Jerrod darted toward the monstrosity and struck a fencing pose directly in front of it. Byron stared, horrified, as Jerrod saluted with his rapier, then quickly parried away the shoggoth's swiping ebon claws. With a deft lunge, Jerrod's sword pierced one of the shoggoth's larger eyes, a pale yellow globe that spurted stygian fluid from the wound. Byron felt a surge of hope, which curdled almost immediately as the shoggoth knocked Jerrod across the room. Jerrod crashed awkwardly into a bookcase, and the shoggoth writhed after him.

Byron's fingers felt numb around the haft of the axe, and his stomach churned miserably, as if he had just woken up from a night spent doing Jaeger bombs until dawn. He willed his legs to push him across the room, raising the axe over his head as he neared the shoggoth. He brought the weapon down on the abomination's back with all his might, and the heavy blade sank satisfyingly into the murk-swirled flesh.

The shoggoth twisted around reflexively, hissing through its fleshy fangs, turning the majority of its insane constellation of eyes on Byron. Its four upper limbs were drawn back to strike. Byron tore the axehead out of the shoggoth's central mass and swung for the nearest arm, severing it from the body in a burst of beetle black gore. The shoggoth hissed again, but a new pseudopod budded from the spot and began to reform the dismembered limb at once.

"Oh, come *on*," Byron muttered.

"*Tekkhkhkk...*" the shoggoth began, before the point of Jerrod's rapier emerged from its open maw. The sword tip wiggled back and forth as Jerrod twisted the hilt against the back of the shoggoth. For all Byron knew, Jerrod was trying to saw the monstrosity's head in half. The shoggoth never gave Jerrod a chance, snapping the length of its entire body like a shimmering black bullwhip and driving Jerrod upwards into the ceiling. Jerrod went limp and tumbled off the shoggoth as the creature spat out the rapier.

"No!" Byron shouted, charging and swinging the axe, tearing a chunk of flesh from the shoggoth's underside. Byron swung again, and again, and again, leaving deep, suppurating gouges in the creature's hide with every chop, but the wounds had little effect on the shoggoth. As Byron made another attempt to hurt it, the shoggoth distorted its own shape, squirming out of reach, then slamming Byron's chest with its head like a hellish battering ram. Byron stumbled backwards and crumpled to the floor.

"*TEKELI-LI!*" the shoggoth roared, a nightmarish assault on Byron's ears that made him wish he were already dead. He curled into a ball on his side, waiting for the killing blow to fall. After a few seconds, he opened his eyes to see what the shoggoth was waiting for. The first thing his eyes focused on was the ceremonial bowl, still faintly glowing. With sharp pains shooting through his neck, Byron turned his head toward the beast.

The shoggoth had returned its attentions to Jerrod, lying

motionless on the floor. Byron wasn't sure why the monster was fixated on Jerrod. Maybe it considered Jerrod's attempt to stab it through the brain to be a greater indignity than Byron's flailing hacking at its midsection, even though both efforts seemed equally ineffective. Maybe it consumed souls when it ingested bodies, and Jerrod's was a more appealing source of nourishment. That made a certain amount of sense to Byron, although he also suspected he might be nursing a minor concussion.

Byron tried to stand, felt the world tilt on rolling wave of vertigo, and braced himself on his hands and knees. He crawled toward the bronze bowl, pushing the axe along in front of him. The shoggoth was still advancing on Jerrod, but slowly, savoring the moment. Byron flipped the bowl upside down, clutched the haft of the axe, and rose to his knees. Arms trembling, he raised the axe, bringing it down in a savage executioner's drop on the base of the bowl. The bowl cracked, splitting nearly in half with a warbling metallic peal that sounded to Byron both too loud and too much like a shriek. Byron hammered the bowl with the axe again, the blade slicing into the side and shearing off a smaller fragment. The remainder of the damaged vessel skittered away across the floor.

The shoggoth's entire body suddenly stiffened, then convulsed in paroxysms as it struggled to croak *"Tekeli-li! TEKELI-LI!"* over and over. The six lower legs merged together as they were absorbed into the central mass of the body, which tapered to a point like an inverted waterspout being drawn down an open drain. The shoggoth sprouted new tendrils of slick onyx that tried to latch onto any anchor point they could find, even as the creature's body continued to warp and dwindle. Its eyeballs imploded, one by one, and then the shoggoth was abruptly gone, its otherworldly voice silenced.

Byron stumbled toward Jerrod, dropping to his knees beside him. He pulled Jerrod's head onto his lap, stroking the hair away from Jerrod's forehead. Jerrod's eyelids twitched, opened.

"What happened?"

"It's gone," Byron answered.

"You killed it?"

"It's gone," Byron repeated. "And I don't think it'll be back. Are you all right?"

"I'm banged up, but I don't think anything's broken," Jerrod said. "Except for most of our stuff. Cleaning up this disaster might be what ends up breaking my back."

"I'll give you a hand," Byron offered. "If you let me take you out for dinner after."

Jerrod smiled, with a knowing look that promised more than a shared meal.

"I'd like that."

They collected everything with blood or ichor soaked into it and stuffed it into the forges to burn. The salvageable items were gathered and stacked or righted in their proper positions around the room. The local all-night diner they visited afterwards had homemade fried chicken and biscuits, and they were delicious. Jerrod and Byron ate enough to make life feel worth living even after the worst day imaginable, overstuffing their bellies in the hopes that food comas would make their sleep dream-free, and keep away nightmares of slavering fangs and tentacles and hideous profusions of eyes. But just to be on the safe side, when Jerrod and Byron went to bed that night, they went together.

THE DEMON WRESTLER

THIS IS HOW YOU WILL ENTER the towns. You will ride your
wagon through the front gates, if the town has them, or come
down the main street, if not. You cannot control whether or not a
town has gates, or what direction those may face, but if the town
has none, then you can control the direction from which you
approach. If there is no gate, you will ride into the town from the
north, or from the east, never south or west. But if the town has
gates, you will always arrive at those gates, and you will ask for
permission to enter.

You will arrive at the town in the late afternoon, well before
sunset, but long enough after the sun has passed its highpoint that
the townspeople have started to feel the darkness coming. They will
not be aware of this feeling, and you will not speak of it to them.
But it will be there, in their hearts, all the same. As the light slants
lower and the indigo seeps into the sky, the sense of the night will
be in them all the same. This is when you will make your entrance
into the town. If your horses bring you close to the town before the
afternoon has begun to fade, you will wait some ways off. If your
horses draw the wagon within sight of the town as the sun
approaches the horizon, you will sleep on the ground, beneath the

stars, and wait for the next day. You will wait for the appropriate time.

You will make your way to the center of each town. If there is no town square, you will find the town market, and if there is no town market, you will find the space that the townspeople think of as the center. You will never go to the church. In these towns, you will find that even if the church lies on the crossroads of the widest thoroughfares, the people no longer go there.

As you pass townspeople on the streets, you will nod at the men, and you will tip your hat to the ladies. You will meet the eyes of the children. You will not smile at them. When you reach the heart of the town you will stop your wagon and you will tend to your horses.

The number of people who approach you will depend on how sizable the town is, and how long it takes you to reach the center and see to your animals. As time passes, some of the townspeople will already have gone to their homes for the night that has yet to come, and the number remaining on the streets will shrink the closer the night comes. The very fearful will not greet you. The very proud and the very dull will avoid you. But some will seek you out.

This is how you will receive them. You will shake their hands and you will ask their names. You will give them a name only if they ask for yours, but most of the time they will not ask. You will suggest that you know the town has seen more than its share of troubles. You will do this with your eyes, and the sound of your voice, and the set of your jaw. You will not do this with words unless the townspeople have had so many troubles they will not say the words themselves. It is always important for them to say the words themselves if at all possible.

You will listen carefully to their tales of trouble and let them be told howsoever the tellers wish. If they are slow to speak, you will give them time. If they are angry, you will weather it in silence. If they cry, you will not comfort them, but let the tears flow. Their stories will take shape, and you will mark them well. You must.

When the troubles have all been told, you will nod with great understanding. You will wait for one of them to ask if there is anything that can be done.

You will tell them what you can do. As the sun sets and the moon rises, you will tell them what you can do. Not what you will do. You will not presume so much. You will speak of possibilities, and you will let them decide.

If you do all these things, they will always decide that it should be done exactly as you say.

They will insist that you spend the night, and you will not protest. They will feed you, and you will eat, even if it is the most putrid of leavings. They may offer you their daughters, or their wives may offer themselves, and whether you bed these women or not is of no consequence. You will sleep, but you must rise ahead of the dawn.

You will go to where they have put up your wagon and your horses. In the time before the sun comes up, you will work quickly and quietly to move the sacks and reveal the proper hatch in the back of the wagon.

This is how you will know which hatch to open. If the people tell you of mutilated livestock, or missing children, you will open the first hatch. If the people tell you of wild women, wives who run off in the night, or daughters who pay no heed to their parents, you will open the second hatch. If the people tell you of poisoned wells or blighted crops, infants dead in their cribs, or unexplained diseases, you will open the third hatch. And if the people tell you of anything else, you will open the fourth hatch.

You will open the hatch and you will let out what it holds under the wagon. You will close the hatch and rearrange the sacks. You will return to your hosts before the sun comes up high enough to banish the moon.

When the sky is light you will rise again. You will make sure you are seen rising, and you will return to the center of the town. You will be left alone, if the people have any wits about them at all. If they try to engage you in nervous talk, you will ignore them, for they will soon lose interest if they are not encouraged.

You will see them gathering near as the sun begins to go down. This will be at almost the same time of afternoon as when you entered town the day before. They will appreciate the rightness of this, how the warm, low sun first welcomed you, and how the same warm, low sun now gathers them all together. There will be more of them than the day before. Not all of the town, but more than before.

This is when you will begin to ready yourself. You will remove your shirt, and you will do so slowly, far more slowly than you would want. It will seem strange to you, but to those who gather to watch you it will seem only proper that they are given the time to observe your every movement. You will don the mask and tie its laces behind your head. If there are children gathered they may find the mask fearsome. You will hide your face behind the visage of the mask and you will wait for the sun to set.

When the day yields to the night, the demon will come. If you have entered the town from the north, the demon will come from the south. If you have entered the town from the east, the demon will come from the south. The townspeople will see the demon drawn into the heart of their town, drawn to you, and you will face it, and you will beckon it closer still.

The demon will snarl at you, and it will hiss, and it will gnash its teeth, and its claws will twitch, and its eyes will burn. The demon will lunge at you, and snatch at you, and bring all of its hate to you. The townspeople will see their fear in the flesh of the demon, but they will see hope, for the demon will not look at them or try to bite or flail at them. The demon will see only you.

You will catch the demon in your arms and you will lock your hands behind its back. You will scream from the pain of touching its unholy flesh but you will not let go. You will lift the demon off the ground, and throw it down. You will pin the demon to the earth with your knees and you will humble it, and you will grind the demon's head into the dust. You will fight until the demon yields and you prevail.

When the demon lays still in the center of the town, you will lift it up in your arms as you would a slaughtered animal. You will tell the townspeople that your time is short, for you must carry the demon to your wagon and ride out of town, to take the demon far away, so far that it will never trouble the town again. The townspeople will not argue. They will feel nothing but gratitude. For they told you of their mutilated livestock and missing children, and you summoned the slavering werewolf and laid low its savagery. Or they told you of their untamed wives and daughters, and you summoned the green-scaled snake woman and triumphed over her venomous insinuations. Or they told you of their plagues and pestilence, and you summoned the lean gray vampire and overcame its fangs and its dark hunger. Or they told you of any multitude of other afflictions, and you summoned forth the chalk-white skeleton like Death itself and refused its power.

You will carry the demon, in whatever form, to your wagon and lay its body across the sacks. You will hitch to your horses and you will ride for the gates, if the town has gates, or for the edge of town where you entered the day before. The townspeople will follow you to the gate or to the edge of town, drowning you in gratitude. You will wait at the gate or the edge of town until your payment is brought to you. You will take the gold when it is offered, and you must take it with humility. You will not count the pieces, not until the town is behind you.

You will drive the wagon until the town disappears. Then you will halt the horses and climb down and walk out into the desert to find a lizard or a rabbit or a small bird. You will bring the animal back to the wagon, alive. Unless Dagoberto lies in the wagon, and then you will snap the neck of the animal as you walk back.

You will go to the rear of the wagon. You will offer the animal to the demon, and you will let the demon feed. When the demon has finished its meal, you will help the demon back through its proper hatch to its resting place under the wagon. If it is Maurico, you will take care to mind his knees and his hips, for the old vampire is as afflicted with pains in his joints as I am these days. If you jolt him he will snap at you, and it will hurt even though his teeth are not as sharp as they once were. If it is Graciela in the back of the wagon, you will hold the hatch open for her but you will not touch her and you will not help her in any other way, for she is a proud and vain snake-woman. It will take her some time to ease into her resting place, especially if your wrestling was prolonged and wearying. If it is Ezequiel in the back of the wagon, you will groom his wolf fur, you will wipe the blood from his muzzle and you will brush the dust and dirt from his hide. He will be sleeping while you do this, or close to it, after he has eaten, and if you shove him into his resting place it will not rouse him. But if you do not clean his fur first his stink will overtake the entire wagon. If it is Dagoberto in the back of the wagon, you will leave the dead animal at his side and you will wait in your seat at the front. The skeleton will let itself into its own resting place after it has fed, and when you hear the sound of the hatch opening and closing you will urge the horses forward.

You will ride as far as you can before you need to sleep. You will sleep, and you will ride, and you will sleep, and you will ride, until you find another suitable town. But most towns will be suitable. All towns have problems, and more towns than not will believe that demons are the cause of their problems, or will be made to believe it. And you will listen to their tales of trouble and offer the solution, and when they accept you will release Maurico or Graciela or Ezequiel or Dagoberto in the night, and they will hide outside of the town until sundown, and you will wrestle them into submission and carry them off, and you will feed them and care for them, and you will take them to the next town, and the next.

For years those old demons have served me, and they will serve you, and you will always have gold in your pocket, if you do these things. All that I have told you is how to give people what they want, and how to show them what they want to see. It will be enough.

RENDERED BY HER DEEDS

THE FUNERAL WAS GRANDIOSE, as only state functions for the royal family could be. Every pew in the cathedral was packed with mourners, every marble tile of the outer floor accommodated those who stood, and every stained glass window was darkened by those who crowded against the exterior when not another soul could be admitted. Rafters draped with a hundred thousand garlands of wildflowers shed green leaves and yellow petals like tears. Statues of holy martyrs occupying alcoves around the periphery were shrouded in black stoles, redolent with incense. The Most Venerable performed the ceremony with grief-stricken solemnity, his voice filling the space even as it struggled against outright despair.

Conspicuous in their absence were the traditional tapestries woven to celebrate the lifetime of the departed member of the royal house. For a king, the funereal tapestries would have depicted battles won and peace defended, wise judgments and favored patronages. For a queen, acts of mercy and benefice, children borne and glories reflected. But what imagery could be drawn from the life of an eleven-year-old princess? Princess Roisia's favorite color had been yellow, as the wildflowers reminded the mourners.

She had adored her pony. She had begun learning to play the harp two years earlier, but had not mastered it, never would. And she had been beloved.

The kingdom's grief was doubled by the loss of all the princess's tomorrows, her potential and promise. Men and women keened, for no words could measure their sorrow. The central aisle of the cathedral remained clear, respect and decorum maintained even in the face of horror. Running through the sea of disconsolate faces like an open wound which might never heal, like the yawning gulf between what the princess's life might have been, and the point at which it ended.

When the last of the mourning hymns concluded, King Tericius rose from his throne. He descended from the dais and traversed the empty central aisle in silence. He held his head erect even as his eyes welled with unspeakable pain. Queen Jivonne followed a respectful span of steps behind him, a mute shadow in her flowing black ermine robes, her head bowed.

It was imperative that no one see her smile.

Tericius stared through the window of the royal carriage. "The people will expect another heir be produced quickly. But I... I will need time," he said.

"Of course, my love," Jivonne gave a demure nod. "Of course." She looked out across empty fields, and felt no need to appease the tenant farmers who had flocked to the funeral. Nor did her husband, she knew. Tericius would prostrate himself to the will of the Most Venerable as he did in almost all things.

The first time she had met the Most Venerable, Jivonne had only recently been elevated to king's consort and installed in quarters befitting her new station. A knock at the door of her opulent apartments momentarily dispelled the thoughts in which she envisioned herself in the king's even more luxurious private chambers, an honor reserved for the queen.

She opened the door. "My lady love," Tericius bowed slightly.

The formality should have warned her, but she was still floating on a silken, perfumed cloud in her mind. "Will you favor me with your presence, for an audience with the Most Venerable?"

"Of course, my liege lord," she curtseyed. "I will send for my handmaids and join you in the throne room hence."

"Not the throne room," Tericius corrected her. "The palace gates, where the royal carriage awaits."

"Yes, my lord," Jivonne said. Tericius took his leave. She shut the door and pulled the golden bell cord to summon her handmaids. Minutes later, the carriage was oppressive with Tericius's uncharacteristic quiet as they rode to the cathedral.

The Most Venerable was seated in his holy throne, elevated behind the altar. After the funeral of Queen Avesia, Tericius's first young bride, Jivonne had not expected to return until the day she became queen herself, marrying the king. Tericius climbed the dais steps like a supplicant commoner, his boot heels echoing in the cavernously empty cathedral. Jivonne had no choice but to follow.

The king genuflected and kissed the jeweled hand the Most Venerable offered to him. Before Jivonne could determine whether she was supposed to mimic the action, the Most Venerable spoke. "No king with a living heir has married the royal consort since time out of mind."

The king bowed his head, but his voice was strident. "It has been long, Most Venerable, some twelve generations past, but not out of mind, not to the historians of the royal archives. King Bardulf the Bright had three sons by Queen Clere, who was slain in the Siege of the Blood Pledge. Bardulf later made his consort Millotte his queen."

"Hundreds of years ago," the Most Venerable sneered, "the church was young. Many of the revelations were yet incomplete. Now with our surety in the will of the Divine, we know better."

"Most Venerable," Tericius beseeched. "The revelations cannot…"

"Millotte was consort for fifteen years before she was queen," the holy man interrupted the king. "Nor did she become consort until five years after the heinous murder of Queen Clere." The Most Venerable looked pointedly at Jivonne. She knew that look, though she had only ever seen fleeting glimpses in commoners' eyes flashed at her just before they dropped their gaze and stared humbly at the ground. The Most Venerable wore the look haughtily: disbelief, disgust, branding her a cold-blooded ghoul. She wanted to meet it, to defy it, and she felt more than ready for the challenge. But she remembered herself, remembered her king's expectations, and dropped her gaze, lowering to her knees behind the king.

"Most Venerable," Tericius said, "may I ask a question?"

Jivonne risked an upward glance through her eyelashes, seething at the smug self-satisfaction on the Most Venerable's face. "My purpose in the mortal world is to serve the Divine, and share the wisdom which derives from the Divine. All who seek answers from me shall find them."

"We all serve the Divine. You provide an exemplary model, sharing your wisdom and guiding our worship," Tericius agreed. "How then may a king best serve the Divine?"

"The head of the church is the instructor, while the head of state is the protector," the holy man said, warming to the extemporized sermon. "Most subjects will never understand the smallest fraction of the revelations and mysteries. They cannot hope to attain any understanding at all of their proper relationship to the Divine if they are distracted by mortal fear. The king keeps the kingdom strong, and keeps his people free from want and harm, so that they in turn may turn their hearts toward spiritual matters. In this, the king may best serve the Divine."

"So if there is peace, the king must honor it," Tericius said. "If there must be war, the king should do all in his power to defeat his enemies swiftly. If there is famine, the king must feed his people. Unrest, he must quell."

The Most Venerable nodded sagely with each of the king's pronouncements. "It is nothing less than your most sacred duty."

"And what if the unrest is within the king's own heart?" Tericius asked. He remained on one knee, his arm resting on the opposite thigh, and the tilt of his head rose slightly. His voice, however, took on an edge of menace. "If the king suffers pangs of longing for companionship, if loneliness assault's the king's very sanity with an army of ill thoughts every night, must not the king protect himself, as well?"

The Most Venerable's smile curdled into a sour grimace. "Matters of companionship and matters of state are not ..."

Tericius cut him off. "Or should a king ignore such inward threats? Even if they should drive him to distraction, or to death by his own hand? Should a king deny these perils, until he is powerless to resist them? Must a king then forsake this world, entrust his kingdom to his young and untested heir? Would that protect his people, make them feel safe to seek out the higher mysteries of the Divine, to beg for wisdom from the lips of those who denied their king one request to forestall his doom?"

The Most Venerable's mouth hung open in shock, unaccustomed to being questioned. "You ... I ... they would not ... the commoners would never assume ..."

Tericius shrugged, a small yet potent gesture. "Who can say what a king driven mad by his isolation might say, to those who would listen, while he still had breath with which to speak?"

Jivonne had wanted to smile, to cry out with laughter, when the Most Venerable had realized that Tericius would heap infamy upon him if the church did not sanctify their marriage. At the very least he would lose worshippers, and at worst he might find himself deprived of property, liberty, and possibly life at the hands of rioting peasants or invading hordes, if the king carried through on his threats of self-harm. The Most Venerable had acquiesced, grudgingly, and Jivonne and Tericius had been wed in a spectacle of pageantry in the cathedral. They were not summoned for a private audience again.

Four years had passed, and now Jivonne felt a familiar tremble at the corners of her mouth, the laughter that could not be permitted release. Not on the day of Princess Roisia's funeral. Not until she was alone in her private chambers. She held her tongue. Outside, doleful bells tolled from every tower. The queen's head ached from the sound by the time the palace was in sight.

As the carriage rattled across the drawbridge, few servants met their arrival. Most had been given leave to attend the funeral and grieve in their own fashion for the remainder of the day thereafter. Gern, the halfwit kennel boy too dim to even understand that the princess was never coming back, opened the carriage door. Yuzat, captain of the guard too grizzled to ever show emotion, offered his arm to the queen.

Jivonne made her way toward inner gate, never looking back to see how closely the king followed her. But Yuzat's shouted "Your Highness!" gave her pause. As she halted and turned to peer over one shoulder, a granite gargoyle crashed in her path, shattering to bits and cracking the courtyard flagstones it impacted.

Tericius and Yuzat rushed to her side. "Are you well?" the king asked.

"I … am fine," Jivonne answered, splaying her fingers against the hollow of her throat. "Captain, we owe you a great debt."

"Only doing my duty," the captain said gruffly.

The queen looked up at the battlements above the gate, where the gargoyle had formerly crouched. Jagged masonry marked the perch, glittering with flecks of minerals within. Above, the sky seemed heavy and menacing.

A fortnight after the princess's funeral, Queen Jivonne was as foul-tempered as she could ever remember feeling. She had expected a trial to be endured, but this went far beyond impatience and insincere grieving. She could not sleep, could not eat, could not cast off the suspicion, the near-certainty, that her own demise was imminent. She had narrowly avoided death four separate times, counting only the most obvious incidents.

An errant linen basket left in the palace courtyard overnight had spilled its contents, and a rain-drenched sheet had been snatched by a gust of wind and plastered over the chimney venting the queen's quarters, filling the room with soot and smoke while she slept. A foreign emissary had offered an exotic delicacy which proved to be almost fatal to anyone not exposed to the ingredients since birth. A stray arrow from the palace guard's archery practice had come within inches of piercing her breast as she walked the ramparts. Three dressmakers competing for the queen's favor had nearly strangled her in their haste to ply their most extravagant designs, wrapping her in mantuas and stays brocaded in precious metals and festooned with gemstones.

Jivonne knew, deep in her heart, that this was a kind of justice, retribution from the Divine. She had taken pride in poisoning Roisia with an elixir replicating a fell childhood malady, rare but not so uncommon to arouse suspicions. Her plans meant nothing if they came to fruition under the clouds of rumor and doubt, yet she should have known that fooling the healers, even duping Tericius, meant nothing to the Divine, all-seeing and all-knowing. More importantly, all-powerful. The Divine might act through the weather, through seeming accidents, through the unknowing or rash mistakes of others, subtle strokes of fate that made her poisoning look like addled pantomime in comparison. None would ever suspect a guiding hand, except for the murderess herself.

She rose the morning after the suffocating dressmaking incident and dressed quickly, without summoning her handmaids. She hurried from her tower to the stables, to her stallion Carnelian. The horse twitched its long black tail but was otherwise motionless as she rested her head against its neck and inhaled the comforting smell. She would ride as far as the stallion would take her, tarrying as long as she could. There was no place she could truly escape the will of the Divine, but she knew not what else to do. Perhaps the Divine had concentrated the possibilities of reprisal within the palace, and the surrounding countryside would be safer. Perhaps the Divine would eventually lose interest in balancing the scales. Perhaps the world would end in the meantime.

"Your Highness?" a voice startled Jivonne, her nerves wound

tighter than snares. She whipped around to face Lajos the tackmaster, who regarded her with nothing more than curiosity mingled with reverence. "Does the Queen wish to ride this morning? I was not informed, forgive me …"

"You were not informed, because I only chose to ride upon waking, not long ago," she said.

Lajos bowed. "Your steed will be ready in but a moment, Your Highness. And I will summon the royal escort riders at once."

He turned away, and she scowled. She wanted no escorts, who would only thwart her attempts at passing unnoticed into some hinterland sanctuary. Yet now there was no way to avoid them. She would be forced to wait for the riding companions, just as she was forced to admit that she did not know how to saddle Carnelian herself, and needed the tackmaster's assistance to ride at all.

With the sun still low in the early morning sky, Queen Jivonne and six armored guardsmen cantered out of the palace courtyard and onto the open road. Pedar, the detachment leader, asked his queen their destination; she indicated that it would suit her for now to ride for the eastern foothills. Much of that land was uninhabitable, with stony soil and the nearby mountains full of hidden dens for both wild beasts and bandits. Some called the area godforsaken, and Jivonne hoped against hope they were right.

The foothills rose up around them, and the riders continued eastward. Queen Jivonne did not indicate that they should turn around, nor give any clue as to what their new destination should be. The road became a trail, and then a narrow ledge of rock that switched back and forth up the face of a mountain, forcing the horses to proceed single file. Pedar, in the foremost position, dismounted to lead his horse on foot, unable to spur his mount forward from the saddle. The beast reluctantly continued the ascent with the guardsman walking before, and the rest of the horses dutifully followed.

The mountain pass rose so high that Jivonne could see their entire journey behind them, over the foothills and the fields, all the way back to the palace. Suddenly, Carnelian reared and pawed at the air, whinnying wildly. Jivonne clutched at the reins, even as she heard the other horses stamping their hooves and snorting, guardsmen shouting in confusion. Carnelian threw her from her saddle, and the queen fell, past the edge of the pass, down into a crevasse so deep it all but swallowed the sky, leaving only a pale sliver of blue that taunted Jivonne from impossibly far away.

She struck the bottom of the ravine, wind knocked from her lungs. She could not draw air, and rolled from side to side clawing at the sheer rock walls, feeling like a fish hooked from the pond. She could hear the guards calling down to her, but she could not answer them. Gradually, she regained the ability to breathe, one shuddering lungful at a time. She could have raised her voice back to the guards, but felt no desire. Finally, the divine retribution had come. She had fallen into a dark tomb of the earth, and would die a solitary and lingering death, balancing the scales. She yielded to her release from torment.

The stone beneath her, untouched by the sun, was ice cold even through her garments. She waited for the discomfort to abate, but instead it grew worse, the chill spreading along her skin, sharp points of rock digging into her flesh. Jivonne sat up, her eyes slowly adjusting to the gloom of the crevasse. The edges of deep shadows stood out, revealing the striations of the mountain, severe cuts scored by a well-honed knife.

Something, heard but not seen, moved towards her.

A scream caught in her throat. Her feet kicked, searching blindly in the dark for purchase to push herself away from the apparition. Her hands slapped stone behind her, and one palm felt the sting of a splinter of bone, as it came down and crushed a pile of animal remains. She cried out in pain before biting her lip.

"Poor woman," a rasping voice emerged from the shadows. "All alone, all afraid, all powerless and lost."

"Who are you?" Jivonne demanded.

"If only you could see."

"Show yourself!"

The voice did not respond. Jivonne saw a slender shape drop

from the sheer rock, disappearing in the impenetrable dark of the ravine floor. Then she felt a gentle, insistent weight on her left foot, a slithering up her leg, swishing atop her robes. The insinuation rounded her knee and continued into her lap, and a serpentine head rose up, its hard glittering eyes of gold meeting her own. Jivonne exhaled a breath she had not realized she had been holding. "I am beyond the fear of a lowly pit viper," she said. "If you are the instrument fated to send me to oblivion, so be it."

"If only you could see," the serpent repeated, "oblivion need not be your fate."

"The Divine will see to it that it is," she said.

"The Divine," the serpent said, the words wrapped in a sibilant, reproachful sigh. "No man or woman can oppose the will of the Divine, nor escape punishment once condemned. Not even a queen."

Jivonne said nothing.

"If only there were other celestial forces a woman might appeal to," the serpent continued. "Others that might condone what the Divine would condemn."

"The Divine is the sole highest virtue..." Jivonne quoted the scripture automatically, before her voice began to falter, cut off by an angry hiss.

"If only man had not forgotten. If only man had not believed the church of lies, lies that spoke of the Divine as the only wellspring of virtue, rather than one among many," the serpent said. "If only man remembered that once, before he was domesticated, forbearance and compassion and propriety were not supreme. Fortitude and cunning and avidity were virtues, once. If only they could be again."

"If they could … if they were …" Jivonne felt an ember of hope she scarcely dared acknowledge. "Those virtues could be … rewarded?"

"If only the wellsprings of those virtues had power to mete," the serpent said. "If only man had not fallen away from their worship."

"I worship you," Jivonne whispered with fervid passion. "Strength and dominance and obeisance, I have always worshipped you!"

"If only the worship of one woman were enough to restore the former balance," the snake said.

"I am queen," Jivonne said.

"Queen of a people who mindlessly worship only the Divine," the snake said. "If only a queen were able to show her people another way."

Jivonne contemplated in silence. "If only I were not trapped in this crevasse."

"Follow," the serpent said, slithering from her lap to the ground.

She rose to her feet, and the serpent led her along the bottom of the ravine, up its side, down again, through narrow cracks in the stone that she would have thought impassable, into a left branch here, a right fork there, and maze-like twists and turns until finally she stood at the bottom of a rockslide which towered over her head but above which she could see the blue of the firmament once again. Jivonne climbed up the pile of rocks, her movements awkward in her garments but her will undeterred. At the summit of the rocks, she scanned the surroundings, confirming that no peasants were about to see their queen clumsily descending down the heap of stones. She worked her way down the outer face of the rockslide, unwatched by any eyes save those of the serpent still hiding in the shadows of the crevasse.

Once her feet touched solid ground again, Jivonne looked around the foothills, trying to identify a landmark that would show her the way home. She did not recognize the landscape at all. She turned around to ask the serpent for help, but saw only a flash of its golden eyes which quickly disappeared into the darkness.

"Remember those who would protect you," the serpent's voice sounded unnaturally close to her ear. Then, she knew, the beast was gone.

She heard strong hoofbeats, spun toward them and saw Carnelian galloping toward her. She exhaled in relief. The stallion drew to a halt at her side, and she mounted to the saddle once again. A slight kick of her heels set Carnelian into motion, and the horse's unerring instincts carried her back to the palace.

Queen Jivonne's return was greeted with a relief so deep it threatened to transform into a festival of celebration of its own accord. King Tericius decreed that Pedar should be freed from the dungeon, to receive twenty lashes and then be reinstated for duty immediately, commuting the sentence of a month of forty lashings every sunrise and sunset he had received after returning without the queen. For her part, the queen retired to her chambers and took dinner in bed. She had skirted death once again, but now knew what she must do.

"So it is true," the Most Venerated said. "You are here."

Queen Jivonne did not look up. She knelt in the pew, hands clasped, forehead resting against her thumbnails, in the same place and position she had maintained for four days.

"If you seek absolution, you should know that the Divine is unmoved by such displays," the Most Venerated intoned gravely. "The heart of a man or woman cannot be hidden in the sight of the Divine, and the truths within that heart make all the difference."

"I am quite sure you are right," the queen said deferentially, her eyes remaining closed.

"Then, what is the meaning of this?" the Most Venerated demanded.

"I am praying for a sculptor to finish what will surely be his masterpiece," the queen said.

"Sculptor? What sculptor?"

"I do not know his name," the queen admitted. "Only that his work will endure, and improve the world in which we live. If the Divine wills it so, of course, and for that I pray, have prayed for days and will pray for as long as it takes. Although if I know my husband, it will not take much longer."

"What has the king to do with it?" the Most Venerated asked.

"I had a dream four nights ago, a powerful dream," the queen explained. "And when I awoke, I told my husband the vision I beheld in that dream, and that I knew it was meant to be immortalized in stone. I asked my husband to make arrangements, and then I came here, to pray for the success of the endeavor. My husband greatly desires my return to the palace, I know this because he sent guards here at nightfall that first day, but I sent them back after making it clear I would not return until the vision had been realized in stone."

"What is this vision?" the Most Venerated pressed. "Some new blasphemy …?"

"No, Most Venerated," Jivonne answered, but she would say no more, resuming her contemplative silence.

The Most Venerated retreated to the altar, immediately beginning a ceremonial purification. The ritual gave him an excuse to remain in the cathedral, something to do while he watched the queen and waited for her resolve to break, for the facade of piety to crumble and reveal the heathen beneath. But the queen knelt and prayed without wavering, until a palace guardsman arrived and strode down the aisle to her pew.

"My queen, it is finished," the guard announced.

Queen Jivonne rose to depart. From the aisle, she looked up at the Most Venerated and bowed her head in farewell. She followed the guard out of the cathedral, leaving the Most Venerated to wonder why the queen had spent four days kneeling beneath the apse. She hoped his inability to understand would torment him to the point of ruining his sleep for at least four nights.

Her vigil served three purposes. First, as she boasted to the Most Venerated, it ensured that her husband, once he realized she had no intention of leaving before the statue was completed, to use every ounce of his wealth and royal influence to bring the project to fruition. Second, it reminded the people who heard of the vigil that she was pious. And third, it provided a temporary respite from the wrath of the Divine, who surely would not strike her dead while she engaged in the act of worshipping him in his own house. Or so she had hoped, and as she returned to the palace in the royal coach, she seemed to have been proven correct.

The palace servants gathered for dinner at dusk, allowing time for one large communal meal before dark, when the king and queen and their court would be served the nightly banquet. They clustered in small groups and made their way to the kitchens, passing the garden nearby. There, the new statue had been erected, depicting the princess with a full-grown timber wolf on one side and a baby deer on the other, the defender of innocence, the bringer of peace. Standing before the sculpture, almost as motionless as the stone, was Queen Jivonne.

The servants murmured to one another, none daring more than a few hushed words of observation as they passed the queen. Louder opinions were expressed and detailed theories were advanced out of earshot over the nightly fare of stew and brown bread. By the end of the meal, the matter had been exhausted as a topic of conversation. Yet when the servants departed the kitchens an hour later, Queen Jivonne remained where they had last seen her.

Brunna, the oldest and longest-serving of the palace laundresses, broke away from the two maids she had been walking with and entered the garden. The maids stopped and stared after her, unable to comprehend why Brunna would forget herself and approach the queen unbidden, equally unable to follow after her and break their own habits of avoiding the queen unless summoned. Brunna approached Jivonne respectfully, until they stood side by side. For a few moments, as the sky above hurried from the fading spectacle of sunset to the deeper darkness, neither spoke.

Brunna broke the silence. "I ... Your Highness, I beg pardon, but ... I saw you here and ... I lost a son when he was twelve, almost the same age as the princess. 'Twas many years ago, but I still think of him, often."

For a long interval, it seemed as if the queen would not deign to respond, but when she answered, Brunna was surprised by the unassuming emotion in Jivonne's voice. "I would not wish this kind of loss on anyone," she said. "Not my worst enemy."

"Nor I, Your Highness," Brunna agreed. "'Tis a strange sorrow to bury a child."

"Strange?"

"Strange and large, too big for us, too big for this world," Brunna explained. "At first, it swallows up all the joy the child ever brought us. But, in time, the sorrow becomes less, and the joys return. You will see."

Jivonne cast a sidelong glance at Brunna, a limpid shimmer in her eyes. "Thank you, good woman."

A man in a hooded, mud-daubed cloak edged along the low stone wall that bordered the garden. With an inhuman yowl, he lunged toward Queen Jivonne, one dirt-streaked upraised hand clenching a dagger. The hood flew back, revealing a poxy face dominated by wild eyes and a snarl of rotten teeth. Queen Jivonne stepped back, her face defiant, while Brunna fell to her knees and began to shriek as if the madman were coming straight for her.

A dark blur of motion from atop the wall sped toward the would-be assassin, barreling into the madman's back. A black wolf pinned the queen's attacker to the ground. With one savage snap of its jaws, it tore off the hand holding the dagger in a crunch of bone and spray of blood. Brunna continued to wail, the agonized screams of the madman mixed with hers. The black wolf regarded Queen Jivonne briefly, then bounded back up and over the palace wall.

The palace guards arrived on the run; several of them took the madman, woozy and weak from blood loss, into custody. The remainder escorted the queen back to her chambers, leaving Brunna alone in the garden. When she gathered her wits and was able to rise to her feet once more, she made her way back to the kitchen. She returned to the garden shortly with a pair of sheep's leg bones. Most of the mutton had been stripped away for the servants' stew, but she had snapped them in half to expose the glistening marrow within. Brunna laid the broken bones on the statue's plinth, beneath the head of the marble wolf at Princess Roisia's side.

The Most Venerable walked the length of the throne room, his robes whispering against the carpet. Although they were the finest raiment the Most Venerable possessed, they were not as resplendent as they had once been. The golden thread no longer sparkled, and the fur trim was thinned along the bottom hem, discolored along the collar. There was a gap now between the collar and the Most Venerable's neck, as the church leader had shed some of his former plumpness.

In front of the raised throne where Queen Jivonne sat, the Most Venerable stopped. "Is King Tericius unable attend this audience?" he asked.

The queen said nothing. She stared down at the Most Venerable, expectant and unsmiling.

The Most Venerable gazed back at her, then bowed his head. A moment later, he began to awkwardly lower himself to his knees, gathering his robes and bending stiffly. "Forgive me, Your Highness," he said.

Once he had abased himself, the queen spoke. "My husband is ill, Most Venerable, as you know. He does not find long periods in the throne suit him, and he only holds audience on matters of greatest importance."

"Your highness," the Most Venerable protested, "what could be of greater importance than the fate of the Church, which the king has always loved and served so well?"

"My husband has dedicated his life to serving the Divine," Queen Jivonne said. "While I am sure that he appreciates that you, also, serve the Divine, I do not recall our king ever pledging service to the Church."

"None … nonetheless," the Most Venerable stammered, "the Church needs the king's aid. Our coffers are nearly empty, without more funds we shall …"

"And why is it that the Church finds itself in such dire straits?" the queen interrupted. "It is not the duty of the king to provide alms to the Church. Do all the faithful no longer make donations?"

"They … do, Your Highness," the Most Venerable said. "But they … they are fewer than they once were. Attendances at ceremonies are smaller. There are more seats empty than filled in the cathedral of late."

"But surely if the congregation to which you minister is smaller, then less monies are required?" the queen asked.

"A candle's cost is a candle's cost, Your Highness," the Most Venerable said, "whether it is lit to give light to one hundred gathered together, or one alone."

"True," the queen nodded. "I seem to recall that the candles in the cathedral were imposing columns of perfumed beeswax, inlaid with gilded patterns. Perhaps the Church should consider smaller, simpler candles, to minister to the one rather than the hundred. I also seem to recall that I never saw a candle lit in the cathedral without a virgin white wick touched to flame. Does the Divine forbid you to reuse a candle? The peasants could show you how it may be done."

"My la—Your Highness," the Most Venerable scowled. "The cathedral has always been considered one of the blessings bestowed upon the kingdom. If King Tericius could only …"

"My husband and I are of one mind on the subject, and it is our decision that the Church will not receive further gifts from the royal treasury," she said.

"I do not think …"

"No, I am aware that you do not think, Most Venerable," the queen said. "You talk and talk and talk. Instead of talking to me you should talk to the Divine. Pray for more worshippers, or pray for the worshippers you retain to contribute more of their own wealth. Pray for the Divine to miraculously fill your coffers with treasures which fall from the sky. But leave your king and your queen out of it."

A storm of fury gathered across the Most Venerable's brow, only to break in confusion as the queen rose from the throne. By standing, she signaled that the audience was over. The Most Venerable could make no more arguments or entreaties, as by the codes of court protocol they would fall on deaf ears. That all of his previous attempts to persuade the queen had already fallen on deaf ears made no difference.

Queen Jivonne descended the stairs of the dais and walked past the Most Venerable without deigning to look at him. She held her head high. She smiled.

The queen sat in her bedchambers, perched on a divan alongside a large, arched window. The spot was one of her favorites in the castle, and she spent many pleasant afternoons simply gazing upon the scenery in solitude. The beveled glass panes were open wide on their iron hinges, affording the queen a majestic view of her kingdom, the lands beyond the palace courtyard, the fields and roads and the distant forest where many reports indicated that the population of wild boars was flourishing.

Tericius spent almost all of his time in bed now, in the grips of an affliction which filled his lungs with fluid, sapping his strength and, increasingly, his lucidity. His only relief was lying as still as possible, as any movement would trigger a choking cough that produced gobs of the vile, murky fluid. Jivonne visited him from time to time, but briefly, as the king's healers advised him not to speak. She missed her king's attentions, now and then, but there were benefits to his infirmity. The people of the kingdom were afforded a generous span of time in which to accept that Queen Jivonne effectively ruled the land, while her husband clung to life and bestowed her reign with legitimacy. She was glad she had selected an elixir with such dilatory effects to dispatch the king. The question of Tericius siring an heir was now moot, as well, which suited Jivonne perfectly. She intended to rule unrivaled for years and years to come, without creating the temptation to cast her aside for a younger member of the bloodline. Questions of succession would wait until she had reached the hereafter, when they would no longer affect her.

She spied two figures approaching on foot, men in robes as gray as cold cinders. They were supplicants from the cathedral, making their monthly visit to the palace, where they were permitted to station themselves at the gates to beg for alms from the passersby, the merchants and functionaries and servants who came and went performing the bidding of the king, at the behest of his queen. Jivonne did not begrudge the holy men their attempts to exhort charity from her subjects. She knew they would not collect much for the church, which fewer and fewer people attended or believed in each year. But they were welcome to try, to see the results for themselves. If anything, she preferred it that way.

Jivonne watched as the holy men's steps converged on those of a father, mother and young son going the opposite way. The supplicants stopped to make their humble appeal, but while the trio hailed them amiably enough they never slowed. The father carried a sizable bundle across his shoulders, doubtless an offering for one of the celestial wellsprings. A shrine to the fleetness of the fox had been erected a little further up the road, and one dedicated to the prowess of the eagle beyond that. Offerings to the animal avatars became more popular every year and now were commonplace. The results were more immediately gratifying, which appealed to the commoners far more than meek contemplation of the abstract, unknowable Divine. Perhaps life was a bit more cutthroat, a bit less genteel, at least among the rabble. But at least none of them persisted in questioning whether or not it was fair that the previous heir, the young princess, should have died in childhood. No death was untimely when they were all seen as nature's way, allowing the strong to survive and the strongest to thrive.

The queen felt a tickling along her hand, resting on the warm stone of the windowsill. She glanced down to see a spider crawling across her skin, one slow step at a time. The spider's legs were as thin as a cat's whiskers, and its body was bright crimson. Pinprick spiders, they were called, because their legs were as slender as pins and their bodies resembled ruby droplets of blood, but they were far more dangerous than the prick of a pin. Despite their small size, their venomous bites could paralyze the mice they hunted, and could cause a grown man to lose feeling in an entire limb for weeks. But Jivonne was not afraid, merely fascinated as the tiny, deadly predator made its way across her hand.

The holy men arrived at the gates, and the queen realized that one of the gray figures was none other than the Most Venerable himself. He looked much older, his eyes sunken in purpled cavities, still double-chinned but wearing the excess flesh in sagging, deflated folds. Today, he was mortifying himself by begging at the palace gates, rather than sending an underling out in his name. Perhaps there were no more underlings to send.

Queen Jivonne raised her hand, bringing the pinprick spider closer to her face, serene, contented and grateful. She lowered her hand to the windowsill and allowed the spider to continue on its way, in search of its next sustenance, its next victim. The queen respected the spider's path, and that it was true to itself, just as she was true to herself. She would never change. When all had seemed lost because she had risked too much, a transgression too far, she had been inspired to change the rules of the game. She had seized control of a world where ambition was castigated, and now she ruled a world where risk was rewarded for its own sake. It was a world she far preferred, and it was good to be its queen.

A Haven For Talismans

MOST OF THE STORES AND RESTAURANTS in the upscale retail district went to great lengths to draw attention to themselves, from the huge cement urns overflowing with colorful peony blooms flanking the front door of the Bouquets By Kaylee flower shop, to the controversy-courting wooden Indian standing sentinel at the entrance to the Smoke Signals tobacconist, to the painted mural of an archipelago at sunset on the window of the Far Horizon Travel Agency. The wrought-iron lampposts lining the street were hung with banners that changed every other week, advertising upcoming festivals or announcing the change of seasons with thematically appropriate imagery, and the herringbone pattern of the brick sidewalks seemed to point pedestrians ever onwards to the next slate standee advertising daily specials in a pastel chalk rainbow, the next book store hosting a local author signing books at a bunting-draped table, the next combination art gallery and wine bar giving away samples of tempranillo to lure people in to the exhibit of black and white photography.

So the overabundance of signage and statuary was maintained in a self-perpetuating endless cycle, like an arms race, or the biological evolution of more and more extravagant mating displays. The lone exception was three storefronts east of the corner of Cockrell Lane and Aster Road. The front window was covered by heavy curtains hanging inside, velvet which had once been black but had been leached to indigo by years of exposure to sunlight. There were no placards or swinging shingles marking the place, no neon in the window or beveled lettering bolted to the masonry above. The entrance to the establishment was set back from the sidewalk in a recessed alcove, a plain dark wooden door with another curtained window occupying the top half. Painted on the door window in golden script were the words "PHYLACTERIUM APTUS PORTUS", surrounded by a circle of interlocked shapes and sigils in cobalt and silver.

Standing on the shadowy step of the entranceway, Ajax Masterson nodded his approval. The shop was easy enough to pass by, to dismiss as unimportant or unworthy of attention. Only the true initiates of the higher mysteries would recognize the quiet, abiding power of the place. In that sense, the shop and Masterson had much in common. Tall, but not remarkably so, spare framed, with dark wavy hair swept back from his forehead, hazel eyes, and no distinguishing features. He wore a tailored suit, navy blue with subtle pinstripes, and a pearlescent gray shirt and tie. He carried an ebony walking stick, the head of which was shaped like a primitive depiction of the sun, a spherical face ringed with geometric rays.

It had taken Masterson years of research, exchanging information and favors and following leads that mostly turned out to be dead ends, before he had finally determined the exact location of the Phylacterium, and that followed only after earlier years' laborious efforts to ascertain whether or not the shop even existed and what it was called. But it had all been worth it, now that he was here. Or rather, it would be worth it assuming he successfully transacted the business that had brought him here.

Masterson straightened his shoulders, took a deep breath, and twisted the doorknob. As he stepped into the dim interior of the shop, he smelled the sharp tang of burning incense and the deep earthiness of potted plants. In the moment it took for his eyes to adjust to the near darkness, the olfactory notes were all he could process. But as his vision came back into focus, he saw a small amount of space arranged to display as many wares as possible. Wooden shelves ran around the walls, the lowest two feet above the floor and the highest only inches from the ceiling, all jammed with objects of great interest, old books with cracked leather spines, clear glass jars filled with murky liquids, clay pots, some painted and glazed handsomely, others the color of dried dirt. Under the lowest shelf there were baskets and boxes and crates and a set of drums. In the center of the store was a square of shelving, reaching nearly to the ceiling and overflowing with more items. There was only enough open floorspace for a single person to pass between the shelves on the wall and the rack in the middle. The front door opened into a corner of the floor plan so that a visitor could only walk straight ahead or turn to the right. Along the wall to the left was a glass display case which also supported an old-fashioned cash register. The shelves behind the register no doubt contained the more rare and powerful items for safekeeping. In the corner directly opposite the front door was another doorway, hung with a tapestry painting of the Sephirot.

There had been no bell or chime when Masterson had entered the store, so he simply turned to the right and perused the items on display there. What he needed was a decoy, some object which was potent but not too powerful, thereby allowing him to demonstrate that he knew how to separate quality from dross. Once he brought the object to the shopkeeper, he could inquire after his true aim, which he suspected would not be anywhere a curious browser might openly, randomly encounter it.

He picked up a small charm, an upward-pointing triangle on a chain. The materials were cheap, tarnished brass and inlaid stones which were semi-precious at best and much more likely paste glass. But the workmanship was admirable, and as he lifted it in his hand he felt a ripple of energy across his skin, enough to raise the hairs on his forearm. It was probably only a good luck piece, with no specific application, but it was something. Masterson kept the charm in his hand as he continued his circumnavigation of the store.

"Can I help you?" a voice floated through the air. Masterson stepped past the central shelves and saw there was now a woman standing behind the glass display case. She was every bit as unremarkable as the facade of the shop. Straight mouse-brown hair parted in the middle and bound in matching pigtails at the base of her skull. Large frame glasses over brown eyes, a button nose, thin lips, and no makeup on her face. She wore a white linen peasant blouse and a dark turquoise skirt that brushed the floor, an outfit which showed she was neither overweight nor voluptuous nor skinny, merely average in every proportion.

Having taken the measure of her, Masterson made a show of returning his attention to the shelves as he sauntered toward the front of the store. "You have a remarkable little shop here," he said, not bothering to look at the woman.

"Thank you," the woman said. "Is there anything in particular you are looking for?"

"I've already found something which piques my interest," Masterson said. He had reached the display case, and he laid the talisman on the glass top.

"Lovely," the woman said. She smiled. "You have a good eye."

"Thank you," Masterson replied. "I do however wonder if I might be able to find something a little more … empyrean." There it was, the secret shibboleth, the unlikely word that would indicate the he, Ajax Masterson, was no novice, no New Age dilettante. He had connections, and he had cajoled those connections into sharing the passkey with him, essentially vouching for his credentials.

"What exactly do you mean, Mr…?" the woman asked.

"Masterson. Ajax Masterson," he gave as his name. It was not his true name, of course, and he hardly expected her to believe that it was. His real name was Alan Meyrowicz, which he knew was a difficult name for many to take seriously, particularly in the spheres of ancient mysticism which he had dedicated himself to gaining entry. And one of the earliest yet most important lessons he had learned was to never give other practitioners of the arts, be they human or entities from beyond, his true name, for that was a surrender of power easy for others to exploit.

"Mr. Masterson. I'm sorry," the woman said, "can you be a bit more specific?"

She wasn't responding to the shibboleth the way Masterson had expected her to. Was she testing him? Trying to determine whether or not he had simply overheard or stumbled upon 'empyrean'? He poked idly at the chain of the talisman, rearranging it into an undulating wave of tiny brass links. "This trinket is well wrought, and I have no doubt that it can fulfill its intended function. But that function itself, is, shall we say, somewhat mundane? It channels and redirects effects which are already co-aligned with our world. And as we must live in this world, day to day, there is prudence in possessing such a thing. But what I truly seek is transcendence. Something more metaphysical than physical. Something sublime. As I said, empyrean."

The woman nodded, more in polite understanding than in signal of having received a coded message. "Perhaps if you could give me a specific example?"

Masterson's patience was too thin for him to participate in whatever coy game the woman was playing any longer. "For example," he said brusquely, "an Eggja stone?"

The woman behind the counter considered Masterson for a moment, during which he cursed himself inwardly, sure that he had misplayed his hand. When the protocol he had been advised to rely upon had failed, he had simply resorted to his customary bluntness rather than attempting anything with more care and finesse. He kept his face a mask of composure, daring the woman to challenge why he would want an Eggja stone in the first place.

But the woman only smiled and said, "I can look around in the back. Wait one moment, won't you?" And before Masterson could so much as clear his suddenly dry throat, she had whirled through the Sephirot tapestry and disappeared.

Masterson blinked. Perhaps a show of self-confidence was the real passkey, or the necessary other half of it. He congratulated himself on the victory.

The woman returned in less than a minute with a bundle of cloth in one hand. She set it on the display case and unfolded the fabric, revealing a stone about the size of an apple. It was a flat trapezoid with smooth rounded corners. The face of it was carved with an animal totem of some kind; Masterson expected it was a wolf. The woman turned the Eggja stone over to reveal rows of finely inscribed runes on the obverse. "This is what you consider empyrean?" the woman asked.

"Indeed, it is," Masterson sighed. His mind was reeling. The Eggja stone was before him, so close, and all he needed to do was take it. "How much?"

"Make me an offer," the woman said.

Masterson thought for a moment. For the Eggja stone he would pay anything. He had several credit cards in his wallet with thousands of dollars available on each, but he doubted a shop like this would be able process electronic payments. He had brought fifteen hundred dollars in cash as well against just such an eventuality. If he were going to haggle with the woman, he would need to leave himself negotiating room. "Eight hundred," he said.

The woman nodded. "And I'll throw in the talisman for another twenty-five," she said. She was already pushing buttons on the cash register, each one triggering a muted ch-chunk of gears inside the old device. The drawer did not so much spring open as slowly extend like the jaw of a yawning lion.

Masterson pulled out his wallet in a near daze. He thumbed through hundred-dollar bills, counted nine of them, and handed them over. The woman counted them again, slid them into the drawer tray, and drew out three twenties, a ten, and a five to hand back. "Thank you, Mr. Masterson."

He nodded numbly. That was all there was to it, the Eggja stone was now his by right. The transaction had been fair and honest. He stuffed the talisman in a pocket and refolded the fabric around the Eggja stone, cradling it like a newborn puppy. As he walked toward the exit, he was already envisioning making use of the stone, using it to sharpen the steel point of his walking stick, which in turn would bind warrior spirits to the metal and make the weapon increasingly more formidable, just as king Hrolf Kraki had bound berserker souls to his legendary sword Skofnung.

Reaching for the doorknob, Masterson was overcome by the urge to unwrap the stone and gaze upon it again. It occurred to him that some details of the binding were still unclear to him. Actually acquiring the Eggja stone had been his greatest obstacle so far, to the exclusion of other considerations. Was the blood of the warrior meant to be applied to the metal before sharpening it on the stone, or to the stone itself? Did the warrior have to die before his soul could be bound, or would using the blood of a living man in the ritual kill the man? What kind of man counted as a warrior in this modern world? Soldiers, of course, and policemen. Firemen? Boxers and wrestlers? Gang members?

Masterson hesitated at the threshold, agonizing in uncertainty. He had so many questions, and while he was sure he could research the information, he had potential access to many if not all the answers in the proprietress of the shop. His impatience battled with his pride, until he realized the one thing holding him back was a fear that he would be deemed unworthy of the stone if he displayed the slightest sign of ignorance. But that was foolish vanity. The transaction was complete, the Eggja stone was his now and nothing could reverse that against his will. If he posed his questions to the woman, at worst he might suffer a few moments of social discomfort under her withering scorn. But the stone would remain his, and he would be no further away from the answers than if he walked out now. And at best, he might save himself precious time and effort. The reward far outweighed the risk.

He reversed himself, finding the woman once again gone. He walked to the glass display case. "Pardon me, madam?" he called out. Silence answered him. "Excuse me? I meant to ask one thing before leaving?" he tried again. The Sephirot tapestry did not so much as stir. "Hello?"

Masterson edge around the display case, expecting the

proprietress to finally answer at any moment, but no response was forthcoming. He approached the tapestry, took hold of its soft, fraying edge, and drew it aside. He stepped into the back room.

The storage area was even darker than the sales floor, small windows near the ceiling painted over opaquely, a single bare lightbulb providing limited visibility. Here were more shelves, arranged not for display but for storage, crammed with slatted crates and cardboard shipping boxes. Each corner of the room was occupied by utilitarian racks, creating cruciform aisles between them. Masterson could see to the end of the aisle running from the doorway to the far end of the back room, and the proprietress was nowhere to be seen. He walked to the midpoint, to look down the perpendicular aisle in both directions.

He spied the woman, squatting on the floor at the end of the aisle, her back to him. She was hunched over a bundle propped against the cinderblock wall which looked approximately the same size as her. Masterson took another step closer and saw that it was, in fact, another woman, just as a pink Styrofoam peanut squeaked beneath the sole of his shoe.

The noise drew the proprietress's attention, her head swiveling swiftly. Masterson froze in his tracks as he stared at the visage turned upon him. The woman's hairline had drawn back to the apex of the skull, and the flesh of her face had parted like a curtain. A grotesque aggregate of features protruded from the rend, beady black vulture eyes and a long scarlet snout, with backswept spines lining either side like saw-teeth, as if the horror had cut its way free from inside the woman. But that was not the case, Masterson realized, as his blood turned to ice, draining from his head to leave a howling hollow feeling and pooling in his belly as cold, heavy dread. There was no woman, and there never had been, there was only this fiend which had worn a mask of humanity and then sloughed it off.

The fiend hissed, an animalistic sound which made Masterson think only of territorial aggression, but when a black, forked tongue emerged from the serrated snout it accompanied a voice.

"You should have taken your prize and made haste away from here," it snarled.

"You should have chosen somewhere else to feed," Masterson said, somehow keeping his voice much steadier than he felt. He was certain that he had crossed an invisible line the instant he had seen the creature's true face. He would have to fight his way to freedom or he would die here in the backroom of the Phylacterium, and if he showed fear he would only encourage the creature to attack more ferociously.

The fiend made a gurgling sound that might have been a humorless laugh. "You think you have only interrupted predation for sustenance? You think you are the only one who seeks the secrets empyrean?"

It was not a question that Masterson had been expecting, yet the intense curiosity it stirred in him somehow focused his senses and made the mortal terror recede. "What secrets can a dead woman reveal?" he asked.

"The woman is not dead," the fiend growled. "Not yet, though she will meet her end tonight, in the darkest and most baleful hour. The bloodletting of one of her kind will consecrate a ritual to unfetter ..."

Masterson did not wait to hear the remainder of whatever arcane upheavals were promised and prophesied. He lunged forward, leading with the steel tip of his walking stick and heaving his entire weight behind it. He had only just obtained an Eggja stone for purposes of enchanting the implement, but he always kept it savagely sharp as a matter of course.

The steel tip bit into the midsection of the creature, and Masterson could only hope that it sank completely through the human-skin disguise and found purchase in the fiend's own flesh. He was encouraged by the fact that the fiend roared in what sounded like pain and rage, but then the fiend was upright, standing to its full height of eight feet tall. The skirt that had brushed the floor now swished in the air above dark, crooked legs that seemed to belong to some kind of scaly goat. The forearms had split apart like overcooked sausages, revealing bony talons tipped with claws like scythes. The fiend slashed at Masterson, who was already staggering backwards, and caught the side of his head, a glancing blow that drew blood Masterson could feel running down his cheek and neck.

Ignoring the bright stinging pain, Masterson tightened his grip on his walking stick. He readied himself for the fiend to press the attack, and did not have to wait long. As soon as the looming monstrosity took one step forward, Masterson darted closer and drove the steel point into the top of the fiend's scaly foot. Without abandoning his momentum, Masterson spun around the side of the fiend and positioned himself behind its back. The creature's now-elongated neck presented itself as a clear target for Masterson's two-handed overhead thrust.

Once again the walking stick punctured the distended human skin, and Masterson hoped for an accompanying spray of ichor with the force of a ruptured pipe. But while the fiend shrieked, it was neither paralyzed nor laid low by the wound. The fiend swung an arm behind, knocking Masterson aside with the back of its bony hand. The force sent Masterson reeling, vaguely aware that had it been the claws striking him with such power he would have been eviscerated rather than bludgeoned.

Masterson's mind raced as he lay sprawled against the struts of shelves. The fiend was savage and cruel and more than physically capable of tearing him apart. What had been the point of the earlier ruse in the front of the shop? If the fiend needed the woman for some dark ritual, why had it not already removed her to the profane site? A notion began to form amid Masterson's chaotic swirl of questions.

He gathered his wits as he rose to his feet. He braced his fists one atop the other near the head of his walking stick and ranged across the floor, brandishing the accessory like a sword and meeting the soulless gaze of the fiend without blinking. The fiend, wary of Masterson's advantage-seeking, waited like a coiled spring. Masterson cocked the walking stick over his shoulder and strode forward, and immediately the fiend caught hold of Masterson's jacket and shirt and tie in one tangled handful and lifted him off the floor. The fiend slammed Masterson's spine against the cinderblock wall near the ceiling. "Take comfort," the fiend insisted, increasing the pressure on Masterson's ribcage, "that your death will spare you the knowledge of the many and varied ways in which I defile your corpse afterwards."

"Kind of you," Masterson wheezed. He transferred the walking stick to his left hand alone, allowing it to slide through his fingers until he held the steel tip and the beatific sun dangled near his feet. He swung his arm up, the walking stick slashing a wide arc through empty air until the sun struck the painted pane of the window over his shoulder. Glass shattered and fell to the floor and sunlight streamed through the jagged hole. The beam struck the fiend's arm and the flesh sizzled into noxious red vapor.

The fiend yowled piteously and dropped Masterson. He swept his walking stick through the fiend's ankles, upending the creature. Its legs flailed in the daylight and scales crackled and smoked as if held to a branding iron. Masterson ran around to the fiend's head and grabbed the long brown hair of the human skin. In fits and starts, while the creature bucked and thrashed, he dragged the fiend toward the patch of sunlight on the floor. The fiend twisted in a paroxysm of agonizing terror, until Masterson stabbed the steel tip of his walking stick into one of the skin's human ears, pinning it to the ground in the center of the day-lit area.

The fiend jerked its head from side to side, widening the gash of parted human skin down the centerline of its throat, but the shining sun was already taking its toll. The fiend's eyes boiled and popped, oozing down the sides of the sawtooth snout in oily black rivulets. The fiend extended its serpentine tongue only for it to flake apart into ash as it undulated in the light. The fiend's clawed talons shielded its head for a brief instant until the limbs sublimated into clouds of discorporate matter. With a final desperate screech, the fiend gnashed its maw while it burned away into charred embers that glowed incandescent orange before fading to lifeless gray.

Masterson's shoulders slumped. He leaned heavily on his walking stick, drawing deep breaths until his heartbeat no longer hammered in his ears. Once he could bear to open his eyes and raise his head again, he looked to the woman against the wall, who had been all but ignored during his confrontation with the fiend.

Masterson crouched beside the woman and tentatively felt for a pulse in her neck. He found it, proving the fiend had at least been truthful in that regard. In fact, the woman seemed altogether uninjured as Masterson guided her to a sitting position. "Madam?" Masterson asked, tapping the woman's cheek. "Madam, can you hear me?"

Her eyelids fluttered. She moaned once, shook her head, and looked quizzically at Masterson. "What … who …?"

"Madam, are you all right?"

She tilted her head from side to side experimentally. "I think so," she said. "I don't … the last thing I remember is opening the shop this morning, coming back here and …" She struggled to make sense of the memory.

"I believe you were attacked," Masterson supplied. "By something … unnatural."

"Is it still here?" she asked, looking past Masterson's shoulder with apprehension.

"No. I hazarded a guess that the creature had invaded your shop last night, waylaid you in the morning as you seem to suggest, and was waiting until nightfall to abscond with you. I surmised this was because the creature was averse to sunlight, and I dispatched it accordingly. I apologize for damaging your window," Masterson said, gesturing to the broken pane.

The woman looked up at the window, shaking her head. "No, no, you … you saved me. You have nothing to apologize for. If anything, I'm in your debt."

Masterson stood up and offered a hand to the woman. "Think nothing of it," he said as he helped her to her feet.

"I insist," the woman said. "If it's within my power to reward you in any way you see fit, I'd like to."

Masterson considered the woman. The fiend in human skin had evidently not been trying to mimic her. The true proprietress of the shop was short, with soft features that gave her an ageless quality, like a prepubescent child with near-adult proportions. Her hair was a halo of blonde ringlets, the curls across her forehead dyed bright pink. She wore what looked like a vintage bowling shirt with the sleeves cut off, revealing various tattoos on her upper arms, drab cargo pants and t-shirts. Her earlobes, neck and wrists were decorated with a riot of clashing jewelry. Chaotic as her attire and accessories were, it was her eyes that commanded Masterson's attention, waiting patiently for him to answer.

Masterson reached into his pocket. "I wouldn't ask for recompense," he said, "but I would consider it a great favor if you could answer a few questions about this Eggja stone."

The woman looked at the object he held out to her. She glanced up after a moment to read his face. "This … isn't an Eggja stone," she said.

Masterson blinked. "What else could it be?"

"A grave ward, of course," the woman said. "Protection from grave robbers and evil spirits. You came here looking for an Eggja stone?"

"Only to be deceived by your captor," Masterson frowned at the grave ward. "Still, better to learn of the chicanery now and set it right."

His eyes flicked to the woman expectantly, only to find her expression had hardened in severity. "Eggja stones are conduits of darkness and corruption," she said. "I'd never keep such a dire relic in this store, let alone hand one over to a complete stranger."

"Even a stranger who saved your life?" Masterson challenged her.

"Even so," she rebuffed. "I think it'd be best if you took your leave now. I won't detain you, even though the intentions revealed by what you seek are troubling at best. Consider the scales balanced."

"*You* won't detain *me*?" Masterson repeated in disbelief. He meant to step forward, to encroach upon her space with his superior stature and his righteous anger, but in that moment he could feel the woman's innate advantage over him. There was power within her, long-abiding and hard-earned, slow to stir perhaps but too terrible to withstand if roused. She met his glower, unafraid, until he spun on his heel and stalked away.

He was back out on the sidewalk and two doors down the block before he was aware of anything more than the crimson storm thundering behind his eyes. He could scarcely reconstruct the whirlwind of events that had buffeted him from success to near death to triumph to humiliation in the span of a single afternoon. The day that had begun with such high hopes was now fated to end seeing him utterly empty-handed. He was worse off than he had been at the outset, his wallet lighter by nearly a thousand dollars, his clothing irreparably damaged, and the proprietress of the Phylacterium now a skeptic of his worth if not an outright adversary.

Still, Masterson consoled himself, he could not count the episode a complete loss. He had the grave ward and the luck charm, and while neither was the prize he had sought, each might have their uses, their value to others with which he could bargain and barter. No setback could deter him from his ultimate ambitions. If his ascent must continue in slow, minuscule increments, so be it. It would continue all the same. One day he would reach the goal of his empyrean quest. He could be delayed but never denied. And on that day, when his power was more than a match for any other, perhaps he would again pay a visit to the Phylacterium, with a different outcome. He looked forward to it already.

REQUITAL

Someone help me, please, I'm begging, anyone
Her desperate thoughts soaked in cold sweat
She cannot undo, what's done is done
Bleeding, life ebbing, forcing legs to run
Away from the man with the eyes of jet
She's begging, someone help me, please, anyone
Splashing mud, gnarled root, her flight undone,
Branches crisscross overhead a trapping net
No one can undo, what's done is done
He closes in, murderous, final act begun,
Hatchet in hand, a slavering red threat,
Still begging, please, someone help me, anyone
Spirits rooted here, victims in their own season,
Aware of the terror the preyings beget
They cannot undo, what's done is done
Ghost green hands wresting free his weapon,
Drag him down to a grave cold and wet
Help me, please, he's begging, someone, anyone
She shudders, awed by her salvation,
Witnessing her attacker's fate without regret
She cannot undo, what's done is done
Fading, get a doctor, call for help, she's won

A chance, at least, to see tomorrow yet
I'm begging, anyone, help me, please, someone
But their purpose is pure, lethal mission,
Taking life for life to pay bloody debt
We cannot undo, what's done is done
Dying, she joins their choir of fallen
And will the next victim's reprisal abet
Someone begging, please, help me, anyone
They cannot undo, what's done is done

RECLAMATION RUN

WHEN THE DASH DISPLAY for the return beacon lit up green, indicating successful deployment, Jeffries flipped the switch for the secondary windscreen. Smoky polarized glass retracted smoothly into the body of the tanker above the cockpit, granting Jeffries and Mariotta an unobstructed view through the primary windscreen. The process always reminded Jeffries of something he had read about back in grade school, how some birds and lizards had third eyelids, extra protection for their optical organs. The primary windscreen was the lens of the eyeball, Jeffries and Mariotta were the brains inside the skull, and when the extra lid slowly blinked open they were able to get their bearings as to what kind of hellscape they had been sent to this time.

By definition, every reclamation run took place in a hellscape, what the brains of the operation would call a "hazardous environment", and over time the huge swaths of devastation had begun to blur together somewhat. One killing field full of corpses looked much like another, no matter the cause of death; one blasted arid wasteland closely resembled the next, the source of the ruination notwithstanding. The landscape unspooled in front of the tanker now was noteworthy merely because it looked so normal, a sea of yellowing grass, prairie in the dry season. But the sky here was menacing, dark low-hanging clouds that looked like puddles in a heavily trafficked asphalt lot, with scrims of oily, iridescent discoloration. The dome above was overcast with poison from one horizon to the other.

Mariotta, as usual, said nothing and keyed the engine to life. The tanker gave its customary rumbling growl, which settled to an angry muttering. Mariotta coaxed the tanker forward through the brittle grass, toward a fenced line in the distance.

"You think this one went out peaceful?" Jeffries asked.

"Hope so," Mariotta grunted. "Be nice to clock out early."

Jeffries agreed with Mariotta, silently, inside his head, since Mariotta's tone indicated no interest in making small talk. Not that Jeffries had any plans for after their shift, but he hoped this world's civilization had expired quietly because that would make the task at hand that much easier. Sometimes the end of the world was a reasonably orderly affair, a slow winding down that allowed people time and space to put their affairs in order before either setting out on some doomed quest for a reprieve, or seeking a quick and painless exit on their own terms. On those worlds, the trappings of civilization were abandoned ghost towns. But sometimes the end of the world was an utter shit show, a tumult of chaos and panic that arrived without warning and flared up in a frenzy before burning out, leaving an unregulated slaughterhouse floor amongst the works that endured. Either way, the reclamation runners would get what they came for. It was just so much less effort when they didn't have to dig through too much death and needless destruction first.

The tanker crawled slowly across the prairie on its long chain tracks of steel plates. The sheer size of the vehicle's body, a hundred fifty meters long and twenty meters in diameter, had awed Jeffries the first time he had seen it, and he had wondered how the behemoth was able to move at all, particularly once it was full. But he had never bothered to ask anyone to explain it to him. He was no engineer versed in the underlying principles, just as he was no economist able to determine the precise amount of resources that could be reclaimed on what exact schedule to maintain stable world markets. He was no politician responsible for deciding who had access to the reclaimed resources, and no theoretical physicist with the capacity to devise a means of transiting from one parallel quantum universe to another. He wasn't honestly sure if he even had the words 'parallel quantum universe' in the right order. He was just a roughneck, glad to have a job at a time when so many others did not, grateful for the hazard pay whether or not he fully understood the dangers.

"Do you ever feel bad about it?" Jeffries asked aloud.

"Huh?" Mariotta grunted.

"This job," Jeffries said. "I mean, it's basically grave robbing, isn't it?"

Mariotta shrugged. "We need the fuel."

"That doesn't make it not grave robbing."

"You rather have it the other way?" Mariotta challenged him. "Rationing? Then riots? Martial law?"

"No," Jeffries said diffidently. He was thinking of another lesson from his schooldays, this time a fable about grasshoppers and ants. Random bits of the formal education of his early years kept leaping to mind, but that was hardly surprising. The lead story in the news that week had been that the country had officially declined below fifty percent capacity at schools nationwide; no school could keep the lights and air conditioning on five days a week, and some couldn't manage it at all. One more reason on the pile of justifications for reclamation runs in the first place. "But doesn't it feel like taking advantage of someone else's work instead of doing our own?"

Mariotta actually turned to look at Jeffries. "You think this isn't hard work?"

"No, no, of course it is," Jeffries shook his head. "But my point is, we got ourselves into our own situation, and now we're solving it by stealing …"

"I know you're not calling me a thief," Mariotta said warningly. "I know you're not."

Jeffries's mouth snapped shut.

"Grave robbing? What does that even mean? You can't steal from a dead person, they don't own anything. And you definitely can't steal from a dead world where there's nobody left. Should we just let it all go to waste? If you're starving to death, would you help yourself to some fruit you found just lying around, or no because you weren't the one who planted the tree it grew on?" Mariotta demanded.

Jeffries felt that Mariotta wasn't making a fair comparison, but he couldn't quite articulate why, and so he remained silent.

"Look," Mariotta went on, "it's not like we're fighting wars with anybody over the stuff. Or like we're picking on somebody too weak to defend themselves and screwing them over in the process. The probes find the dead worlds where there's no anybody, and there's no somebody, there's just nobody …" Mariotta seemed to realize he was drifting into nonsense, and stopped talking.

Jeffries let it go. He knew Mariotta had heard all the same speeches and soundbites he had, all the promises that scientists and engineers had found the way forward, the way out of all the shortfalls and stagflation, thanks to "the ultimate inexhaustible resource." The human race had discovered the previously unimaginable, and used that new knowledge to keep doing exactly what they had always done, in a slightly different way. Progress without change. Who wouldn't accept that?

The tanker continued its forward crawl, with Mariotta making only slight adjustments to its direction, until it approached a gate in the fence. Mariotta dropped the tanker's engine into neutral, and the behemoth shuddered to a halt. Without a word or a glance at Jeffries, Mariotta flipped the hood of his coverall suit—Level 4 Mission Oriented Protective Posture gear—over his head and fastened it, then opened his door and stepped out of the cockpit.

Jeffries followed, and by the time his thick rubber boots hit the ground, Mariotta had already walked up to the gate. It was unsecured, which was par for the course on a world that had gone quickly, and Mariotta let himself through and into the sprawling, fenced facility. Usually Mariotta and Jeffries discussed whose turn it was to scout ahead and find the access point to the fuel cache, and whose turn it was to haul the siphon line from the tanker, but apparently Mariotta had made up his mind and left the latter task to Jeffries.

Jeffries walked around the front of the tanker; the siphon line housing was on the driver's side of the vehicle. He unlatched the front panel and grasped the heavy collar at the end of the hose, lifting it from its cradle as he turned away from the tanker. The hose fed out behind him as he followed Mariotta's path into the facility, expanding seemingly without limit. Another miracle of molecular engineering, something to do with a graphene coil fiber weave, another wonder he lacked the advanced studies to understand. Pulling the gray umbilicus longer and longer, Jeffries made his way to the spot where his partner stood waving.

As Jeffries came within arm's reach, Mariotta held out his caliper key. Jeffries took it and slotted the USB plug end into the port on the siphon line collar. The measurements Mariotta had taken were electronically transferred to the collar, which began to autonomously reconfigure itself to the proper gauge. While the micro-adjusters clicked through their mechanical dance, Mariotta said, "Sorry for jumping down your throat."

Jeffries shrugged, although how visible the gesture was through the bulky folds of the MOPP suit was anyone's guess. In any case, Mariotta continued, "I got an earful of that same crap, almost exactly the same, from my kid the other night. Oh no, it's not really solving the problem, oh no, it's just band-aids, and oh no oh no, what happens when we run out of dead Earths to plunder?"

"What did you tell him?" Jeffries asked.

"Told him if he wants to go live in some dirty hippie commune, with no refrigeration and no indoor plumbing, chewing on leaves in the dark, he could be my guest," Mariotta snarled.

Jeffries nodded, unsure if he should poke at it any further, but ultimately could not resist. "What about the running out part?"

"Big brains say there's infinite Earths we can transit to," Mariotta said. "And that's good enough for me. Infinite means we never run out, right?"

Jeffries supposed Mariotta's conclusion was correct; he too had heard scientists remarking on the infinite quantum universes they were probing and cataloging, usually while lamenting that their funding dictated their focus exclusively on worlds like this one: resource-rich and uninhabited. The collar had finished its self-adjustments and Jeffries handed the caliper key back to Mariotta. Mariotta hooked the tool to his belt and Jeffries attached the siphon line to the valve Mariotta had already opened. Once the seal was airtight, the suction pump within the tanker automatically engaged, and the reclamation extraction was underway. The rushing sound of fuel flowing through the siphon line filled the air, undercut by a scratchier, rasping noise. A rasping Jeffries had never heard in his life.

"You hear that?" Jeffries asked, turning in place to look back at the facility lanes he had traversed, and the tanker still idling outside the fence. He continued to rotate, back to facing Mariotta, and then he saw it: tiny crystalline grains in a pile a few feet behind Mariotta. The pile was growing, as if the bits were rising up out of the ground, like an hourglass running in reverse. The crystal bits were white with irregular red streaks, like blood that had seeped into snow. The pile behind Mariotta grew and grew with alarming speed, and by the time Jeffries had taken in what was happening the pile was as tall as Mariotta and cresting, falling forward like a wave of red and white particles toward Jeffries's partner. "Look out!" Jeffries yelled, lunging for Mariotta.

Jeffries grabbed for Mariotta's arm, to yank him out of the path of the crashing swell, but Mariotta inadvertently pulled his arm just out of Jeffries's reach, as he spun around to see what Jeffries was yelling about. The mass of crystals smashed into Mariotta's midsection, knocking him off his feet and backwards into Jeffries. Both men went down in a tangle of limbs and joints bruised by the impact with the unforgiving concrete.

"What the hell was that?" Mariotta demanded.

"Don't know," Jeffries said. "Some chemical residue?" From

some frightened, instinctual part of Jeffries mind came the idea that it was no synthetic compound, but rather flecks of human pain and death, the red of blood, the white of bone. Jeffries kept this thought to himself.

"Where'd it come from?" Mariotta asked, rolling off Jeffries and climbing slowly to his feet. "How'd it come flying at me?"

"Maybe we disturbed an air pocket underneath it," Jeffries suggested.

Mariotta said nothing. Jeffries rose to his feet and looked at the fuel cache and the long gray hose connecting it to the tanker. He wanted to go back to the siphon line housing to see how far the needle had moved on the gauge, but knew that Mariotta would object to being left alone waiting for another chemical burst. Or worse, Mariotta would insist that he go and check the gauge while Jeffries stayed behind, alone with the red and white grit on the ground.

Mariotta actually took a few steps toward the fuel cache. He swept his boot over the ground, generating the scratching sound again. "Looks like … salt," Mariotta observed.

Salt and bone and blood, Jeffries thought. Before he could think of a more fitting response, however, the pale, red-streaked crystals moved again. They did not bubble, or jump, or scatter as if acted upon by an outside force. They coalesced, gathering and pooling, animated by some internal will of their own. It happened very rapidly, and only because Jeffries was a few paces behind Mariotta could he see it and make some sense of it, as the grains swirled in an ever-increasing mass, like a flock of birds or a swarm of insects, then extruded a single flail that slashed across Mariotta's chest like rubied lightning.

Mariotta screamed, in shock and pain, but Jeffries was no longer witness to what happened to his partner. He turned on his heel and sprinted back toward the tanker, legs pumping as fast as he could force them under the heavy burden of the MOPP suit. He could hear the scraping, scouring sound of the ever-growing mass of salt and bone and blood pursuing him, but would not allow himself to slow and look back over his shoulder, no matter how much the cold, nauseating weight in his stomach insisted he must.

By the time Jeffries reached the tanker, his skin was entirely slicked with clammy sweat, his every muscle trembling. He reached for the door handle and could not find purchase with his shaking, gloved fingers. He made a whimpering noise in the back of his throat and tried again. This time he was able to grip and pull the handle and swing the door wide. He climbed up into the cockpit, only to feel a rough push on his hip from behind. "Move it, MOVE!" Mariotta bellowed.

Jeffries half-leaped, half-collapsed into the cockpit. Mariotta climbed in behind him and slammed the door shut. By the time Jeffries had regained his balance, Mariotta had thrown the tanker's transmission into reverse and was stomping on the accelerator pedal. The tanker was not built for speed, but rumbled backwards away from the abandoned fuel depot at the limits of its earth-shaking power, while Jeffries settled into his own seat.

The fuel depot disappeared, along with everything else, as a deluge of white flecked with red assailed the windshield. Jeffries pushed himself back in his seat, grinding his teeth to keep himself from screaming. The salt and blood and bone continued to throw itself mercilessly at the windshield, and tiny cracks bloomed near the edges. Then the tanker slowed and stopped.

Mariotta let out a howl of rage, kicking at the accelerator. In response, the tanker slewed to the side, with the relentless rasping flood of crystals continuing against the windshield and the roof of the cockpit. "We're tethered," Jeffries said.

"What?" Mariotta roared.

"Tethered by the siphon hose," Jeffries explained. "It's still hooked up. We're anchored to the fuel cache."

Mariotta grunted in disgust and rammed the gearshift into drive. He hauled on the wheel, turning the tanker to the right as it snarled ahead in a forward arc. The tanker was slow, but moved faster forward than backwards. The steel-treaded leviathan slowed again as the siphon hose went taut, but this time the forward momentum of the tanker prevailed. The coupling to the tanker's intake valve or the coupling to the fuel cache, Jeffries could not tell which one, broke loose and the tanker surged forward. Mariotta remained in full grapple with the steering wheel, like a deranged sea captain navigating a hurricane by sheer force of will, only allowing the wheel to spin back and the tanker to clamber forward in a more or less straight line when it was once again pointed toward the return beacon.

The abrasive cacophony of the salt and blood and bone receded. Mariotta slumped back in the chair and Jeffries took a good look at him. Mariotta's MOPP suit had been slashed open in at least three places, across his chest, down his left forearm and over his right knee. Each of the ragged holes in the suit showed the slick red of weeping wounds behind them. Behind his clear faceplate, Mariotta's eyes were hard, bright pinpoints of terror and rage, bulging out of sickly pale flesh.

"I am taking this out of someone's ass," Mariotta muttered, his voice rough. "I already know what they'll say, they'll say the damn probe didn't find out about that ... that ... thing ... but that isn't good enough, not by a long shot ... they had to know something, not like they didn't have all the other worlds in creation they could've sent us to instead..."

"All the other worlds?" Jeffries asked. "Or most of them?"

"I am taking this out of multiple someones' asses," Mariotta said, with a steely sidelong glance at Jeffries. "You keep talking if you want to be the first."

Jeffries fell obligingly silent. The tanker rumbled on, finally arriving at the very coordinates where it had touched down on this parallel quantum universe's version of Earth. The return beacon stood where it had been deployed, yellow diode at its apex blinking intermittently. Mariotta put the tanker into neutral and Jeffries pressed the dashboard's square yellow button for retrieval. The diode on the beacon stopped blinking and shone with a steady light. The hyperstring signal was sent to the reclamation base, and in a minute the gateway would open again for the return trip.

Jeffries wondered briefly what consequences he and Jeffries would face from returning with less than a full tanker, and a damaged siphon hose in the bargain. Expectations had been so high for this reclamation, tentative return runs to this Earth had already been marked out on the work shift scheduler. What if no one believed their story of being attacked and fleeing for their lives? Although surely, between Mariotta's injuries and the erosive damage to the tanker's exterior, no one would accuse them of lying …

The beacon diode began to blink again. No gateway had appeared. Mariotta and Jeffries stared through the windshield at the beacon, then turned and stared at each other. Jeffries pressed the retrieval button. The diode shone steady for a few seconds, then resumed blinking on and off. Jeffries slumped down in his seat.

"Hit it again," Mariotta insisted. When Jeffries remained limp and unmoving, Mariotta leaned over, reached across him and pushed the button. Steady, then blinking. He pushed it harder, slammed it, punched it repeatedly. The steady, then blinking pattern of the beacon diode persisted. "Where the hell is the gateway?"

"All the other worlds?" Jeffries breathed. "Or most of them?"

Mariotta glowered at him. "What the hell are you back on that for?"

"You said they had all the worlds in creation to choose from," Jeffries said, eerily calm. "They send probes first, and sometimes the probes come back and say it's too dangerous. Too much background radiation. Too much electromagnetic disturbance. Too many pathogens they don't want to risk bringing through the big tanker gateway."

"So what?"

"Do the probes ever come back and say it's too safe? That the world still has people living on it? That civilization still exists and people are still using the resources and we can't just roll in and take what we want?"

"Of course not," Mariotta spat, sounding more angry than confident. "They don't even send probes to those worlds in the first place." He stabbed the square yellow button again, with predictable results.

"Because they have some master list somewhere that lets them narrow down the possibilities?" Jeffries pressed on. "How could they, how could that exist? Parallel quantum universes were only discovered nine years ago, and reclamation runs started not long after."

Mariotta shook his head, his lips pursed sourly. "I don't know what you're getting at."

"What seems more likely?" Jeffries asked. "That in all the worlds, sometimes human civilization keeps going, and sometimes it collapses, fifty-fifty chance give or take? And, on top of that, with a fifty-fifty chance of every new quantum parallel universe containing an Earth where civilization collapsed and left behind usable resources for us, we beat the odds and just happen to find one of that kind, a hundred percent of the time?"

Mariotta scowled silently.

"Or does it seem more likely, does it make more sense, to say that almost all human civilizations eventually collapse? That a nuclear war or a plague or whatever else is basically inevitable? And so every time we check another quantum parallel universe, we find a depopulated Earth because that's so overwhelmingly common?"

"You know what? Fine. I don't know if that's right or not, I don't care, but let's say it is," Mariotta spat. "What the hell does any of that have to do with our beacon not working and our gateway not opening up?"

"Well, at some point you have to ask yourself," Jeffries said. "What makes our universe so special?"

"I don't know," Mariotta said.

"Neither do I," Jeffries said, holding up both hands placatingly as Mariotta's face reddened and he loomed aggressively toward his partner. "That's what I'm getting at, is all. There's nothing special about ours that I know of. Because it isn't special. It's just as likely to end in a total collapse as anyplace else. It's inevitable. It could happen any time."

Mariotta looked out the windshield, at the mindless blinking of the beacon diode.

"It could have already happened," Jeffries finished.

Mariotta said nothing. He reached over and mashed the square yellow button with the heel of his clenched fist, again and again and again, to no avail. Finally he collapsed back into his seat. A gust of wind threw a scatter of dust across the windshield. No, Jeffries realized, not dust, not flecks of dried earth, but granules of salt and blood and bone. The red-streaked white crystals pooled across the windshield as if it were the bottom of an hourglass. The scratching hiss of it all around the tanker was pitiless.

Vitriol

"This is good," Jeff said with lip-smacking emphasis.

"Thanks," Angela said.

"No, I mean, really good," Jeff insisted, after another swallow.

"I think so, too," Angela said.

"Like, call off the dogs, all good." Swallow. "Don't-change-a-thing, you-far-surpassed-my-expectations-which-were-admittedly-high good." Swallow, swallow. "You can do this again, right? You wrote it down?" Jeff asked. He tucked a hank of long hair behind his ear, a tic she'd known well ever since they had met in organic chemistry sophomore year in college.

"I wrote it down," Angela said.

"Excellent." Jeff held up his glass, smiling at the sardonyx liquid. "This is it! This is what's going to make our name. Name … does it have a name?"

"Batch three dash oh two four," Angela answered.

Jeff shook his head. "It needs a proper name. Something catchy, memorable, strong. Let's brainstorm."

"Okay."

"Hmmm. How about Barley Legal?" he offered.

"Gross," she made a face as if she had discovered putrefying garbage in the back of a closet, not dissimilar to the expression she had worn when Jeff had first shown her the basement where they now sat: ceiling festooned with cobwebs, walls musty with mold, the floor gritty with dead bugs and rodent droppings. But it had the gas line for a stove and the plumbing connections for a utility sink, and after a thorough cleaning and supply stocking, it had become the place where Angela spent most of her free time. "Also, no puns," Angela reminded him.

"Fine," he shrugged. "Liquid Gold."

"That is a macaroni and cheese tagline."

"Okay, not gold. Amber. Fly in amber. Superfly Amber?"

"That doesn't make any sense."

"Thunderbrau."

"I think you mean Donnerbrau."

"Perfect for dinner parties!"

"Next."

"Chuck Norris Tears."

"Physically impossible."

"Hmmm. Hummmm. Hum hum hummmm. Okay, how about Humbaba?"

Angela pressed her lips together, inhaling deeply through her nose. "That's the first one I don't immediately hate," she said.

"That's a start," Jeff grinned.

"Of course, I don't know what it means, either," she said.

"It's mythological," he informed her. "Akkadian. Birthplace of beer, you know, Mesopotamia."

"Nobody knows if that's true."

"No, but nobody knows it's not true. We can get behind the theory, at least."

"Was Humbaba a beer god?"

"No, not a god actually, more a… like a giant servant of the gods."

"So the beer connection…?"

"Nothing," he confessed. "He's pretty badass, though. And it's fun to say. Humbaba. Humbaba-humbaba-humbaba!"

"You have a lot of strong opinions on this for it just popping into your head," she said.

"Fine, you got me," he said. "I did some research, planning ahead. I was going to save Humbaba for like our third or fifth or twelfth variety, whichever one was worthy, after we did our house lager and obligatory stout and obligatory I.P.A...."

She stuck her tongue out. "Blech. I don't want to do an I.P.A."

"I know. You hate I.P.A.s."

"I don't hate them," she said. "I just don't count 'aggressively herbaceous' among my favorite flavors."

"Well we might never have to do one, now!" he pointed out. "Another differentiator for us. Everybody else does I.P.A.s, but a beer like this... I really think you nailed it on the first try. This will get people's attention. Might even win first prize at the Small Brewers' Festival."

"Last year something called Funky Stein's Monster won," Angela recalled.

"I know," Jeff nodded. "A mediocre beer with a silly name."

"A terrible beer with a terrible name."

"You're making my point," Jeff said. "We've got far and away the superior beer now. Give it a non-terrible name, and …" He left the tantalizing possibilities dangling.

"So we lead with Humbaba, dive right in with a pseudo-claim on beer's origins and a deeply obscure mythological reference," she summed up.

"Heck yeah, we do. In fact, I already know how the label would look, check it out," he said on his way to the blackboard. Angela had wanted to get a proper whiteboard for the work area, but Jeff had insisted on the blackboard because real pubs worked in chalk and slate since time out of mind. Angela should have known he would name the first beer something grandly archaic.

Jeff grabbed the chalk and drew a large circle, with HUMBABA arcing along the top, and in the center a crude face.

"Is that a … yak?" Angela asked.

"What? No, it's … well, it's supposed to be a lion with bull's horns," Jeff waved the chalk at it.

"That's weird," she said.

"Yeah, okay, I can't argue with that," Jeff shrugged. "But the general idea?"

"Assuming we get an actual artist to do the horned lion rendering... " She nodded assent.

"Deal! A toast!" He fetched another glass and filled both. They chimed glasses together, spilling frothy brown ale onto the floor, and took their victory sips.

The beer tasted different to Angela now. She was not sick of beer, never could be, but she had been working so long to perfect this recipe, she feared her palate was losing capacity to appreciate subtle pleasures. With Jeff's approval and the naming of the beer, the pure enjoyment of tasting it had returned. She supposed that was some kind of full-circle turn in their friendship. Beer had never touched her lips before she and Jeff met, when the goofy white boy had flopped into the seat beside the shy black girl in the lecture hall's back row. Jeff made dumb jokes under his breath during class, entirely for Angela's benefit, no matter how many withering glares his puns earned from her. Angela started making jokes back, confidence boosted by knowing hers couldn't be worse than his. Jeff invited her to hang out at a bar, and on the first night in a year and a half that she had been anywhere outside her dorm room after ten p.m., he introduced her to beer. Creating his new favorite beer returned the favor, and Angela savored it.

Pounding on the door at the top of the stairs resounded through the space, less request for admittance and more battering ram. Angela and Jeff exchanged confused looks.

"Expecting someone?" Jeff asked.

"No, you?" Angela replied. When Jeff shook his head, she asked, "Did you lock the door?"

The door crashed open. Angela screamed as she and Jeff leapt up, backing away from the stairs as far as they could. Heavy footfalls echoed across the upper landing.

With their first glimpse of the intruder descending the stairs, Jeff spread his arms instinctively and Angela positioned herself behind him. A tiny part of her marveled at immediately falling into the damsel in distress cliché, while a much larger part insisted that she wake up from this alarmingly lucid nightmare. The ponderous reptilian foot on the first step looked prehistoric, broadly splayed digits ending in hooked claws. Its counterpart's toes curled over the second step's edge. Its lower legs were covered in dark silver dollar scales, each a wicked horn-shaped barb protruding from the flesh. Once it reached the sixth step, it was clearly walking upright on two legs. The sinuous tail growing from the base of its spine thrashed angrily. The oversized hands, muscular arms and broad torso were humanoid, except for their covering in squamous horns.

The visitor, standing ten feet tall, barely cleared the basement ceiling as it reached the last step and turned to Jeff and Angela. Jeff's sketch had put the idea in Angela's head, so a lion's face was what she saw. The mane was composed of fleshy coils, dark splotchy tubules unspooling and doubling back like intestines. Elongated baleful red orbs, shaped like a cat's' eyes, sat above a wide, blunt beaklike nose. Its lipless mouth parted, unsheathing fangs and letting loose a furious bellow.

The next several moments were a blur, as the creature wreaked havoc in the basement. It strode past the stove and swept two large stainless steel brew pots off unlit burners, sending them flying across the room. One pot bent in half colliding with the sink, while the other smashed into two carboys and a box of beer bottles, unleashing jagged blooms of flying glass shards. The creature snatched up a plastic bin full of hop pellets, knocking spoons, funnels and strainers off a wire rack bolted to the wall, and hurled the bin. It smacked a smaller table's leg, split open and knocked the table over, dumping the grain mill and bench capper. The creature tipped over a metal cabinet, spilling jars and canisters in every direction amidst the thunderous crash.

"Stop, stop, stop!" Jeff yelled over the din, breaking the paralysis of shock and fear.

"I have come," the creature announced, surveying the damage done.

"You have," Jeff said. As usual he sounded unflappably in control. "And now you can go. This is a private party and you ... whatever the hell you're supposed to be ... are not invited."

"Do you deny I was summoned?" the visitor asked. "My name was spoken." It pointed toward the blackboard. "My likeness was invoked." It swept its hand down, a gesture encompassing the spilled beer pooling across the floor. "Libations were poured out. I have come."

"Your name?" Jeff repeated. "What name?"

"I am the Monstrous and Most Terrible, son of Utu, guardian of the Cedar Forest by the will of Enlil. My roar is the flood; my mouth, death; my breath, fire. I am Humbaba."

"We don't need any floods or fires or deaths, thanks," Jeff said.

"The summoning, let's just consider that a wrong number. So like I said, you can go. Humbaba, begone!"

Humbaba stared at them. "I cannot depart until I have fulfilled my duty."

"What duty?" Angela asked.

"Terror," Humbaba answered.

"I'm terrified," Angela said, in complete earnest.

"Terror of the heart is not enough," Humbaba snarled. "Death is the price of my release from the underworld. If I do not slay a single human to claim its soul for Manungal, I will be accursed."

"Then I challenge you!" Jeff shouted, suddenly inspired. "I summoned you, I set the terms! Our prowess against yours. If you can beat us, we will surrender to your radiant terror."

"That's laying it on a little thick," Angela muttered.

"Kill us both, we won't resist," Jeff went on, ignoring her. "But only if you win. If you lose, leave this place, never to return. Agreed?"

"Very well," Humbaba seethed. "Name your challenge."

Jeff smiled. "Drinking contest."

"Jeff ..." Angela protested.

"Trust me," he whispered. "Just like old times."

"A contest ... to the death?" Humbaba asked.

"Let's say, to the point of no return," Jeff countered. "If you die, certainly you lose. If you fall unconscious, or if you vomit, you lose, until only one remains who has avoided all of those."

"I accept," Humbaba said.

Jeff righted the table and chairs. He went to a cabinet for three cups and a pitcher. He filled the pitcher from the tap and returned to the table. He gestured for Humbaba and Angela to sit down, poured an inch or two into each cup, and set the pitcher in the middle of the table.

Humbaba settled onto his chair, which creaked under the weight, and lifted his cup, but Jeff held out a warning hand. "Whoa, whoa, whoa," he said. "I don't know how they do drinking contests where you come from, but my house, my rules." He reached into his pocket and pulled out a quarter, holding it up for Humbaba to see. "Gotta sink it before you drink it."

Humbaba scowled. "All coins sink. What has this to do with our contest?"

"I'll demonstrate," Jeff promised, pushing his cup an arm's length away. He held the quarter by the edge between his thumb and middle finger, bobbed his hand up and down three times. He brought his hand down sharply and bounced the quarter off the table; the coin traced a parabola through the air and landed with a splash in the cup. He proffered the cup to Humbaba. "Drink!"

Humbaba drained off the cup, setting it down on the table empty.

"I hope you didn't drink the quarter," Jeff said. "I should have mentioned that's not part of the game."

Humbaba spat the quarter out. "Now I must mimic your actions?" he asked.

"Nope," Jeff shook his head. "It's my turn until I miss." After replacing the beer in his cup, he took another shot, which caromed off the rim. "Shee-it. Okay, fine, now it's your turn."

Humbaba picked up the coin, balancing it with surprising delicacy between two talons. He struck the coin against the table, but it hopped straight up and down, nowhere near Humbaba's beer.

Jeff chuckled. "Okay, her turn."

"This contest is between you and me," Humbaba growled.

"I'm pretty sure her life is on the line, too. That was the deal, two souls versus your eternal punishment," Jeff pointed out. "She has as much to play for as you or me. She's in the game."

Humbaba sullenly slid the quarter over. Angela snapped it smartly into her cup, and handed off to Humbaba. He drank, spat the quarter out.

"If you could not get the coin in your mouth, just keep it in the cup, that would be great," Angela said.

"How?" Humbaba demanded.

"Close your teeth a little when you get close to the bottom?" Angela suggested as she refilled. She picked up the quarter and flipped it in with a satisfying bloop. She handed the cup to Humbaba again.

"This is cozening," Humbaba grumbled. "You stack the odds in your favor, two against one."

"All right, new rule," Jeff suggested. "You can't make the same person, or demon, drink twice in a row."

Humbaba nodded, satisfied, while Angela looked at Jeff doubtfully. He fixed her with a wide-eyed but encouraging look, the same look he had favored her with when he had taught her to play quarters and discovered to his awestruck delight that she was a natural prodigy. He motioned for the beer and drank it, showing Humbaba how to get the last drops without swallowing the quarter. Angela made two more shots, then badly banked the third, cursed, and slid the quarter to Jeff.

The next round, Jeff sank three shots in a row, giving the first and last drinks to Humbaba. Humbaba overshot, but came closer than before, the quarter nearly falling into the cup after barely clearing the far side. He passed to Angela.

Angela shot, sank, and handed the cup to Humbaba. As her next shot plopped into the beer she winced involuntarily. She slid the cup to Jeff, who drank without complaint. Angela made another shot, passed to Humbaba, then missed wide to the left, so that the quarter came to rest before Jeff.

Jeff shook his head slowly and gave Angela a fleeting yet dark side eye. He made two shots, then missed and surrendered the quarter. Humbaba bounced the coin into his cup, then looked back and forth thoughtfully between Angela and Jeff. He gave the drink to Jeff. His next shot was overconfident, and the quarter sailed wide, clinking onto the floor. Jeff pushed himself to his feet to go after it, weaving slightly as he traversed the distance. He returned the quarter to Angela.

Angela shot, sank, made Humbaba drink. She hesitated for a moment when the quarter came back to her, until Jeff coughed loudly into a fist, making a beckoning gesture with his other hand

under the table. She made the shot, and Jeff nodded approval as he drank. Angela made a dozen shots before she finally missed.

Jeff exhaled through lips flapping like a horse's snort. He lined up his shot, took it, missed. He was done, Angela knew. He might make another lucky shot here or there, but was basically no longer competing. The group activity had become a duel, and Humbaba picked up his weapon, the quarter.

Humbaba made his shot, pushing the cup to Jeff. Humbaba made four more shots before finally missing. Angela made a half dozen of her own.

On his turn, Jeff closed one eye, raised the quarter above his head and dropped it, making a whistling sound like a cartoon bomb. Angela tried not to grimace visibly at Jeff's desperation move. Amazingly, the quarter rebounded off the tabletop and wobbled into the beer, which Jeff promptly sloshed toward Humbaba. While the demon drank, Jeff winked at Angela. The coin and cup returned, Jeff tried another bombardier shot, but missed. He passed the quarter.

Humbaba looked back and forth from Jeff's face to Angela's to see if mimicking Jeff's overhead shot was expected, but found only blank stares. Humbaba took his shot in the normal fashion, made it, and made Jeff drink. The demon sank another and passed the cup to Angela. When she went to refill the cup the pitcher was empty. Jeff pushed himself to his feet and carried the pitcher to the tap.

The demon shook his head. "This game takes too long," Humbaba said.

"Tell me about it," Angela muttered.

"What do you mean, too long?" Jeff called back over his shoulder.

"Throwing coins into cups to take sips, one by one, pfah," the demon spat. "This may well take all night, or never end at all. If you are attempting to forestall your doom, your trickery will not succeed."

"It's not a trick," Jeff insisted. "And there are ways to accelerate the game. It ends when either you go down or you're the last one standing, all right? And you are going down."

Humbaba looked skeptical.

"All right, all right," Jeff sat down and pushed the refilled pitcher to mid-table. "New round, new target! Is that better?"

Humbaba considered the pitcher. "Better," he agreed. He bounced the quarter toward the pitcher. The coin clattered off the side.

Angela took the quarter and adjusted her shot to clear the taller height. She overcompensated, sending the quarter sailing over the pitcher. She cursed and handed the quarter to Jeff.

Jeff rolled the quarter down his nose. It fell, sprang up sharply, and tumbled into the pitcher. Angela wanted to jump for joy and squeal with delight, activities which she usually left to Jeff's natural proclivities. But Jeff declined to celebrate, merely pushing the pitcher towards Humbaba. The demon hoisted it like a tankard and drained it in five seconds. When the pitcher was lowered, the quarter was between Humbaba's bared fangs. He pushed it free with a forked tongue.

Jeff staggered toward the tap to refill the pitcher. He returned and took another nose shot, but missed. He gave the quarter to Humbaba, who lined up and made a normal shot. The pitcher slid toward Jeff.

Jeff raised the pitcher in a mocking salute toward Humbaba before drinking from it. Angela cringed; her beer was not swill to be chugged. For some reason Humbaba's guzzling hadn't bothered her, but seeing Jeff suck down the same ale he had been praising only minutes ago, albeit minutes that now felt like part of a distant past life, was dispiriting. Jeff stopped halfway through, let out a loud gurgling belch, and continued to pound until the beer was gone. He flipped the pitcher toward Humbaba. "Thissstime you refillit," he slurred.

Humbaba obliged. "Jeff, what the hell am I supposed to do if Humbaba makes the next shot?" Angela asked frantically. "I can't chug a whole pitcher, I'll die!"

"Iffff you don' chuggit, weeeboth die," Jeff answered, squinting at her with one eyebrow trying to arch to the top of his forehead. "Buddon' worry, you wohn hafta."

"What do you mean?"

"When issss yerturnnnn … jusssss. Dohn. Missssssssss."

Humbaba returned and set the pitcher down. As he lined up his shot, Jeff began to chant "Missssss miss miss miss misssssss." Humbaba glared at him; Jeff glared back and chanted louder. Humbaba missed his shot.

Angela took the quarter, lined up her shot, made it, gave the pitcher to Humbaba. He drank. She made another shot, started to push toward Humbaba again. The demon laughed, crossing his arms over his chest in refusal. Jeff leaned across the table and took the pitcher. "Worth a try," Angela said.

"Youuuuuuu knowhat?" Jeff said. "I dohn like thissss getting up an gettin a new pitcher erry dingdang shot." He grabbed three more pitchers and filled all four, carrying two in each hand back to the table. He pushed three to the edge and one into the central playing area.

Angela prepared her shot. Humbaba chanted, "Miss. Miss. Miss." Angela looked at him in disbelief. "Anything he does, I may do," Humbaba said defensively. Angela made her shot anyway.

Humbaba drank.

Humbaba remained silent as Angela lined up her next shot. She sank it, sending the pitcher to Jeff once again. Jeff finished the beer and sat back. He listed to the side and fell from the chair. "Jeff!" Angela cried.

"He is no longer playing the game," Humbaba said. "And thus he need no longer concern either of us."

"Looks like it's just you and me, then," Angela said.

Humbaba nodded. "You. And me."

Angela lined up her shot. Her eyes darted to Jeff's prone form on the floor, looking for some sign that he was still breathing. A few stray hairs from behind his ear fell across his sagging open lips, fluttering in his exhalation. Angela squeezed her eyes shut, trying not to cry from sheer relief, trying not to cry from frustration and fear because the remainder of Jeff's life would be brief if she could not vanquish the demon sitting across from her. Humbaba stared at her, sneering through his fangs, hissing, "Miss. Miss. Miss. Miss. Miss."

Her eyes felt hot and raw, but the tears dried up, boiled away by pure anger. She was tired of being underestimated. Tired of being taken for granted. Jeff was her best friend, mostly because he had never made her feel like there was anything wrong with her and never let her walk away from a challenge saying she couldn't. Now it was her turn to believe in Jeff. This had been his plan, and it might have been stupidly reckless, but she owed it to him to see it through. She slammed the quarter into the table, maintaining furious unblinking eye contact with Humbaba. She did not watch the quarter's flight, but heard it plop into the pitcher. Humbaba drained the beer.

Angela centered the third pitcher, shot, sank it. Humbaba drank. She repeated the motions for the fourth. She didn't know why she had ever been worried. She could do this all night. All she had to do was not miss, and she wouldn't. She was good at this. Humbaba rose, one huge taloned finger threaded through the four pitchers' handles, and crossed the room to refill them, the protocol by now tacitly understood. As Angela watched him, inspiration struck, followed immediately by a problem. She continued to ponder as Humbaba rejoined her, bobbing the quarter in the air idly as her mind raced.

Humbaba growled impatiently. Angela sent the quarter flying to its target. As Humbaba drank, ideas revolved rapidly in her mind. She wanted to pound the side of her skull with her fist, her habit whenever her brain was stuck, but that might put Humbaba on alert. She rolled the quarter's grooved edge over the pad of her thumb. She moved the second pitcher into place, made her shot. The beer disappeared down the demon's gullet, and Angela was certain he was drinking faster now, on purpose, as if he knew she were playing for time. She made another shot, and Humbaba quaffed the pitcher in two epic gulps.

There was nothing else for it. Angela's next shot missed the pitcher, wide right. Humbaba laughed cruelly as he slapped his hand atop the errant coin and pulled it toward him. He bounced it off the table. It wobbled through the air, and for a moment Angela feared it wouldn't clear the pitcher. But the coin flipped against the lip and slid down the inner surface. Angela closed her eyes, took a deep breath, and pulled the pitcher toward her.

She drank the pitcher without putting it down. She paused occasionally, slamming closed her glottis and breathing through her nose, but resumed drinking as soon as she could. She could feel herself growing light headed, but powered onward. Once the beer was gone, she rose to her feet, gathered up the pitchers, and crossed to the priming bucket.

Angela stumbled and fell to her hands and knees, sending the empty pitchers chattering across the floor. Humbaba grunted with amusement but said nothing. Angela crawled around retrieving the pitchers from the debris Humbaba had scattered in his rampaging arrival. She filled the pitchers quickly.

Realization crashed down on her as she returned to the table. She had given up her last shot to Humbaba so that she could be the one to refill the pitchers. But since he had made the shot, his turn continued. As Humbaba's shooting hand approached the table, Angela shrieked wordlessly in frustrated desperation. Humbaba released too early and the quarter dribbled along the tabletop.

Humbaba glowered at Angela. She batted her eyelashes innocently and reminded him, "Anything I do, you can do, too." She picked up the quarter and readied her shot.

Humbaba barked as she let fly, but Angela was already back in the zone. The quarter found its way unerringly into the pitcher. Humbaba drained it and let the quarter fall. Angela positioned the next pitcher and shot again, with Humbaba unleashing a bestial howl to distract her, to no avail. Humbaba drank the beer as quickly as a spring breaker throwing down a tequila popper. Humbaba slammed the pitcher to the table and spat the quarter at Angela defiantly. It thunked off her chest, leaving a smear of spit behind, but she picked it up unfazed.

She lined up her shot, the most important in any quarters game she had played in her life, in any game anyone had played in history. She allowed herself to hear nothing except her own steady breathing, allowed herself to see nothing except the surface of the beer in the pitcher, a sea of henna with golden foaming shores, a splashdown target a mile wide. She dropped her hand toward the table, with Humbaba's roaring reaching her ears from a vast distance. The quarter rose, peaked and plunged into the beer, as if the eagle emblazoned on its obverse were diving for prey.

Humbaba snatched up the beer and drank it off in a heartbeat. He dropped the pitcher, which banged noisily onto its side and rolled until the handle braked its progress. Humbaba held up a massive, horn-scaled fist, with the quarter throttled in its clench, and opened his mouth. Perhaps he meant to threaten Angela, perhaps merely to insult her, but his speech was lost in an acidic torrent rushing up from his gut. Angela pushed her chair back as the vomit wave crashed across the table so forcefully it knocked two empty pitchers to the floor. Even after distancing herself several feet, a few foul-smelling splatters dotted her arms, stomach and lap.

But Angela smiled. "You lose," she said.

"What?" Humbaba roared

"You agreed to the rules. If you pass out, you lose, and if you vomit, you lose." She rose to her feet. "That makes me the last one standing. So go, get banished."

Humbaba's red eyes widened in disbelief and a yowl of indignant rage tore from his fanged maw. He stood up, sending his own chair skidding noisily. At the same time, smoke tendrils rose from the demon's hide, like wisps of burning incense, filling the basement air with the smell of cedarwood and cloves. Humbaba's inchoate screams warped from anger to fear as flesh sublimated to dark fumes swirling toward an unseen vortex, until the demon was more mist than solid substance, and finally disappeared altogether.

Angela collapsed, shaking. She took several steadying breaths while the basement spun merrily and mindlessly around her. When the speed at which her surroundings were rotating dropped from unsafely operated tilt-a-whirl to children's carousel, she crossed to Jeff, kneeling beside him.

"Jeff," she said, shaking his shoulder. "Jeff, come on, talk to me. Look alive. Be alive," she pleaded.

Jeff blinked slowly. He let loose a huge belch, at which Angela turned her head, squinting and wrinkling her nose. She told herself that her eyes were watering entirely due to the rank smell of his breath. "Angela?" Jeff said. "What ...? Where's ...?"

"Gone," she answered.

"You drank him under the table?" he asked, awed.

"No," Angela admitted. "I got him to DQ himself on the reversal of fortune rule."

"That explains the smell," Jeff said. "But how?"

"Blue vitriol," she said.

"Come again?"

"I dumped some blue vitriol into the pitchers," she explained. "Cupric sulfate, you know, the fungicide I stocked up on in case we need to store berries for a fruit batch. It's an emetic. I mean, it's toxic, too, not really medically recommended for inducing vomiting anymore, but I wasn't too concerned about that, honestly."

"So you salted the beer, and Humbaba didn't notice?"

"Nope. I got him pretty angry, too, so he was rage-drinking too fast to figure it out until ..." She stuck her tongue out in a fair pantomime of copious regurgitation.

"Angela," Jeff said in amazement, "you cheated."

"Hey, don't hate the player, you ungrateful jerk."

"I'm grateful to be alive," Jeff said. "But for our brewery, I'd call tonight a setback."

"True. But I learned something."

"And what might that be?"

"Better to slap a dorky pun on a beer label than to accidentally summon an avatar of chaos and death," Angela said.

"Cheers to that," Jeff said.

MOTHERS AND DAUGHTERS

WITH MY MOTHER, IT WAS CATS. Because she loved them ever since she was a little girl, she assumed all little girls loved them, and I must as well. But I never really took to the creatures as she did. I vowed if I ever had a daughter, I would never impose my predilections on her. The other day my daughter came home with a severed hand, dripping still-warm blood. She wanted help salting the relic. I smiled to myself, knowing she was asking to please herself, not me. Young witches should be free to follow their own crooked paths.

RED SCREAMY

I'M PICKING UP ISABEL'S TOYS in the living room when I find a weird fiber I can't identify. It looks like a single bristle from a broom, except that it's dark red rather than a woody yellow-brown. I try to visualize our broom and whether its bristles are a uniform color or if there's a scatter of earth tones. It's not coming to me. I should check the broom later, figure out if it's getting so old that it's shedding bristles on its own, or if Isabel just capriciously decided to start plucking them out while I wasn't looking. And if it's not from the broom, I should figure out where it came from. On second glance it reminds me of the shaft of a feather, with all the soft barbs stripped off. The last thing I need is to find out Isabel's been digging around in animal nests in our yard without me knowing about it. Or to be accused of failing to be aware of it.

"Mommy," Isabel sings out to me from the dining room, interrupting my train of thought. "I'm bored!"

When Isabel was younger the bristle might have set off choking hazard alarm bells in my brain, but she's three now and doesn't put everything in her mouth as a matter of course, so I stick it in my back pocket and immediately forget about it. I reach the dining room and find Isabel sitting on the floor with her head all the way to one side as she stares up at me expectantly.

"You're bored, Iz?" I ask.

"Uh huh."

"And what is Mommy supposed to do about it?"

"Draw monster!"

I look at her for a couple of seconds and don't do a very good job hiding the indecision on my face. She takes my hesitation for something else, flashes me her best smile, tiny perfect teeth making a grin so big and wild, adds a "Please?" Her gorgeous thick eyelashes spread wide; when she learns how to bat them we are all doomed.

Josie and I are trying to teach Isabel manners, now that the novelty of her speaking English rather than pointing and grunting has worn off, so I find it hard to say no to her when she remembers the magic word all on her own. Politeness wasn't the reason I paused to begin with, but never mind that now, as she reaches out for my hand and guides me toward the kitchen table, the same way I've guided her toward countless meals ever since she got too big and independent for me to carry her.

As always, a pile of paper and a box of crayons await on one corner of the table. I sit down and lift Isabel up onto my lap. "Okay, what kind of monster?" I ask.

"Green!"

"Green," I agree, shaking that crayon out of the box. "What else? Big? Small? Skinny? Fat?"

"Ummm … small. And fat. And big ears."

"Big round ears?"

"No, pointy," Isabel insists, a note in her voice implying that it was a pretty dumb question. Of course the monster should have pointy ears.

I brace my left hand on Isabel's chest and start drawing with my right hand. I've learned by now that if I don't hold Isabel back she'll lean so far forward I won't be able to see what I'm doing, and I'm good but I'm not that good. So I hold her against me and draw with the green crayon, something that looks like a half-melted dollop of pistachio soft serve, with pointy ears that reach up to the top edge of the paper.

"How many eyes?" I ask.

"Four, no, five! Orange eyes!" Isabel informs me. I swap crayons and start filling in little orange orbs inside the crown of the green blob, at the points of an upside down pentagon. I'm tempted to sketch in a pentagram to connect them while Isabel decides on the next detail, but I know that Josie would take that as a provocation. Which it kind of would be, as if this little game between Isabel and me weren't enough of one already.

Isabel saves me from myself by yelling out more instructions. "Do the arms, Mommy!"

Since she hasn't specified I decide to make the arms blue, and draw them as stubby little appendages that don't even clear the width of the monster's ample hips. "Longer!" Isabel giggles. I extend the limbs, one straight out to the side and one bent at the elbow as if it's waving at us. "Now do the claws!" Isabel commands.

We're not exactly making monsters who live in a sedate multicultural neighborhood on public television here. Isabel is into what she calls "real" monsters, the scary kind; she probably has more synonyms for claws and fangs and barbs and spines in her vocabulary than most pre-schoolers. Well, her mommy is pretty into scary monsters, too. One of her mommies, at any rate. I give the monster three needle-sharp light blue talons on one hand, and a single wicked meathook on the other.

"Don't forget the mo-outh," she admonishes me, sing-stretching out the last word, ding-dong. I dump all the crayons out to get at the black one, as always the most worn down, hiding at the bottom of the box. I give the monster a big frowny maw.

"Do you want this one in your room?" I ask.

"Yeah!" she agrees. "Can we put it up right now?"

"Sure," I tell her. She slides off my lap without being asked, so I can get up and grab the tape. She carries the drawing of the monster, held out in front of her, admiring her prize. We go up the stairs, me following her.

Her bedroom closet door is covered and surrounded by drawings, a few by her, most by me, all crazy monsters. She walks up to the closet and holds the drawing against the wall where she wants it, and I tape it in place. "Okay?" I ask.

She nods, but she's already communing with the menagerie in her own way, touching each monster in turn with her thumb and humming a little song I don't know the words to. I'm not sure if she does, either. I leave her to it, head back downstairs to see what we have in the house I can make a reasonable approximation of dinner out of. I think there's ground turkey in the freezer, and hopefully the peppers in the crisper I'm thinking of stuffing haven't gone mushy.

"I see Isabel has a new beastie in her collection," Josie says that night as we're both getting ready for bed. Isabel's bedtime was hours ago, and Josie was the one who spent twenty minutes getting her settled and tucked in, asking her questions about her day, answering questions about whatever popped into Isabel's head in the moment. It's something like the fiftieth night in a row that goodnight detail has fallen on Josie, per Isabel's request. Josie and I used to take turns until one day Isabel started asking for Josie every night.

"She sure does," I answer. I try to make it sound casual and not passive-aggressive, but as soon as I hear my own voice I know I've failed and basically begged Josie to come at me.

"Mel," Josie's voice takes on the timbre of someone convinced they're being the reasonable one and wishing her irrational partner could admit that. "Don't you worry that she's getting a little bit … fixated?"

"Not really," I shrug. That's twice now I've spoken without even trying to look at her, so I force myself to meet her eyes, standing on opposite sides of the bed, neutral creampuff expanse of duvet between us. "She's three, babe. She'll be on to something else before too long."

"And if she's not?" Josie throws back. "I mean, do you even try to guide her, even a little bit? Do you ever say, hey, why don't we draw cats or airplanes or … or …"

"What is the big deal, drawing things that aren't real?" I ask. "So Isabel has a big imagination, isn't that a good thing?"

"Not if she's imagining frightening, violent things," Josie shakes her head, looking down as she ties the drawstrings of her pajama pants.

"She's not going to turn into some psycho killer," I shoot back. "When I was little I wanted to be the dragon from Sleeping Beauty, and I don't go around burning things down now."

"No, but …" She cuts herself off as her eyes flick guiltily toward me. I hold my tongue somehow, turn away, disappear into the bathroom and start brushing my teeth. There's a little blood in the toothpaste when I spit, because scourging my gums is better than venting my spleen all over Josie. I clean up the sink and splash my face with cold water. By the time my face is dry and I'm back in the bedroom, Josie is in bed, under the covers, her back to me. I know we won't talk any more until morning, and even then it won't be a continuation of the conversation that just imploded.

I turn off the light and slide into bed on my back, not letting any part of my body touch any part of hers. She knows better than to hope that I don't know what she was about to say. No, I don't live out violent fantasies, but I still get a kick out of them. I like horror movies and action movies where people get shot and stuff gets blown up. I like the really old comic books from back before most grown-ups were paying attention, with the axe murderers and the cannibal ghouls. I find Scandinavian death metal bands with complex Satan-worshipping systems included in their album liner notes hilarious. I always thought Josie accepted that as harmless fun, my little mental release valve.

Harmless for me, but not for her daughter. Our daughter. Ours when she needs disciplining or gets sick or outgrows the clothes we just bought her three months ago. Certain other times, Josie's and Josie's alone.

The next night Josie works late and doesn't get home until Isabel's already in the bath. Josie stops in the doorway of the bathroom as I'm leaning over the tub and washing Isabel's back with my hands, while Isabel carries on a conversation with her purple unicorn-shaped washcloth.

"Oh, are you and the unicorn taking a bath together? Does the unicorn like getting clean?" Josie asks.

Isabel turns the washcloth around to face Josie and says, "I like bubbles!" in a high-pitched voice that's supposed to be the unicorn's.

"Aw, that's nice, I like bubbles, too," Josie says. I know this is being put on for my benefit, Josie's demonstration of her own appreciation of whimsy. She's not merely into realistic vehicles and animals, no, she's totally down with unicorns, very open-minded. "I forgot we even had that washcloth," Josie addresses me, finally.

I should give her credit for trying but I can't help myself. "Yeah, I was actually looking for the kraken washcloth, but I couldn't seem to find it."

"Nice," Josie rolls her eyes. I'm not looking at her, I'm pouring a cupful of water down Isabel's back to rinse her off, but I can hear the eye-roll all the same. Josie walks away and I know that by the time I have Isabel out of the tub and dried off and in her jammies, Josie will be changed out of her work clothes and ready to take over the bedtime ritual. I also know once Isabel is down for the night, her mommies aren't going to have a very pleasant bedtime conversation between them, if anything ends up being said at all.

Isabel was conceived from one of Josie's eggs and IUI, but sometimes, and I'm not proud of this, sometimes I wish Isabel had been IVF. Because sometimes I wish I could throw that in Josie's face, that for all we knew Isabel was the result of some mix-up at the lab and no more biologically Josie's than mine. Not that I'd be able to make a convincing argument beyond that. Isabel looks like Josie, at least some reasonable combination of Josie's DNA and our kindly anonymous sperm donor's. She has her mother's protruding blue eyes, the same pout to her lips, the same dainty bone structure.

Isabel has Josie's temperament, too, and likes a lot of the same things, although that argument could come down to nature versus nurture. Bottom line, though, Isabel is even more outwardly girly-girly than Josie. Isabel wears her hair long with naturally curly bangs, and every day when she gets dressed has to pick out clothes that either have ruffles, bows, sparkles, or shades of pink or purple, preferably two or more in combination. I think left to her own devices, Josie would want to present in the exact same way, but her job dictates a more sober wardrobe and sensible grown-up haircut. Josie's hair is still feminine, of course, and nowhere near as short as mine.

For a long time after Isabel was born I didn't know how to bond with her because I didn't know how to relate to her. Sounds stupid to talk about relating to a newborn who can barely focus more than eighteen inches away from her own face, but I couldn't help but feel the absence. There's an animal love that human beings feel for their family, their children, and I never felt at a loss for that with Isabel, not from the first moment I held all six trembling pounds of her in my arms in the hospital. But then there's another level of connection, or sometimes there is anyway. Mutual understanding and respect and common interests, all the things that determine if you would consciously decide to like this other human being if she weren't directly related to you. Newborns don't have any interests except what their parents project onto them, and I suppose I felt guilty that Josie had been through nine months of pregnancy and twenty hours of labor and so I stepped back and let Josie chart the course. If Josie wanted to make Isabel her precious little princess doll, and she so clearly, so desperately did, then I didn't have boo to say about it.

And I didn't see how Isabel getting older would necessarily change or solve anything, once the groundwork had been laid. I did my share of midnight feedings and rockings and diaper changes the first few months, and when Josie went back to her old schedule at the firm it was just me and Isabel at home together five days a week. I read to her, I played with her, I kept her from licking electrical sockets when she learned to crawl. I did not watch horror movies while Isabel played with stuffed animals in front of the TV. I did not crank up my Sepultura and Morbid Angel albums in the car when we drove together to the store. Much as I loved her, I didn't think we'd ever have anything in common. It was like she was a porcelain trinket of Josie's that I was entrusted with while Josie was at the office, and I was always half-terrified of breaking her.

I finally relaxed one day when I was reading Isabel a big picture book of wild animals, and I put a little extra something into making the animal noises: the hooting gorilla, the roaring lion, the hissing snake. Isabel went crazy for it, I had a blast doing it, and she didn't have night terrors about being lost in the jungle or anything. I realized maybe she wasn't as breakable as I feared.

But still, the very first time my daughter came to me wanting to draw monsters, I was so thrilled. Because it came out of nowhere, or more to the point it came from her. I wasn't projecting anything. She came to me.

"Come sit down for lunch, baby," I say as I pull the folded-over paper towel out of the microwave.

Isabel sets down her family of dolls, none of which have forked tongues or horns. She steps lively to her chair, because she's enthused about what's on the menu today: chicken nuggets, normally a treat reserved for special occasions. Today I bribed her with them. I took her to the store in the middle of the morning and she alternated between trying to run away and grabbing random things and throwing them in the shopping cart until I offered her favorite for lunch in exchange for good behavior. Maybe not the moral high road, but it worked.

"I'm not a baby," Isabel announces proudly as she pulls the chair away from the table. "I'm a big girl." She climbs onto the chair from the side, stands up on the seat, then turns ninety degrees toward the table and lowers herself onto her butt, which today is covered in a flouncy pink skirt with silver sequins.

"You are," I agree with her, setting a small plastic plate in front of her, bearing a half-dozen chicken nuggets and a small pool of ketchup. "You're mommy's very big girl, and I'm glad you were good at the store for mommy." Eventually.

Isabel grabs an oblong nugget, dips it in the ketchup, and takes one dainty bite from the end; one of the reasons she likes this meal is because it's no-silverware-required. I turn away from her and start trying to figure out what I'm going to have for lunch. Soon I have my head buried in the fridge but nothing particularly appealing beckons.

"Mommy, look!" Isabel calls. I straighten up and turn around, looking over the counter to see Isabel holding up a chicken nugget that looks like a solid figure eight, or a snowman. Isabel opens her mouth wide and bites off the head. She dunks the remainder in the ketchup while she chews, then holds the nugget up again. Her eyes and mouth open wide and she fake-screams, while making the decapitated chicken nugget run back and forth in midair, its neck stump a gory mess of Red No. 5.

I clap my hand over my mouth way too late, after I've laughed. Isabel is supremely pleased with herself and takes yet another big bite of nugget. As she chews and swallows a contemplative look spreads across her face and finally she says, "Mama wouldn't like that joke, would she?"

There was a time when Josie and I wondered if we needed to come up with different names for Isabel to call us, and introduce them to her, to avoid the confusion of our daughter calling us both "Mommy". But in the end, Isabel came up with the distinction on her own; Josie has always been "Mama" and I've always been "Mommy". "No, Mama probably wouldn't," I agree.

"But you think it's funny," she beams. "And Mama's not here.

So it's Okay."

"Iz, honey," I hear myself saying, "Maybe … maybe you shouldn't do things Mama wouldn't like, even if Mama's not here. Okay? You just … if you know Mama wouldn't like it, try not to do it."

Isabel barely processes the idea before she gives me a chirpy "Okay" and gets back to devouring her chicken nuggets. I return to the fridge and grab the first yogurt I see, feeling like there's nothing in particular I want for lunch, feeling like it usually matters much more what someone else wants than what I want.

"Did you hear Isabel get out of bed last night?" Josie asks me at twenty past six the next morning. Isabel wakes up any time between 5:30 and 7:30 lately, according to no predictable pattern. Josie and I get up at the same time every day no matter what, and when Isabel's up with us I supervise some combination of playtime and breakfast while Josie gets ready for work; when Isabel sleeps in, Josie and I get to enjoy a little leisurely adult conversation over coffee. Or at least, we enjoy it when things between us aren't tense as hell like they are now.

"No," I answer her.

"We must have both slept through it," Josie says.

"Slept through what?"

"I don't know," Josie says. "I peeked in on her before I came downstairs and the carpet just inside her door had all these pulls and loose threads sticking out. A couple of inches were almost down to the backing. I don't know what in the world she could have been doing."

I'm expected to answer for this because of course it's my fault, the slippery slope from drawing five-eyed fiends to sleepwalking and destroying parts of the house and all manner of antisocial acting out. "Did Isabel look all right?"

"She was asleep in bed," Josie admits. "She was sucking her thumb, had the other hand under the blanket. I didn't want to disturb her."

"I'll check her fingernails when she comes down," I offer. "I'll ask her what she was doing."

"Oh, I doubt she'll tell you," Josie says. She clears her throat right away and tries to recover. "I mean, she wouldn't tell either of us, assuming she even remembers ..."

"I need to get those alternate layouts for the brochure covers done this morning, the sooner the better" I announce, standing up from the kitchen table. Josie doesn't say anything, not even goodbye. I head into the home office, fire up the laptop, and start opening files, but it's not until I hear the door slam behind Josie as she leaves for the day that I can actually start concentrating on the tasks.

Isabel wakes up on the late side and has breakfast, then heads back upstairs to get dressed. I putter around the main floor, cleaning the kitchen and straightening the living room. After a while I notice Isabel's been upstairs much longer than it takes to put together a tunic and leggings ensemble.

At the threshold of Isabel's room I pause and look down to see the damage to the carpet Josie was talking about. It reminds me of when I was younger and my family got a puppy, which my brother Mark accidentally trapped in his room when he closed the door on it once. Eventually we heard Bandit whimpering and let him out, but not before he had peed on the corner of Mark's bed and tried to dig his way under the closed door. Isabel's rug looks a lot like that, but Josie and I have never gotten a dog. She's a cat person, I'm allergic to cats, not much room to compromise there.

Isabel's been busy rearranging her room a bit. She's pushed the kid-scale table and two chairs that usually sit in the corner of her room to the middle of the floor, and cleared all the random toys off, replaced them with her tea set. Josie's old childhood tea set.

"Whatcha doing, Iz?"

"Tea party," she answers, without looking up, because she's

legitimately concentrating on arranging the cups and saucers. Thank god she's too young to be passive-aggressive yet.

"Oh yeah? Who's invited?"

"Red Screamy."

"Ah." My eyes go to a picture taped up at the top of her closet door, one of the first ones I drew for her. Red Screamy. Part vulture, part demon-bat, part alligator, all bloody red. I've toned the pictures down a bit since that one, which even I admit is about as overtly horrific as Crayola monsters can get. Josie tried to take it down once, with no objections from me, but Isabel threw a Kong-sized fit. The picture of Red Screamy stays.

Sometimes when Isabel gets wound up and hyper and runs around yelling to hear her own voice, I call her Red Screamy, which only eggs her on. I'm well aware that Josie hates that, but lately I'm understanding just how much, and on just how many levels.

"Do you want me to get him down for you?" I ask, reaching toward the drawing. "So you can set him in his chair?"

"No, Mommy!" Isabel screams at me, going from domestic Zen to genuinely distraught in a heartbeat. "The chair is for Red Screamy, not for a picture of Red Screamy!"

I hold my hands up like she's a cop who caught me messing with a locked window. "Okay, okay," I say. "He can sit in his own chair. Okay?"

Isabel just nods and I take that as my cue to leave. Poor little thing. At least she didn't try to have her imaginary tea party on the weekend, with Josie home. She'd probably try to guide Isabel away from offering plastic cupcakes to her favorite monster, for fear of … whatever it is that Josie's so afraid of. I wish Josie would just drop the whole thing, for Isabel's sake. We both know our daughter will always be an only child. She'll never even have a pet, most likely. It's going to be hard enough for her as it is, without discouraging her from her fantasies, even the weird ones. Especially those.

Another late night for Josie, and she misses bathtime, and bedtime. Isabel's been down for a couple hours at least when I finally hear the garage door. I'm working in the office, trying to get ahead on a few different assignments, so I don't get up to go greet her or anything. At least, that's my excuse.

I sense her behind me, at the threshold of the office. "Hey," she says.

"Hey." I don't turn around. "Have you eaten?"

"Yeah, we sent out for Thai." She sighs. "Mel, here's the thing. This … you and Isabel, you drawing things for her … don't you think that's stifling her creativity, to some extent? She might very well show some talents of her own someday, but not if you always do things for her. She'll always compare her developing talents to your adult ones and … it's just not good for her self-esteem."

My eyes are locked on the laptop monitor.

"Do you disagree?" Josie asks.

"I'm kind of in the middle of something right now," I answer. "Can we talk about this tomorrow or something?"

"Fine," Josie says, in a register that is the diametric opposite of fine. "Good night."

I'm not sorry that she's gone. I know sooner or later we have to have it all out but I don't know where to even start. There's so many things I want her to know.

I want her to know that it wasn't a choice for me, when I was a kid, not that much older than Isabel. I was the way I was and I couldn't just go along to get along. I didn't choose to be an iconoclast because I was so daring and so into upsetting the order of things around me. I had no choice.

I want her to know there's a world of difference between what I went through and what Isabel may or may not be going through. I gravitated towards the monsters and mutants, the creepy-crawlies and things that go bump in the night, because they were freaks and I felt like a freak. It gave me a focal point for my feelings of disconnection. It was never something I bonded with anybody over, it was just a mental lifeline I grabbed onto by myself. If Isabel is into monsters and wants to talk to me about monsters that means we're making a connection, and the superficial details of cloven hoofs or bloody entrails could not be more beside the point. I want Josie to realize that she's hung up on the trappings and that's all wrong.

And maybe, maybe on some level I want Josie to acknowledge what I've given up for us, for our family, for Isabel. I used to make art, all the time, every day. I used to take my nightmares and my insecurities and my anger and frustrations and, yes, sometimes my hopes and happiness, and I used to bring them out of my head and onto a canvas or a wall. And that was how I first started connecting with people, including Josie, if she'd ever care to remember that. But that doesn't pay the bills, so I do freelance work from home designing the trade dress for technical manuals, and the closest I get to creative artistic expression is deciding if behind the title of Organizational Paradigms for Property Management there should be a free-floating teal trapezoid or maybe just a blue rectangle. And it sucks and it's soulless but it does help pay the bills. But sometimes Isabel wants me to draw a silly monster and for one brief shining second I can flex some artistic emotional muscles and make somebody happy and it feels good. I'm not doing it to warp Isabel into my image and I'm not doing it all for myself but I'd be lying through my teeth if I said there wasn't a little something special I was getting out of it myself.

But that's the sticking point. I want her to know these things, but I don't want to say them out loud. I don't want to tell her, I don't want to have to tell her, I just want her to already know. I feel like she should already know. I know in my head that's not fair, but in my heart I want her to already know. And she doesn't. She has no idea.

So I just keep working on the latest assignment from the publisher, moving a stock photo of street fair attendees back and forth from the upper right hand corner of the layout to the lower left hand corner, trying to figure out which placement truly captures the essence of Maximizing Human Capital and Recruiting. Eventually, very late into the wee hours of the night, I give up and save both versions and decide to let the publisher choose. Nobody cares what I think.

I turn off all the lights on the main floor and mount the stairs, and by sheer chance I'm right outside Isabel's door when I hear the heavy thump of weight hitting the floor coming from inside her room. I remember Mark breaking his collarbone falling out of bed when he was little, even though that was within weeks of him moving straight from a crib to a full-sized bed, and Isabel's been in a low toddler bed for almost a year. The differences between the situations don't matter at all as I throw open her door and rush in, not even bothering to turn on the room lights. Which is why I stumble directly into the tea party table and chairs still sitting in the middle of the room, and I fall ass over elbows to the floor, and I'm lucky I don't break my neck while I'm at it.

I roll onto my side and I look to Isabel's bed and I see the blanket-covered outline of her still safe and sound in bed. But I also see a shape beside her bed, too big to be a pillow or a stuffed animal, bigger even than Rangoon, the huge Gund orangutan Josie's parents sent when Isabel was born.

The shape moves towards me.

I still have one leg half up on the tea table, and I slide it off so that I can get my feet under me and stand up, but that only makes the shape move faster. It's dark in Isabel's room, blackout curtains on the windows so she can go to sleep at her bedtime even in the summer when the sun's still up at eight. The door's partially open but I hadn't bothered to turn the hallway light on as I climbed the stairs, the whole house is dark. My eyes are adjusting, not fast enough, the shape is solid shadow against the other indistinct shapes in Isabel's room. Before I know it the shape is all I can see, taking up my entire field of vision, practically on top of me.

It's alive. My brain is very slow to fully process the fact that there is a living thing in the room with us, but my stomach drops from a great height into an ocean of darkness. And the alive thing is not human, it's some kind of animal, but not any I've ever known. It's close enough now that even in the darkness I can make out some of the details. The snout, nearly touching my chin, glossy beetle-black, the edges of the upper and lower mandibles serrated, edges interlocking like the teeth of a bear trap. A tongue undulating in and out of the open snout, ropy and raspy, like the wayward arm of an octopus. A smell of rotten meat rolls off that naked tongue in waves, propelled by growling exhalations. Eyes triangular, sharp and narrow, watchful, resentful. Segmented legs jutting upward from the body, bending almost double back down to the floor again, insect-like but covered in dense bristly fur, hard to tell the color in the darkness but it looks red, blood red, it's Red Screamy, Red Screamy as big and ugly as life is in my daughter's room and now I'm the one who's going to scream …

"Mommy?" Isabel says sleepily. She's standing at the foot of her bed, between the bed and Red Screamy. She has one arm draped around Red Screamy's spiky ruff, as lovingly as if it were a golden retriever.

"Yeah, Iz," I manage to answer her.

"Is it time to get up go downstairs have breakfast?" she asks, not quite believing it herself.

"No, baby," I tell her. "I just came in your room …" The reasons have flown from my mind. "It's still night-night time. You go on back to bed."

"Okay," she sing-songs, drawing out each letter. But she doesn't move. "Did Red Screamy scare you, Mommy?"

"A little," I admit, because a gibbering part of my reptile fight-or-flight brain insists that Red Screamy will know it if I'm lying. Know, and feel displeasure.

Isabel pats the top of Red Screamy's skull, and it lowers its head submissively. It turns in place with bug-like micro-steps and retreats to Isabel's closet, squeezing impossibly through the small gap in the doorjamb. When Red Screamy is gone, Isabel and I are left looking at each other, our eyes level, me still on my backside like a helpless turtle, her standing. I'm concentrating on taking soft, quick breaths so my daughter won't see me shuddering in the grips of an epic freak-out. She's about three-quarters asleep, swaying with unbothered tranquility.

She breaks the silence first. "Don't tell Mommy," she says. It's not quite a request, or an admonition, or a plea for guidance, although it's also kind of all of those things at once.

"Don't worry," I stage-whisper. "I won't tell."

I finally feel like my limbs have stopped trembling enough that I can get to my feet without pitching over again. Isabel waits patiently for me to put a hand on her shoulder and gently guide her back to her bed. She climbs in willingly enough, and I wait for her to settle herself, rolling onto her stomach and changing the positions of her arms and legs a few times, before I pull the blanket up over her. Her eyes are already closed, her breathing steady.

I close the door of Isabel's bedroom behind me as quietly as I can, then let go of the doorknob as if it's electrified. I slump forward, not far since the hallway isn't that wide, ending up leaning my weight against the opposite wall with my cheek flat against the relatively cool and totally mundane surface of buttercup-yellow interior latex. I hitch a deep breath, hold it in, then let it out with an involuntary "nuuhh" sound. I do that again, and again, I lose count of how many times, and I only push myself away from the wall when the hallway stops spinning.

I'm as existentially certain as I can be that I'm in the upstairs hallway of my home, that I'm awake and lucid and not hallucinating thanks to a stroke or nervous breakdown or marijuana tea flashback.

I have just seen a monster in my daughter's bedroom, an unnatural abomination that can only exist to spread destruction and terror and has confined itself to her closet.

And I've left my daughter with a promise that I would not tell Josie about Red Screamy, which means not telling anyone else, either.

How long has Red Screamy been here? Does the monster have some independent existence, and was it drawn to Isabel by her nature, and her nascent interest in monsters? Or did Isabel somehow bring Red Screamy into existence by force of will, using my crayon renderings for focus? What about the other drawings, do they have equivalent carapace-and-viscera versions co-habitating in the closet with Red Screamy, and how many of them are there, a pack, a small army? Or are they just variations on the theme, an incidental decorating motif inspired by a singular pet horror? What is Red Screamy capable of, and what does it want? Can Isabel really control it, or was I simply lucky? I have a million questions and exactly zero answers.

The uncertainty in and of itself spells danger, if not doom. If Red Screamy, or any other monstrosity, harms anyone, especially Isabel, then that will be on my head, if I knew the threat was present and real but did nothing about it. My daughter is basically harboring a supernatural weapon of mass destruction, I know she is. And she's asking me to help her keep it a secret.

But she did ask me. She trusts me. On some level I understand what she sees in Red Screamy, why she wants to keep it close, just between us, and why Isabel instinctively knows that I have the capacity to understand. She doesn't think that Red Screamy will hurt her, could ever hurt her, and honestly, deep down, neither do I.

I ponder that some night Josie might enter Isabel's room unawares, and trip over Red Screamy, and shriek and wail until Red Screamy rips out her throat with its claws and fangs.

I think, on the other hand, she might not. There's really no way to know.

I say quietly, mostly to myself, "Don't worry. I won't tell."

About The Author

DALE W GLASER is a lifelong collector, re-teller and occasional inventor of fantasy tales. He grew up right on the line between suburban cul-de-sacs and unspoiled wilderness, and has been known to get up to mischief in the woods late at night from time to time. He is a small town boy made good, the small town in question being one built entirely out of Tinker Toys and Lincoln Logs and populated by off-brand sword and sorcery action figures, alien finger puppets, and wind-up robots. He needs air, food, water and stories in order to survive, not necessarily in that order. His lifelong love of written words has manifested as a devotion to the English language almost exclusively, which is probably just as well because if he were to master any of the dead tongues that conceal ancient mysteries and invoke malevolent forces, we'd all be in trouble. He currently lives in Virginia with his wife, their three children, and a small menagerie of rescued pets. Follow his blog and find links to all his published works at https:// dalewglaser.wordpress.com/

www.ingramcontent.com/pod-product-compliance
Lightning Source LLC
Chambersburg PA
CBHW020139120726
47903CB00007B/2324